# ANTHOLOGY OF SHORT STORIES
## BY
# YOUNG AMERICANS®

# 2003 EDITION
# VOLUME LXVII

Published by Anthology of Poetry, Inc.


©*Anthology of Short Stories by Young Americans*®
2003 Edition
Volume LXVII

All Rights Reserved©

Printed in the United States of America

To submit short stories
for consideration in the year 2004 edition of the
*Anthology of Short Stories by Young Americans*®,
send to:  poetry@asheboro.com  or

>   Anthology of Poetry, Inc.
>   PO Box 698
>   Asheboro, NC  27204-0698

Authors responsible
for originality of short stories submitted.


The Anthology of Poetry, Inc.
307 East Salisbury • P.O. Box 698
Asheboro, NC     27204-0698

Paperback ISBN: 1-883931-43-6
Hardback   ISBN: 1-883931-42-8

*Anthology of Short Stories by Young Americans*®
is a registered trademark of
Anthology of Poetry, Inc.

It has been said that a reader can take from a story what the reader brings to the story. Arriving with only a reader's perspective, what more could the reader learn than what is obvious? However, arriving to the story broad-minded, and willing to enjoin the writer's perspective, there is good chance for even greater discovery.

To see past the written page, to not only taste the crème that has risen to the top, but to dive deeply through the levels of drama, is to experience the story with all five senses heightened and receptive. For it is down through the dimensions of the story where the reader will find the writer's heart. And it is from the heart of the writer that the reader returns with a chest full of treasure.

Welcome to the Anthology of Poetry's 2003 edition of the *Anthology of Short Stories by Young Americans®*. Young writers from across the country have opened their hearts, emptied their pens, and delivered to us imaginations woven to words, and spun into story. We tried to present the short stories as the authors wrote them, in their format and punctuation. We congratulate all those who participated, and we are grateful to bring you the latest collection.

Settle in and open up. Enjoin the writers and be entertained. Upon your return find happy treasures that no earthly king could ever provide.

The Editors

# MY FIRST AND SECOND STITCHES

When I was five years old I lived in Idaho. One day my brother and I were jumping off of his windowsill on to his bed. I jumped, while he was still sitting on the bed I hit his head on my chin. I could feel the skin peeled open. I could see, and taste the blood, it was really, really gross. I started to cry! My mom came in and she picked me up. She set me on the counter and got frozen peas. She put them on my chin. She told my dad to get the car started, we were on our way to the hospital. When we got there I was put on the emergency table. The doctor came in, he started to put the stitches in, but before that he numbed it. The numbing really, really hurt. It was like peroxide. I thought he only put five stitches in but he put eight stitches in. My mom told me to be careful. I did go to school the next day. That is my first story of stitches.

## Here Is My Second Story Of Stitches

When I was in Loveland, CO, my brother and I were playing with my dad. We were riding our bikes and we were pretending that we were hurt. It was my brother's turn to tell my dad that I was hurt. I was too chicken, so I started to pedal as fast as I could. I hit a rock, my front tire got stuck and my back tire flipped me. I hit my chin on the curb, my dad came out. He called my mom at Wal-Mart. She told him to meet her at The Orchards Medical Center. We met her there and I was in the emergency room again just like four years ago in Idaho. I got five stitches but, I recovered quickly and I went to school the next day.

Molly Wilson
Age: 10

Tim Dawson a twenty-one-year-old, woke up, thinking it would be just a normal day. But who would guess that he would be drafted by the Washington Mad Hatters, a Junior A ice hockey team. After hanging up the phone with the coach, he energetically began to pack his stuff.

Since he lived in Erie, Colorado he had to live in a dorm room with Ryan Joseph (not related to Curtis Joseph a NHL goaltender). They became good friends and did everything together. They carpooled to practice and to games and classes together.

Ryan was a twenty-two-year-old who lived in Detroit and is the team's first line center. Ryan and Tim after practice would work out together and would get on the ice and skate.

Once their games started they would do a ritual together. They would each smack an egg over each other's head. Supposedly it helped them in the game.

After a game against Omaha Ice Lancers they both went out and got drunk. Once they left the bar and they were in the car, Ryan was driving drunk as they were driving back to Washington. The car started to go out of control, they were weaving back and forth between each side of the road when they were at a light they ran it and didn't see a semi-truck coming at them! They tried to dodge the truck but the truck swerved the same way and hit them! Their car was totaled. Ryan suffered a major injury to his legs, which kept him from playing hockey for the rest of the season. But Tim suffered a sprained right arm, and a concussion.

When they got picked up by their coach in a bus they got lectured about drinking and driving and almost got kicked off the team. But by the mercy that he showed them, he let them stay, but he moved Tim back fourth line defense. Since Tim got moved back he decided to work even harder at his hockey. He started to get better grades and would work out by himself, just to get better so that maybe he could be on first line defense. He was motivated, and nothing could stop him. Ryan's injury made him realize he should play every game like it could be his last.

Tim would talk to Ryan all the time about his personal life. He liked this girl in his class named Stephanie. He told him that she had blonde hair, blue eyes and worked at an animal shelter. He told him that he just didn't have the guts to ask her out. He was afraid that he would get turned down. But since he was so motivated, he worked hard to impress her. So now he had more than one thing motivating him.

Soon, she became his girlfriend. Everything was coming together for him. He started to move up on his team and is now on the second line of defense. Now he is a straight A student and has a great personal life.

Even though everything is coming together for him, he still feels empty inside. So one day he decided to go to a church. He sat there and wondered... after a couple of minutes of just wondering about life, the priest came up to him and asked what was wrong. He told the priest that he just didn't know what to do. Tim said that his life was coming together and everything else but he still felt empty. The priest talked to him for a little while and the priest asked him if he wanted to become a Christian. Tim said yes. The priest and him prayed for a couple of minutes.

Now Tim is a Christian with very strong faith. Now he decided to try and convert Ryan and Stephanie. After a couple of weeks of trying to get them to believe he finally got Stephanie to believe. But Ryan rebelled and it took a lot more than Tim to make him believe. But he finally did!

The Washington Mad Hatters, Tim's team, were now twenty-four wins and six losses, well on their way to becoming Junior A champions. They had four games left until the playoffs. Now Tim has moved up to first line defense. After his hard work, he deserves it. He has fourteen goals and twenty- one assists. He is fifth on the team in points.

They needed to win one of their four games to go to the playoffs. But they won three out of four games. So they were sixth going into the playoffs. So they had to play the third seed team. Their game was an upset. They beat their opponent 7 - 1. Now they have to play the first place seed. They also upset them. They needed to win their next game to go to the championship game. It was a close game all the way up until the last three minutes, and then the Mad Hatters broke away and scored three goals in less than a minute and a half! They were now first place in their bracket. So now they go to the championship.

The team they played for the championship was a team they could not beat all season. They were the New York Tama-Hawks. Since this team was a team they could not beat all season the coach had to build up their confidence. So he gave them a big pep talk before the game. At the end of his pep talk Ryan ran into the room with his gear on. Tim, Ryan's best friend did not even know that Ryan was out of a cast. But Ryan was, he was healthy and ready to play.

It was an exciting game full of great hits and awesome goals. But the Mad Hatters were down at the end of the second, 4 - 2. They went into the locker room down. But when they came back out they had an energetic spirit. They tied it up with three minutes to go. With a minute to go, the Mad Hatters called a time out. They put their five best players on the ice. Ryan and Tim were about those five. When play started again, Ryan took the puck into the zone. He waited behind the net very patiently and finally when Tim got open, he gave Tim a pass. And Tim one-timed it, top left corner for the winning goal!

Tim got the MVP of the last game. After the game Tim, Ryan, and Stephanie went out to celebrate at a local Texas Road House this time none of them got drunk. In the middle of having dinner Tim got down on one knee and asked for Stephanie's hand in marriage. She accepted.

At the wedding Ryan was Tim's best man. At the after-party Ryan made a toast to Tim and his new wife and they have a happy and faithful life together and that their life is full of love in God.

Ryan and Tim kept in touch through the years. Tim and Ryan got drafted into the NHL at age twenty-three and twenty-four. Ryan got drafted to the New York Islanders. And Tim got drafted to the L. A. Kings. They both led great Christian lives for the rest of their lives.

Justin David Lee Slavin<br>
Age: 13

# A DIARY OF CRYSTELLE

### June, 1939

France has been declared an ally and Germany is occupying our streets and back roads. All the German soldiers say "How lucky you are at fourteen, to die in a war." Ohhh, I'm really starting to hate this war!

My mother has just given birth to my baby brother, Henri (on-re). She almost had a miscarriage because, she thought she might have to go to a concentration camp. Henri is crying so I must go. I hope tomorrow is better.

### July, 1939

Mother has gone out to get some medicine for Henri. He was very sick last night. It has been three hours. I must go and find them.

### Later

They have been arrested! The Nazi work for Hitler and they don't like the Jewish so they arrest us. I must find somewhere to hide!

### September, 1939

Today Marseille was bombed. I've made a plan to save Mama but the Resistance wrote to me and said "Your Mama has died in this war Crystelle (qui-sel). So has Henri, you will soon be captured and brought to the Nazi. Then you will die in a war, too, if you don't escape."

### December, 1940

Today I mourn for my Mama, it is her birthday.

Marie (may-he), my best friend, wrote from Arhus, Denmark. She is a Christian and has offered to take me in so I will be safe. I need to "find a day for fishing" as we would say. So good night for I am very tired.

### February, 1940

I've "found a day for fishing." I'll escape from France and this frantic war, in one month. If I left later, I would be sent to the Nazi.

### March, 1940

Today I am "going fishing" in Denmark. I already have a "cover." My new name is Suzanne (Su-zean) and I am going to be fifteen years old. Tonight I'll go to a funeral in disguise and escape with seven other Jewish people to Christians in France.

### January, 1945

Hooray, hip, hip, hooray!!! Finally this cruel, frantic war is over!!! Marie's parents officially adopted me and today I adopted a baby boy. I named him Henri after my baby brother. I've run out of pages in my diary, so I'll have to say good-bye.

Hannah B. Innes
Age: 10

## THE LONG WEDDING

At my grandma's wedding I was the flower girl. I was so scared I could barely throw out flowers. I saw people looking at me. I heard people whispering about me. My grandma was hyperventilating about what I should look like. She even bought me a gold crown! In the end I did good.

Cortney King
Age: 11

## WHEN MY BROTHER GOT HURT

One day when I was about three, my mom told my brother Zak, my sister Hannah and I that we were going to the park. So we ate lunch and started to get ready. My mom asked Hannah to go and get Zak some socks. My brother wanted to go with her but my mom said no, because she had to change his diaper. The phone rang and he went into his room. I wanted everyone to listen to my mom. So, I went into his room and picked him up. I decided to close my eyes, because I thought it would be fun. All of a sudden I ran into a wall and heard someone screaming. I opened my eyes and saw blood on the wall. I felt my brother's wet tears on my hand. The person screaming was my baby brother. I looked at him and his face was cherry red. I put him down and realized that I had cracked his head open. My mom came running! The next thing I know we are rushing to the hospital. When we were on our way my brother's head had a wet cloth on it. He was screaming so loud I could not hear anything. When we got to the hospital my brother had to get sixteen stitches!

Sarah Griess
Age: 11

I sat in the forest clearing, trying to think. My thoughts kept swirling around and around, unable to form into separate, clear thoughts. More had happened in the past few weeks than I could comprehend. My life had changed more than I ever dreamed possible -- all because of the Colonists who decided that they had no need of the British government! Why did they want a revolution when the British seemed to be governing these people nicely? Why do the Colonists need more land? And why would they want to take land that belongs to the Cherokee People?

It had all started several weeks ago when the British traders who came to my village regularly told us that the British army had been attacked at the battles of Lexington and Concord. They wanted my village of Cherokee people to help the British. While they did their trading, they told everyone who would listen that the rebel Colonists calling themselves Patriots, were wrong and needed to be stopped.

My village has been in an uproar ever since their visit. A few men who had been trading recently at other villages had heard how the British had a tyrannical way of governing their colonies, and that the Patriot rebels were only freeing themselves from this tyranny. Everyone formed his own opinion. The town elders held many meetings discussing these events. No one knew who to believe. People were turning against each other. All of this was happening because everyone was choosing sides about who was right in this revolution.

As I often did when I was confused, I ran to my mother for guidance.

"Mother," I said quietly, "What is going to happen to our wonderful Cherokee Nation if no one can agree on anything?"

My mother remained silent for a moment, then looked away from me as she said, "We cannot disagree forever. Soon this period of argument will pass. In the meantime, we must have faith that the Heavenly Spirits are watching over us and will let no harm come to our people."

"Will it be over soon?" I asked, not quite sure I believed her.

"Yes, Rose Blossom." Then she said determinedly, "We will be a whole people soon."

But our problems got worse. Soon my father and mother were arguing. My father had decided that the British had been the worst of dictators to the colonists who now called themselves Americans. My mother begged him not to take sides in this argument. As long as our people and land were left alone, she often told him, we had no reason to take part in the arguments. He would not listen to her. He always said that when our neighbors are in trouble, it is our duty to help them. He said that the Americans are our neighbors.

I did not know what to think. I really did not care about the battles that were going on many miles away. I cared about the division that they had brought to my usually peaceful village.

Though I had seen my village warriors fight many battles close to my home, they had always worked together-never against each other. Division in my village was a new experience.

As I sat in the forest clearing thinking how things had changed dramatically, I wondered if life would ever be the same. I heard horses galloping near where I was sitting. I wondered if it might be other traders coming to divide my village even more.

I ran back to my home in time to see men step from their horses as they called out that they needed to see the leader of our village. It seemed that they had urgent business to discuss. This worried me. I wondered if it was more news of the war that had divided my village.

It was. When my father told my mother and me about what had occurred, I was too upset to pay attention. The news had made the American supporters even more in favor of the Americans. The rift dividing my village had grown wider.

Later that day, my mother told me to go out and play with my friends. She had seen me moping around lately, doing none of the things I usually enjoyed. She wanted me to forget about the problems of my community.

"These problems," she said, "are no concern of yours. Now go outside and play. You'll feel better."

I went outside. Most of my friends were sitting around discussing the current division of the community. When I saw them sitting at opposite ends of the clearing where we usually played, I had an idea that could possibly bring us together. I got down on my hands and knees, and pretended to be a deer. This was our favorite game. One child, pretending to be a deer had to touch another child. That child was then the "deer."

My friends looked at me. They knew that I was trying to get them to play Deer with me. Then slowly, my friend Bluebird got up. She was one of the fastest of all of us, and she rarely got tagged. She ran up close to me, and as I lunged for her ankle, she darted swiftly away. This game continued for several minutes, and then I grabbed her ankle, and she fell on top of me, and we collapsed in a heap, laughing.

When our friends saw how much fun we were having, a few got up and played with us. Soon all of us were running and laughing like we used to do. We played for so long that a few adults came out of their huts to see what all the laughing was about.

The parents recognized their children and saw that they were playing with children of parents who were on the other side. They watched us all playing together. Slowly, adults who had stayed away from each other for several weeks came together to watch us enjoying our favorite game of Deer. I was running as hard as anyone and laughing the hardest of us all, yet I managed to watch the adults gathering around us.

We played for a very long time, 'til the shadows from the trees grew longer and longer. I saw that the whole village was now watching us. Then I saw my mother in the front of the crowd, smiling and talking to my father. They hadn't talked much to each other for weeks, and it had worried me greatly. I was so busy watching them that I failed to notice my friend Small Bear, who was then the deer. He tripped me, and I fell. Others behind me tripped over us. Soon, all of us were in a tired, laughing heap.

As I crawled out from the bottom of the heap, I saw Chief Great Oak walking toward us. We all stood up as he approached to show proper respect. He looked at us and said in his booming voice, "For weeks since the news of the American Revolution, our village has been divided. I know that all of us have taken sides and openly opposed those who do not agree with us. But I look at this crowd, and I see the entire village present - those who sympathize with the British and those who believe the Americans are right.

"All of us heard the laughter of our children and went outside to see what they were doing that was so much fun," he continued, a little quieter now. Then people who had been avoiding each other for weeks began to talk to each other again. Our children, playing a simple game of Deer, have made us realize that we may have different opinions, but we are still one people. We need to enjoy our time together."

I stood there with a triumphant smile upon my face. Not only had I gotten my friends to enjoy being together again, but I had also brought the community closer together. It was more than I could have hoped for.

In that instant, I knew that life would never be the same for my people or me. Yet, I knew also that if nothing else held us together, our way of life would, and it is strong enough to last through any war. I had no need to fear for the future of the Cherokee People.

Daisy Davis<br>
Age: 15

# THE LOOK OF LOVE

In a kingdom far, faraway lived a peasant girl named Victoria with her mother Millicent and father Barnaby. The unique thing about this young lady was she was the ugliest person you could lay your eyes upon. Her ragged, dirty hair hung down to her shins and her filthy skin was covered by tattered clothing. All the while, her parents had beautiful, flowing hair and soft complexions. Her family was quite poor and worked in the fields of Lord Quintain's manor for a living.

Now the time came in early August for the kingdom's Festival of Love, where young women were to be chosen as wives for the young men of the kingdom.

"Father, I cannot go. This is the fourth time I have dressed myself up and not been chosen," whined Victoria.

"Young lady, you can't give up. Now remember your criteria for a husband?" Barnaby questioned.

"Handsome, wealthy, well brought up," droned Victoria.

"Yes! Now your mother is tailoring your new dress and it should be finished in time for the festival."

Time crawled by slowly and it was finally time for the festival. Millicent, Victoria's mother, helped Victoria into a corset and buttoned up the dress. Now with all the makeup, clothes, and a new pair of shoes Victoria still looked absolutely hideous.

Completely discouraged, Victoria hopped into the ramshackle carriage her father built and rode into town for the festival. Men and women were gathered all around, and the discouraged Victoria hid herself behind a sack of potatoes in the carriage.

"What's wrong Victoria?" asked her father.

"I am afraid of failure and letting you down again," sobbed Victoria. "At age twenty-eight I am afraid that I will never find love and be alone for eternity. I feel I am so ugly even God won't accept me."

"Victoria, keep your head up, stay hopeful and strong, and you will find love, wealthy or not. Just find someone who pleases you," encouraged her father.

Enlightened, Victoria hopped out of the carriage with a bright smile on her face. She walked straight into the crowd and started jabbering with some friends.

The hours rolled by and suddenly Victoria was standing alone on the festival grounds. Sobbing uncontrollably, she stumbled to her father's carriage for the long journey home. Suddenly she heard a voice calling her name. She looked back and saw a young man still standing out in the middle of the grounds. She cautiously walked towards him and they exchanged hello's and started to chat. It was love at first sight.

A few days later Victoria and her companion, Miles, were married in Saint Mary's Catholic Church on the edge of town. They lived happily ever after and loved each other for their inner beauty.

Brooke Caton
Age: 12

# A TOMATO STORY

Twelve-year-old Thomas Hendric was at the supper table eating his usual amount of tomatoes when his father solemnly announced that the family was moving to St. Louis, Missouri. Everyone was upset especially Thomas. Thomas was the oldest of five children and was the only one who went to school. He had only moved once in his life; he moved when he was six months old and he didn't remember. When supper was over, Thomas took two tomatoes up to his room for dessert, as was his routine.

Later that evening Thomas began to wonder what school he would go to and where the school was. He also wondered if he would make any new friends. His dad came in when he was about to get up and ask him if he could reconsider the move.

"Do we have to move to a different state?" Thomas asked.

"Yes, I'm afraid so," Dad replied.

"But why?" Thomas asked in a questioning voice.

"Because, that is where my work is moving me," Dad said in a gruff voice.

Thomas took another bite of the tomato and let the juice run down his chin, which he never did unless he was mad or upset.

"I know this isn't going to be easy for you son, but if we don't move, we may not be able to afford very much. I would probably be fired, if I turned this job down," Dad said. Thomas didn't argue and went to sleep.

Two weeks later they were on their way to St. Louis. Once they settled in, Thomas went to school for the last five months of the school year. On the first day it all went well until lunch, when he opened his lunch box and took out the tomatoes and the salad. Everyone at that table laughed at him. He was confused. He asked them what they were laughing about.

They all said, "You like tomatoes?"

"Well yeah. So what?" Thomas asked puzzled.

No one could answer.

"Did you know that tomatoes are healthier than anything you are eating?" Thomas asked.

All the fifth graders looked at him and then at each other. "Of course we do," they all seemed to say at once.

"Would you like to try one?" Thomas asked.

"I guess," one said.

"They are better with salt and pepper," Thomas said. After that everyone wanted to have some.

The rest of the year went by smoothly. In fact, Thomas became quite popular. He talked to his friends and they all loved tomatoes by the end of the school year. All of his teachers were very proud of him because he made the school healthier.

The next year he made the school cleaner and a better place to go to. He started recycling everything and he got everyone to clean up outside as well as inside.

When Thomas grew up he became president and everyone was happy. He cleaned the U.S. by recycling. He made good decisions, when we could have gone to war he made a peace treaty. And he made a law of no smoking at all.

In 2012 Thomas's parents died of old age. They lived to be 98 years old. In 2051 Thomas died of old age also. He lived to be 100 years old, because of new medicine.

In the end, Thomas was one of the most famous people in not only Missouri, but in the United States as well, because of all the great things he did.

A lot of people say that on his grave there is a big tomato, as that is how it all started.

Alexander Hughes

# THE DAY THE TEACHER DIDN'T SHOW UP

Zeb and I galloped to Ben Franklin Elementary. Then we went into room 9. After that, we waited for some horrible seat work. One hour later, our teacher still hadn't come. We could not believe it! We all were very scared. Where was she?

Zeb shouted to Jenacie that she would be a good teacher. She said," O.K." After that she sat in Mrs. Santistevan's chair. "It is nice and cozy," Jenacie said. "I love this chair! I want to sit in this lovely chair every day!" Then she put her feet on the desk. Splash! A cup of water spilled. We all cleaned it up.

Now Jenacie was giving us directions for seat work. All the papers were wet because of that water. When she made us pass papers out, our hands were soaked. She did not let us dry our hands. The pencils kept falling out of our hands and our handwriting was horrible!

Jenacie yelled so loud that we should have a party. We all thought it was a good idea, so we partied. We got a radio and turned it all the way up. Next, we danced the disco and did the chicken dance.

We were still partying when the substitute came in. She said "Hi," and walked in. We ran to the radio and turned it off. After that, we sat in our seats. We tried to look like little angels, but I did not think it would work.

Then it was strange... she seemed to like to party! So she gave us all of the bobcat bucks and said we were angels. We all were very surprised. Later on, she started to party with us and said her name was, "Miss Party." We once again did the disco and chicken dance!

Larcy Brooks
Age: 8

## A SHOE'S LIFE

Are you feeling down in the dumps, or just plain crummy? If you feel like things can't get any worse, just look on the floor and talk to your shoe. Why, you ask? You might as well, because you're listening to one. People just don't listen or even care about us. My human does. Well at least after I told her about my life. She's at the store buying me some new laces. Since I have your undivided attention, and before you run away because of a talking shoe, I might as well go on with my life's story...

I'm a tennis shoe, and I was bought at K-Mart. I was bought for my human because she liked my style. I'm a pretty lucky shoe, I wasn't thrown in the shoe box, but I got to live on the floor in my human's room. I was worn every day to school. I liked school except for the cafeteria. It wasn't very fun to step in pudding or BBQ sauce, but that's another story. Shoes don't get very much credit, we get stepped on, jumped in, and keep your feet warm and safe, and you don't even pay a penny. I can't complain, I've had some thrills for only being half a year old. I once got to ride an escalator, it was fun! You're moving and you don't have to do any work. I also got to go to the fair. The rides were fun, but I lost my appetite for cotton candy when I saw somebody's shoes get barfed on. Those times were fun, but I still have one dream, to one day go and get a checkup at the shoe repair shop. I think it would be fun to get my scuff marks cleaned off, my soles checked, and best of all, stick out my tongue and say ahhhhhhh.

Well enough of my life, now on to the reason shoes don't get credit. Shoes don't get credit, not even a little because we are always there. We don't just walk off, well at least not without you. Second, we aren't mean, but people think we don't have feelings. And third, people don't like us for the way we are. For example, we may be tight on your feet, or we may keep coming untied. Well, we can't help that, that's the way we are.

My little story is done, and maybe you will be a little bit more loyal to us. Thanks for your time, and if you think your life is rough, just remember your shoes' life, too.

Jennifer M. Johnston
Age: 11

Lizzie and Micci were best friends. They had been ever since the second grade. Lizzie and Micci were known as the quiet, really smart kids in high school. After they had finished high school, they lost touch of each other until they ran into each other at the grocery store while doing their weekly shopping. Micci and Lizzie were both twenty-five years old now. They were built quite similar with long blonde hair and freckles lining their faces. They exclaimed at how long it had been since they had seen each other last and finally departed and went to pay for their things. During their short conversation they had made plans for a weekend getaway on a camping trip. So here they were, unpacking their things in one of the most secluded camping sites in the area.

They woke up in the morning to the call of the blue jays and busied themselves with starting the stove and cooking breakfast. The sizzling bacon and boiling coffee filled the air with its scent and made both of the girls' stomachs growl.

"I am sooo hungry..." exclaimed Lizzie.

"I know! So am I! It should be ready here shortly," she replied.

"Did you hear those noisy people last night? The ones that are camping right through the trees there? They and their noisy dog kept me awake all night last night," complained Micci.

"Yes, I heard them. I wonder when they're going to pack up and leave? It would be much more peaceful," sighed Lizzie.

After their breakfast of coffee, bacon, and pancakes the girls grabbed their fishing gear and headed off. They ended up trudging through about half a mile of mud and weeds so they would be able to reach the isolated beaver ponds. There had been a pond right next to their campsite, but they were afraid that the noisy people from the night before would start fishing there too. Both Lizzie and Micci thought it was well worth it because of all the fun they were having.

"There's some water," said Micci. "That will work just fine for me." The girls settled themselves down on the bank of the beaver pond and reached for their poles.

"Micci, look! It's a beaver," exclaimed Lizzie.

The girls watched intently as the beaver swam slowly through the pond and eventually disappeared beneath the water with a splash of its tail, which resulted in Micci and Lizzie getting quite wet. They had a day filled with fishing and hiking through the bushes. They were both exhausted when they got home and were barely able to make dinner for themselves.

"Well, I hope mac and cheese is OK with you because it is all I feel like making for now," said Micci who had taken on the cook's position of the camping trip.

"Yeah, that is fine with me," replied Lizzie. "And look, those people with their noisy dog must have left when we were gone! Finally, some peace and quiet."

The girls stared silently out into the shadowy forest. The pine trees cast their large shadows into the quickly fading light of the campsite. It was now Saturday night and they only had one more night left. They decided to go on a short hiking trip on Sunday and then return to pack up their bags so that they could return to their jobs on Monday. Then they went to bed.

"Micci, Micci! Wake up. I hear something. I think a car just drove up and at first I thought it might be campers but it is ten o'clock and no one is getting out of the vehicle," whispered Lizzie.

Micci slowly turned over and awoke after Lizzie's urgent shakes. They sat in the darkness while Micci tried to explain that it was probably just a couple of campers that had gotten a flat tire on the way up which had made them late.

"Well, then why aren't they getting out of their car or truck or whatever?" demanded Lizzie.

This question Micci had no answer for and they both waited in the dark with their air horn and pepper spray that had originally been meant for wandering bears. After ten to fifteen minutes they finally heard a car door open and heavy thuds like someone was tramping through the nearby beaver pond. That seems suspicious. People don't usually go camping on their own, thought the girls. Suddenly they heard thrashing sounds and big splashes coming from the direction of the beaver pond.

"What in the world is going on out there?" wondered Lizzie.

"Are they dropping body parts into the water or what?" asked Micci in a terrified tone.

The steps faded, as whoever was out there turned a couple of bends and walked into the distance.

By now both girls had bolted upright and were trembling with fear. It seemed as if their hearts were beating so loud that they could not hear what was going on outside. They discussed what they should do next as several shots from a gun were fired down by the beaver pond.

"Oh my! What is he doing firing a gun in the middle of the night like that?!" they exclaimed together.

The girls felt that they were sitting ducks for this madman and realized that this might be their last chance to escape from the tent. The girls decided to sneak out of the tent and hide in the bushes a little ways away from the tent. They quickly unzipped the tent and bolted for the bushes. Suddenly shadows became dangerous creatures and it seemed as if they stepped on every twig in their path. They waited in the bushes or an undetermined amount of time shaking with fear. After a while they heard the person get back into heir vehicle and drive off. They waited for a while then jumped into action packing up their camp as quickly as person get back into their vehicle and drive off. They waited for a while then jumped into action packing up their camp as quickly as they could. Who would stay there with some madman shooting off a gun in the middle of the night?! It was approximately 1:00 in the morning when they started the Jeep and headed back home, while looking over their shoulder the whole way.

"What was that?!" exclaimed Micci.

"I have nooo idea." replied Lizzie.

"I have never encountered anything like that on a camping trip before..." mumbled Micci.

Monday morning had come and the incident from the weekend had been pushed back into the back of both of the girls' minds. There was just one more thing Micci had to do. Early Monday morning she called the sheriff's department and reported the gunshots and asked if they knew what might have been going on.

"Well, chances are it was a beaver poacher. There have been a couple of other reports of the same type of situation. There are not a whole lot of things we can do. We've been trying to crack down on these guys but we cannot seem to catch them. I appreciate your call. We'll keep trying!" said the sheriff.

Cydney Naill
Age: 13

# JACOB'S STORY

"Catch me if you can," Jacob, a fifteen-year-old teen, muttered. Picking up a wrench, he began thrashing it against the door. Suddenly, the wrench recoiled with a CLANG! It flew back and shattered a window. Uh-oh. A series of searchlights hummed for a second, then flicked on, all of them groping around the darkness for Jacob. He dived into the underbrush, and realizing he didn't have much time, crept through the overgrown vegetation around Texas State Penitentiary, as one wrong move meant that it became jail time for him. Traipsing around the Maximum Security Zone, Jacob fumbled with the layout blueprints as he realized he crept near the disc.

"Got it!" he exclaimed. He sprayed the disc with water to clean off fingerprints, but at the same moment, five search lights zeroed onto him.

"Why am I here?" Jacob cursed, "What did I do to deserve this?"

"If... you... get... caught..," Jacob's father stammered five hours before while smoking a pipe. Jake's father exhaled with a sigh directly in Jake's face and muttered, "I'm expecting just this from you, son. First off, you will be inserted into Texas State Penitentiary, overtaken by inmates. They have stolen a very important disc, that when encoded, endanger all agents of the CIA." He waited a while to let this sink in. "I have broken my leg, and am not capable of this. Grab the disc, make sure it has no wires on it, and get out of there. An extraction van will be waiting at approximately 2400 hours."

Jake stepped into the van, breathing deeply. Abruptly, the door opened, revealing the never-ending labyrinth of the prison. Jacob's father smiled and whispered, "You know what to do from here. Be a good boy." A quick bound from the door and he sprinted off. The first step became getting into the blasted place. Seizing a wrench, Jacob launched it into the door, which gave way and...

Suddenly, Jacob blinked into the present. Searchlights circled around the perimeter. Seizing his scissors, Jacob carefully snipped off the alarm wires on the disc, and high-tailed it out of there. Securing the disc safely in his pocket, Jacob accidentally stumbled on a rock. Men poured out of the prison's confines. Jacob tumbled into the extraction van, meeting his father there. With a pat on Jacob's head, he smiled. "Now that's a good boy!"

Kevin Li
Age: 10

17

It was a sunny morning in my new apartment. New York City, to me, seemed more air polluted than Fresno, California. But nothing stopped me from playing basketball, so I got up out of bed. As I laced up my new Adidas I just got, I thought about what Matt was doing back home. Probably sleeping, since I was three hours ahead. Just then my dog zipped in and started licking me like I was a piece of candy.

My mother laughed and asked, "Xavier, what are you going to do today?"

My mom had to know everything from who my friend was to what I am going to do in my room. I guess she was just trying to be protective, but sometimes it seemed overprotective.

I grabbed my basketball, the brisk feel of the ball giving me a tingle of excitement.

Mother called, "Xavier are you going to answer me?"

I said in an obvious voice, "Basketball probably if I can find a court."

I grabbed my wristband on my way out the door. As I walked out, my mother, as always, screamed, "Be home by dinner!"

I walked down Colorado Avenue towards Jackson Park. As I dribbled the ball, it gave me a feeling of excitement. I saw some basketball hoops on the west side of the park. There was a guy about five foot six inches, dark hair, light skin, and a mad jump shot. As I got closer he did a fabulous 360° dunk. I thought to myself if I want to play him I need magic on my side. He put the ball down and grabbed his water bottle like his life depended on it. I walked up to him and complimented him on his dunk.

He just asked, "What is your name?"

"X-Xavier, what 'bout you?" I replied.

"Mike Elrick, but people call me Mlrick. I am sixteen, you?" he said.

"Sixteen too," I replied quickly.

"Well if you want to play, don't even think about it," he said looking to the right. A big and muscular man with a guy just like him was walking right towards us.

"Yo, Mlick! You want to take me?" the man said with a cocky attitude.

"Yeah, me and Xavier will take you and your boyfriend!" Mike barked back.

"No way! White trash ain't playing on my court!" the man yelled.

"Shut up Jason, I bet he could drive your school bus!" Mike barked again.

So Jason, who was six foot five inches, was challenged into playing. We got the ball first.

Mike drove and slammed the basketball down so hard it was sick. With the score 1- 0 we were up! We trapped J. J., his friend, in the corner and stole the ball. Mlrick passed to me then I pulled up a two... swish! Now it was 3 - 0 and eight more points and we had the win over the jerks of the century. J. J. tried to alley-oop Jason, but missed him by a mile. Mike passed me the ball, I hit another two, two pointers making it 7 - 0. Then Mlrick slammed it down hard four more times in a row. At 11 - 0 we had won and the court was ours.

Jason yells, "How 'bout me versus Mlrick?"

"Watch your back Jason! I'll take you right here, right now!"

Bang! Just like that the game was over. Jason slaughtered Mlrick 11 - 2.

I had to do something so I said "Hey Jason! In one week we will play you in 3 on 3 for the court. A win always gets the court."

"Well... you got a match!" replied Jason.

Mike and I had left but we started thinking... for a 3 on 3 we needed one more guy, maybe even two more guys. Mike said he knew two guys, Jack Harvester and Paul Buddy.

Later that day, I was eating with my mom and she asked what I did today. She was excited that I made a friend. That night I had a dream about being at a funeral, but I did not know who it was for. It really freaked me out. I was scared for it could be my mom. She was all I had and I could not lose her.

A week passed. I went to the park. Jason and his friends were shooting around. Mlrick, Paul, and Jack were talking. Right when I stepped on the court the game began. The game went by quick. It was 9 - 7 in their favor already. It was our ball and I hit a two-pointer then we stole it again. I hit the game-winning two-pointer as Jason pulled out a gun. He pointed it right at me and before I knew it, Mlick dove in front of me. He took the bullet right through the chest.

A cop nearby heard the gunshot and arrested Jason right on the spot. Mlrick was dead and now I know that my dream was about him. The next day I walked the streets and met a kid named Isiah Morgan and basketball has never been the same.

Drew Willeke<br>
Age: 13

# PEPSI ISLAND

On July 2, 1986, John Smith was getting ready to leave to head back home. After three extensive months at sea he was exhausted. He missed his friends and family back in San Francisco. He worked on a boat called "The S.S. Menoe" and made a living fishing for squid. The boat was fairly small and there were six other people with him.

They were dropping off their shipment in east Australia and would stay there for the duration of the week. John was glad to be able to stay in a decent hotel and in a comfortable bed. The captain, Frank Larson told the crew they would be leaving at six thirty in the morning to depart for the United States. The night before they were going to leave he couldn't sleep. It was a cold stormy night and the rain was dreadful. He was looking forward to seeing his family so much he just couldn't wait. "I hope it's a clear day tomorrow, but with this rain there's no telling what could happen," John thought to himself.

The next day John woke up around 5:30 a.m. He lay there listening to the songs of the birds, when the captain quietly knocked on his cedar hotel door. John knew it was time to pack and get ready to leave. He opened his shades and looked out the window. It was a beautiful day, not a single cloud in the sky. It would take them two nights and three days to get to the mainland of North America.

John went down to find his crew enjoying breakfast. The captain lifted his coffee mug and said to John, "Make sure you have a decent breakfast, we have a long few days ahead of us. The news said we might run into some nasty weather in about a day, but I'm not worried about it."

The captain was right. At about seven thirty the next morning, they ran into huge waves and massive amounts of rain. The first day turned out to be fine, but the next day was expected to be worse. The waves were about forty feet high and the boat was only fifty feet long and thirty feet wide. John knew that the boat wouldn't make it.

Suddenly, a bolt of lightning struck the steel mast of the boat. The boat began to fall apart. A large steel chunk struck John straight on the head. He lost his balance and fell down. He realized if he wanted to survive he would have to make his way to the small safety raft. It was tied to the right side of the boat so he crawled on his knees. All of the other crew members were soon washed off the boat. He soon fell unconscious from the blow to the head. The raft floated atop the waves for the duration of the night.

It was early the next day when he awoke. He had washed up on an unfamiliar place, an island. He lay there, shocked, reflecting on what happened the night before. He had a splitting headache and reached for the left pocket of his jeans and pulled out aspirin. He took a few and then he soon fell asleep.

It was late afternoon, around four p.m. before he woke up. He went to go sit on the shore and put his feet in the water. Half buried under the sand he saw an odd piece of aluminum. It was a Pepsi can that had floated ashore. He thought to himself, "I think I will call this place Pepsi Island."

John realized that he had to do many things in order to survive the night, like build a shelter, find food, and fresh water. It was not long before he found large pieces of driftwood and gigantic leaves. He would make the base of the shelter out of driftwood and then make the roof (shingles) of leaves. He began to ask himself, "Am I going to survive?"

John had to clear his mind of everything so he went to go lie under his small hut and again he fell asleep.

He awoke the next day around noon and was very hungry. He began to look around for some source of food. He quickly found some coconuts lying under the tree but they had no milk inside. He took an old coconut from the ground and launched it at the coconuts still attached to the tree. He made contact and both coconuts fell to the ground. He pulled out his large pocketknife and cut a hole in the top of the coconut. After eating two or three coconuts he began to explore the island.

He only walked a mile into the inland before he got tired and began to head back to his camp. The next morning he decided he would explore as much of the island as he could in one day. He saw a few animals on his way including lizards, birds, and many insects. He was around ten miles in when he found a small waterfall. The waterfall ran into a small freshwater pond. He gulped as much of the water as he could. He could tell he was dehydrated. John decided he would build another shelter in that area, so he would have access to fresh water. There would be plenty of coconuts so he would be set for food and water for the next few days.

About three days later he went further into the island. He thought this island had to be a circumference of ten to fifteen miles. He saw a sight that greatly frightened him. At the edge of the jungle was a giant field of sugar cane. In the middle of the field there was a wheat patch in the form of a circle with a wavy line through it. He walked further down the sugar cane field and found a wheat patch in the shape of the letter "P." The further he walked down the field the more patches there were.

At the bottom of the hill there was something he thought he would never see again. A large cement building, a metal tower, and a helicopter. He sprinted towards the building and headed for the door.

As John boarded the helicopter he looked back at the island in awe. He asked the pilot if he might know why there was a Pepsi can on the shore. He answered, "Oh, sometimes they drift off the island and then the current picks them back up again."

John asked "What island did they drift off of?"

Then he saw the wheat patches and knew what the wheat patches said. It spelled out Pepsi in large letters and had the logo.

It would take them three hours to get to San Francisco, but they were expected to hit some nasty weather...

Dylan McIntire
Age: 13

21

"Jeroma a lose," claimed King Edward.

"What?" asked Sage.

King Edward looked at her like she was the one who said the saying "Jeroma a lose."

"Excuse me, "Edward replied, "I mean to say that 'Jeroma a lose' means uh, I think, to take good chances. I think."

Sage, who was confused in a way, and said, "Oh." Edward was sitting at his throne staring off into the distance and said to Sage, "Never forget that."

Sage walked away and mumbled, "Sure," though she knew she would probably forget about it. As Sage's shoes clicked on the marble floor, she thought about what it would be like if she wasn't a princess of the island and country of Gallio.

Sage had blue eyes and dark brown hair, it was a bit stringy, like when longish hair is wet. Sage had bangs but they were down to her cheek. When she smiled, her eyes would light up. She wasn't fat, nor skinny, she was average. Sage went into her room and lay on her bed, which was very comfortable. She was thinking about what year it was and how time goes by so quickly. It was the year of 2092 and scientists say, in her century, that the island was founded in 2015, but Sage thought it was founded in 2004. Sage knew nothing about other countries, 'cause there were no other countries around Gallio. "But how am I supposed to know. I'm only fourteen," Sage muttered to herself. Jerosh, her middle brother, came in the room. "You're talking to yourself again."

"Huh?" Sage said, stumbling out of thought. "What are you doing in here? I thought you went swimming in the lake?" Jerosh was standing in the doorway, trying to look sophisticated. Suddenly, a thought came into Sage's head. "What if I could go and find the history of our country! Nah, that would take days, or months, or even years! I might have to run away, go through the country. Wait, but that would be dangerous, should I?" All these thoughts crammed in her brain.

She looked in the doorway and Jerosh was not there. Sage curiously looked around the stone-candlelit room. Then she got off her bed and ran through the long, dim corridor to her father's throne. "Father," Sage came into view to the king, "Father, since you're the king of Gallio, you know a lot about our country, right?" "No, not really, why?" King Edward asked as he finished his chicken. "Oh, I don't know, I, I want to find out the history of Gallio," Sage said glumly. "Now, you don't really want to find out boring history like that, do you?" The king looked at Sage with one eyebrow up.

Sage looked at him and said "Well, yeah, I want to find out about our country Gallio." Then Sage walked away, discouraged.

As Sage was going up to her room, Puzo, her personal guard came to her. "So, what's the matter?" Puzo said, sounding like he knew what the matter was.

"Do you think I should run away to find out the history of Gallio?" Sage said quickly.

Puzo looked at her and said "That's a good question, 'cause it would be hard to cover you while you're away, and where will you go?" Puzo talked a lot and could talk fast too.

Sage stepped forward to Puzo, and put a hand on his tall shoulder. "Puzo, I think I'm going to run away, to find the history of Gallio, and because I, I, need an adventure, and I w-want to."

Puzo looked at her like he was telling a joke. "Are you sure that you can live and survive out there? I mean, hah, you're going to have to pack everything you will need, in a bag!"

Sage felt a little discouraged again, and Puzo saw that.

"Today, I'll help you get ready on this exploration of yours," Puzo said as Sage hugged him.

As soon as you knew it, Sage and Puzo were packing food, clothes, blankets, a canvas for a tent and a couple of matches to make a fire. All this fit into a deerskin bag.

All the rest of the day Sage was silent. If King Edward asked her what she's been doing, Sage would just say, "Oh, nothing."

Evening came, and Sage got more and more nervous. Soon afterward everyone was fast asleep except for Sage and Puzo.

Sage walked out expecting to meet Puzo there, and he was. Sage looked at Puzo concerned and said, "I'll be okay." Puzo understood. "Someone will meet with you, and you'll know who it is."

Sage was satisfied, and smiled at Puzo. Then she walked off into the darkness. "Jeroma a lose," Sage said, knowing she was taking a good chance.

Meghan Olson
Age: 11

# MARIO IN SPACE!

"It's superior, it's super twentieth century fun, it's... Mario In Space! Hurry and get it now while supplies last!" the reporter said in a hurried voice. He turned off the TV.

"Mommy, Mommy!" Danny O'Iram whined through the gap where his two front teeth used to be, knowing Danny; the little excuse "two kids knocked 'um out" was most likely a white lie.

"What is it my sweet little pumpkin dumpling."

"I want this new game, it's better than Mario In The Jungle, and... and... I really want it!" Danny screeched!

"Well you know we don't have that much money right now!"

"MOM go to the store and get that game right now! Don't you love me?!"

Danny rambled on and on as he walked selfishly into his room overstuffed with toys. He stubbornly sat down and played all his other Mario In Something games. Danny, having his plan all set out, started whining and complaining how boring and old all these games were, until he heard the jingling of keys and the garage door shut!

"Yes!" he yelled! Danny had gotten his way again (this wasn't unusual).

Before Danny knew it he was playing the "Mario In Space" game! Having nothing better to do, he passed almost all the levels, however there was one particular level he couldn't manage to pass Gold Planet. You see in Gold Planet Mario saw gold and things he thought he couldn't live without on Jupiter so it was a trap. Although, it was like Mario had a brain of his own in this level. His head always got stuck in space and he couldn't concentrate on the things that really mattered in the game. So as weeks passed Danny ignored all the things that once mattered in his life like his friends and family. So on the bus home, thinking out loud he stated, "I just have to..."

"Pass the level," he was interrupted by his best bud Margie.

"No Marge!" Danny said. "I just have to get the gold on Jupiter."

"Oh, I see" she said sadly. So his obsession went on.

Nobody did anything about Danny's behavior, until the most unlikely thing happened; it started in the summer of 2003.

The sun barely peeked its fuzzy electric beam over the mountain just as Mario beat level eleven the one right before Gold Planet. Mario had a new saying, he had one every so often. Today's was, "Today will be a day of change." Danny didn't know but as the succulent clone of a perfect orange popped up in the sky Mario was right, it would be a day of change.

Danny had been up playing his game all starry night! He had forgotten about everything that did not exist inside the electronic battery-operated game. That included; that it was the first day of summer and Margie's party. Danny didn't care! He blinked his dreary droopy eyes before taking another shot at beating the level Gold Planet, but as his eyes closed he pushed a button... one that wasn't there before. All he knew was that when he opened his bloodshot ovals he wasn't lying snuggled in his bed! Danny was in Mario In Space or should I say he was Mario In Space!

"A...A...A...!" Danny stuttered as he paced around violently. "Hello out there!" His only answer was a strange creature charging at him. Danny then realized that he was going to have to play and beat the game, from the inside, in order to exit the electronic world! Danny jumped, with sweat bolts streaming down his face, he yelled, "Let the games begin!"

Danny started running, like he'd done so many times before, but this time it was not with his hands frantically working the controls but he was actually in the game. Danny jumped from star to star, dodging spaceships and meteorites 'til he reached Jupiter; there he could see the sparkling glow of the Gold Planet. Since he already had a problem with getting whatever he wanted, he couldn't just pass up the gold that had been his goal for so long. The night in space was getting darker and the timer clock was ticking. Danny leaped over big bubbling red spots and avoided the alien ships that periodically came flying at him out of nowhere. Finally he reached his goal... the gold!!! He slowed to a jog and walked cautiously toward the gold, then his greed took him over and he started racing no one but the wind to get there. Then strangely the gold disappeared turning into hideous looking, gigantic aliens! Danny started to run and doing whatever he could to get away. "Help... Help I'm..." he blacked out! "WOW! What just happened?" he questioned when his eyes flittered open again. He wasn't home yet, but the words flashing in front of him explained it all "two lives left." "Oh no," he muttered to himself, "if I die again, I may not be able to return."

OK, he thought, I'm going to have to pass this level without getting the so-called gold. Danny viciously started to rampage everywhere exploring the blood-red planet. He was fantastic at defeating the alien creatures. That's when he came to a spot that did not look at all desirable to just walk into. This junk field on the planet contained nothing but huge gory giants! Danny realized that he had no weapons; there was no way to defeat them. So Danny, out of fear started to run! Boom! A giant took a swing at him, AAAAA!! Then unexpectedly the giant fell to the ground. "Maybe I do have a weapon," Danny said in a sly voice. He went on screaming, and was loving the temporary earthquake each giant made when they fell. He saw that an oversized giant was right in front of him; he let out an extra big scream, while anxiously waiting for the thunder the ground would make. Danny looked up... only to see that the giant was falling right on him!!! Blackout. "One life left."

When he awoke, he could see the exit porthole. He started to step through it. A robotic voice then came and said, "And where do you think you're going? You still have one last challenge." Then she came on again without giving Danny a chance to talk, "Congratulations, you have made the journey, now accept your last challenge."

"All right, bring it on... but make it snappy."

The robot voice came back on, "It's a riddle; here it is: You have passed this level, indeed you have overcome your greed. You and Mario have relations, that's why I say congratulations. What two connections do you have? First is greed the second is on your behalf."

"What is our other connection? Um..."

Danny O'Iram sat there for a while, his brain frantically searching each capsule of information that might possibly hold the least bit of information for him. Finally his name was the only thing that gave the littlest hint of a link to Mario. The sun was shrinking by the minute, unfortunately when it went down his time was up and he'd have to face another black out, and still the only thing he could think of was his name. Danny O'Iram, Danny O'Iram ran from one end of his brain to the other.

"O'IRAM I get it," Danny suddenly said.

The robotic voice came back on, "Do you have an answer?"

"Yes, yes my last name of course... it spells Mario backwards!!"

"Why yes you are right."

The porthole opened, Danny took one last glance at the world that he once only observed with his eyes and now had run with his feet and felt with his hands. He walked out knowing exactly what he had to do when he got back... Margie's party.

Thump! Thump! Danny was back in the real world and was making his way steadily to Margie's house for her party. He finally made it just as...

"Hey were is everybody going?"

"The party's over, thanks for coming," Margie stated sarcastically.

"I'm really sorry I guess I just..."

"Wanted to get the gold on Jupiter, I know," she finished his sentence weakly.

"Well that too, but that was just greed, I decided to pass it and start paying attention to things that really matter."

"Are you pulling my leg?"

"No!"

"Wow! You're practically changed completely!" Margie said excitedly then she got a stern voice, "so, are you OK?"

"Yeah, but did you know that my last name spells Mario backwards?"

"Yeah, you've just been too into that stupid game to notice. What happened anyway?"

"That's for me to know and you to find out, because next time you're going with me."

They both giggled and walked off into the sunset having the time of their lives!!!

Kendra Hamman
Age: 12

# THE MARINE IGUANA

Hola, me llamo Christobal, la iguana marina. I live on Española Island in the Galapagus Islands, and I'm going to tell you a story about me.

It starts out when I was little and my mom and dad just told me to watch out for cats because they will eat marine iguanas. After they told me that, they said I could go out into the water and eat some algae.

While I was eating, I met a friend named Tyler and he is a marine iguana too. Tyler and I ate for a long time. When we quit eating, we lay in the sun to get our body temperature back because the water is cold and it brings our body temperatures down.

While we were walking home from lying in the sun, we saw a cat. Tyler did not know that the cat would eat him because his parents did not tell him. I started to hit the cat with my tail and it scared him off.

After the cat ran away, I told Tyler about the cats. On the rest of the way home, I also met a prickly pear cactus. I said, "Cómo estas?" The prickly pear said, "No, muy bien." Then I asked him what was wrong. The prickly pear said, "My dad got eaten by a tortoise."

The prickly pear was crying after he said that. So I thought if there was anything I could do. Then I got an idea. My idea was to find a seed from the prickly pear's dad and plant it and so I asked him where his dad had gotten eaten.

After I asked the prickly pear where his dad had gotten eaten, I went there. I picked up a seed and planted it next to the prickly pear. The prickly pear said, "Gracias." Finally, my friend and I went home.

Chris Conroy
Age: 10

# MY TRAMP

When I was jumping on my tramp with my friend he went up in the air so high. On his way down he landed on his back. This launched me up into the air and I almost fell on his head. But he moved really fast so he wouldn't get smashed. The next day we jumped and we put a big red ball on the tramp. We tried not to touch it. But, when it got close to me I tried to jump over it. But it got closer and my leg got caught in-between two springs. It hurt so badly. And it caused me to faint for one or two minutes. Then I got up and I jumped again. And I hope I don't get caught in the springs again.

Charlie Bernal
Age: 9

# THE SCARED CHILDREN

It was a cloudy ink-black Halloween night. My mom, brother, and I just got back from trick-or-treating. My dad was at work. It was getting late. We were watching SpongeBob SquarePants on TV. I was getting thirsty. I looked over but my mom was gone! I didn't know what had happened to her.

My brother and I looked in my mom's room. It was so so dark. We saw a flash of light outside. We tried to look, but my mom had a desk. I tried to get on the desk, but it was broken. I did not know what to do. My brother and I went downstairs. I saw a person outside the window. I was frightened. I didn't want to tell my brother or else he would get scared. Then we heard a freaky noise. I thought it was my brother. It wasn't my brother. Who could it be.

My brother and I looked in the bathroom behind the shower curtains. She wasn't there. I looked all over the place. My brother thought she got flushed down the toilet. I looked in the sink. She wasn't there. My brother and I went to look outside. We were really frightened. We saw the tree shake. I didn't want to look, but I had to. I was scared. I didn't know what to do. My brother and I saw the tree shake again. Then we heard a noise. It sounded like my mom. We looked behind the tree. I held my brother's hand. "BOO" went my mom. My brother and I screamed. I think we woke up the neighbors. Then we went in the house and laughed about it.

Alexis Rae – Jōn Gurule
Age: 9

It was eight months now since Gettysburg, and Charley was heading back home. Back to his ma and brother. Coming home with a rich amount of $88.00. Also coming home with a Confederate soldier's revolver, which he had to use on three Rebel soldiers. Here's what happened. Charley was just walking when he heard bushes rustling around. That led to two or three Rebels bursting through the bushes firing their bayonets. He took my revolver and fired and hit one tall man in the chest, and took a very fat man in the shoulder. So he picked up one of their bayonets and fired at the third. He bit off the paper cartridge and reloaded his gun. But after a minute he realized there were no more Rebels. So he went on walking. But in the distance he saw a little hut, he started to run faster and harder. When he got there, his heart froze. His brother Gabrial was sitting there, playing with a little Rebel's boy. He knelt down, hugged his brother then ran inside and out no mother in either place. He sat down and asked his brother, "Where's Ma?"

"Ma died," said Gabrial. "I live with Jeramiah over there."

"You live with Rebels," he said.

"They're good Rebels, they've not joined war yet."

He broke into a massive hysteria. He was shocked to hear Mother died, and Gabrial lived with Rebels. He was so mad he kicked one of the Rebels off their horse and stole the horse. He rode freely, freely for many miles. 'Til he ran across a postman. He stopped him and asked if he had any mail for Charley Nelson.

He said, "Yes, actually I do. Here it is."

30

When Charley read it, he shook his head in disbelief. What, they want me to be a general in the continental army. It says here, in this letter that if you come back to the grounds of Gettysburg, since you were one of the only survivors. Your rank will be general. So come and fight for an honor, and a privilege. Although Charley just got back, he was on his way to becoming a general. Stopping once a day to buy food and water. When he was halfway there he had $46.00. Along the way he met a nice little girl, who gave him some cake. After one month and two weeks he reached the war tent. When he entered he was greeted many times. When he was walking around he saw many lovely foods. Such as pig, horse, cow, and many fine desserts. He didn't eat much. Mostly just walked around talking to people. But his best friend was the colonel. He said the battle tomorrow would end the war. The next day Charley got up early. He ate like a general, dressed like a general. Even talked like one. When it was time for battle, Charley was ready. It was much better a battle this time. We had two thousand four hundred infantry and two thousand calvary. The Rebels had three thousand infantry. This was it, the firing had begun. Next to Charley, the colonel got his head blown off and it disappeared. NNNNOOOOOooooo. How could this happen? First Massey then the Lieutenant, Nelson, Ma. Now the colonel. So Charley went insane and killed all who would stand in his way. All he saw was arms, legs, heads, and even ribs flying off, and the blood was terrible. It was all over him. That day Charley died, but was honored. Also that day the continentals fought like English warriors. They fought like Americans, and won their freedom.

Marcus Naab
Age: 9

# CANDY LAND

So there I was, sitting in a lame-o Jeep with my twin brother, Ryan. We were seven the last time we visited Candy Land. Apparently King Kandy wanted to give us an award and Ryan forgot the way to the castle.

"It's five blocks up; the first orange."

"No, it's the second orange," my brother retorted.

"You're a blockhead, Ryan! Right there; the sign says Rainbow Trail. Turn!" Great, now we have to go down who knows how many more blocks.

We'd been driving awhile when Ryan abruptly swerved to the left; only to get us stuck in Gumdrop Mountain.

"What was that about?" I asked.

"I don't know," Ryan replied. "I guess I got hungry. The mountains looked appetizing."

"Jolly! Jooo-lly!" my cry for help didn't work.

"What're you doing?" Ryan questioned my rescue attempt.

"See if Jolly will help us. Jol --" Suddenly, Jolly strode into sight.

"Oh, hey Rachael, Ryan. You're in a real pickle -- I mean a gumdrop. Ha ha ho! Seems like you'll have to eat your way out."

"Uh-oh," Ryan rolled his eyes.

"I totally don't think so. Gaining weight is so not 'in'," I informed Jolly.

"Well then, kids, I don't know what you're gonna do," Jolly scratched his head. I saw Ryan trying to think but the gumdrops on his "Simpsons" T-shirt was distracting him. He pulled his foot as near his big mouth as possible. When Ryan found out he wasn't flexible enough to lick his shoe he stomped. Gumdrop goo splattered everywhere which jump-started my brain.

"Hey Jolly! Step right between Ryan, me and the car," I hollered.

"Well what for?" Jolly twisted his face. Though he didn't know why, he stepped exactly in the right spot. Ryan and I were free... from the car. The big gumdrop we were in split and our half started tumbling.

We were finally stopped by a candy cane. Mr. Mint was near a cane and raised his head with a smile. Mr. Mint brought a whistle to his lips and blew a little ditty. When he'd finished, Ryan and I clapped.

"Encore," bellowed my brother.

Mr. Mint's cheeks turned the color of cherries as he bowed.

"My word! Is that you Ryan? Rachael? Well it's been ten long years since I've seen you. Now that King Kandy's back on the throne, everything is minty."

I giggled at his English accent.

When I tried to get a whiff of the Mint Forest I was reminded that we were stuck inside a gumdrop.

"Yeah, we're just on our way to see the king," I began to explain.

"For some award thingy. Hey Mr. Mint --" Ryan cut in.

"Oh, please," Mr. Mint squeaked, "call me Monte."

"OK... Monte. Can you help us out of this gumdrop?"

"Why of course. I'll have you out in no time." Under a candy cane was a striped ax. He picked it up and in just a few mighty hacks Ryan and I were free, sticky, but free.

"Thanks, but we really have to skedaddle." I felt bad about not staying to chat.

"If you must leave, take this." Monte unfolded his hand, revealing the whistle he had just played. "Blow it and anyone in Candy Land will be at your side. They all owe me but let's not get into that."

With our whistle, Ryan and I continued our journey to the castle on foot.

**********

"My feet are totally killing me," I whined.

"I told you not to wear those shoes. We just passed Gramma Nut's house so we're almost there," my brother grumbled.

It was getting dark when a thin man wearing pepper red from head to toe appeared. The mystery man spoke: "Children, you should go this way. It's by far the quickest way to the castle." The words slithered out of his mouth. He bowed, showing us a chocolate tunnel. Ryan hurried to the opening gesturing me to follow. The mystery man had mysteriously vanished.

"I don't know Ryan; that guy looked really... twisted."

"Don't worry about it sis." Ryan punched me in the arm.

**********

We'd been walking FOREVER when we saw a light! Whoever was there had to have food. The light was the sun! Ryan and I had walked through the night! I noticed Plumby's plum trees.

"Whatcha look -- oh," said I. "That 'short-cut' led us the way back to the beginning!"

"Kids!" Plumby's stout figure came into view. "What happened?"

I told the whole miserable story.

"What're you gonna do? Plumby stroked his beard. "How 'bout me givin' you a ride?"

"Great, but first can we have some food?" I asked.

"Pick all the plums y'all want. You can eat on the way." Plumby pointed to some baskets that I quickly filled.

When I had picked all I needed, I jumped into Plumby's Jeep.

"Come on Ryan, Plumby and I are ready." Ryan was going way too slow. I slammed the door. We were off! An hour later, Plumby pulled over.

"What's wrong?" my brother asked.

"Molasses Swamp. Can't drive through it." Plumby turned the key and we hopped out.

"Thanks Plumby." I gave him a hug.

"You guys be careful." Plumby waved good-bye and headed towards home.

Ryan and I hadn't walked far when we got stuck.

"Yuck! The yummy stickiness of the swamp has caught us!" my brother hackled.

"Let's eat our way out." I began to eat away.

I remembered the whistle. I whipped it from my back pocket and blew as hard as possible. Sure enough, Gloppy, the castle guard, came to our rescue.

"What is it this time Monte? Oh, it's you kids. You know it's been so long since I've seen you two." Gloppy smiled.

"Hi, Gloppy. Would you get us out of here?" I proposed. Gloppy got to work. He -- being a creature made of molasses oozed across the swamp and heaved us out.

Gloppy escorted us to the castle. It wasn't long before we saw the ice-cream clouds of the palace. Gloppy opened the massive ice-cream cone door then went back to his post. Inside, leaning on his licorice cane, was Lord Licorice! His long, maroon cape draped in front of him.

"You ruined my plot to take over Candy Land once and you won't do it again!" spat Lord Licorice. He bopped us over the head with his cane.

34

**\*\*\*\*\*\*\*\*\*\***

I awoke to Ryan's barks. We were tied to a lollipop stick with licorice ropes. The room was full of piled sweets. We were still in the castle where the walls were made of waffle cones.

"Eat, Rachael, eat! We can eat our way out." Ryan ripped a chunk out of the ropes with his teeth.

I just looked at him. "Is that your answer to everything?"

"Yup." Ryan gobbled down another bit. I sighed. It was the only way. I nibbled at my ropes.

"Just one more bite!" Ryan stretched to reach the strip of licorice holding his ropes together. He got that bite but started eating the wall.

"Rescue me," I whined. Ryan bit into the ropes. "Not that way. Just rip them!" I bellowed.

"Oh," snapped Ryan. I was finally free! Ryan and I ran up the stairs to Heath Bar Hall.

"Ah, my children!" King Kandy greeted us. "Glad to see you escaped. Lord Licorice's banishing papers are being processed as we speak. Here they are now." A stumpy man in clothes resembling a clown's strutted in.

"Your papers, my liege." Clown-man bowed and handed King Kandy a scroll. He took a quill from his side table and scribbled his signature.

"There, banished. My guards will have him out of the way in no time. Now," the king clasped his hands together, "I believe we have a feast to attend," and led us to the Cotton Candy Ballroom.

Everything was fluffy in there. Fluffy pillars, fluffy tiles, blues and pinks danced across the walls. In the center of the room was a statue of a woman: Charla, the Cotton Candy Queen. Long tables surrounded the splendid figure. Everyone was there: Queen Frostine, Princess Lolly, and Gramma Nut to name a few.

"Sweet." Ryan gazed at the upside-down cotton candy machine ceiling.

We took our seats on either side of King Kandy.

"You all know Ryan and Rachael who have saved Candy Land from the evil Lord Licorice," King Kandy stood up. "For this we thank you from the deepest of our hearts." The candy court clapped. "Please accept our token of appreciation." He held out a candy bar in each hand. "These are an installment towards your lifetime supply of chocolate."

"Aaalll right!!" Ryan sprung from his chair and unwrapped his first bar.

"Oh forget the diet," I opened mine too.

King Kandy showed us to our room. That night I dreamt the sweetest dream: I was happy, engulfed in gumdrops, candy canes, brittle, plums, cakes, suckers, and all that's sugary.

Kaitlyn Jerome
Age: 13

It was as if I had been there before. The smell was like that of a distant memory I couldn't capture. My head ached and when I opened my eyes, I felt like I was opening them for the first time. Although I knew that smell, I couldn't remember how I knew it. The room finally came into focus. The place was somewhere I had never seen before, and yet that smell seized my memory, my shattered memory. I tried to shake it off as someone passed by my door. I rolled over, facing the window. I saw the sun setting outside; I had slept all day. Somehow, something wasn't right, but I didn't know what.

A woman swiftly strolled into my room, smiling, she spoke to me as if we were friends, but I didn't remember her face. She told me she had just come to check on me and quickly left.

I felt lost in a swarm of darkness. Nothing seemed real to me, and yet, it was. I closed my eyes and tried with all my might to remember. Simply remember, but I couldn't. Everything was a blur. Suddenly there was a flash across my eyelids. I saw someone. A man. Tall, dark, strong, but I didn't know who he was. The flash was so brief that it didn't register in my mind. All that the image was to me, was a picture of a man whom I didn't recognize.

The friendly woman came back to my room some time later, and chattered away about the weather and flowers, nothing I was really concerned about. Finally, I asked her where I was, and she simply answered that I was in the Northcreek Falls Medical Center. She left again in a swift motion.

This didn't make any sense to me. I didn't know why I would be in a hospital, much less in Vermont. The last thing I could recall was that I had been in Florida. I couldn't understand why I would now be in Vermont, and how I knew Northcreek Falls Medical Center was in Vermont. I was frustrated and perplexed and fell into an uneasy rest. I had a dream that I was by the ocean, and the man from my earlier vision was there. He wasn't old, maybe twenty-three, and he seemed so carefree. The beach was beautiful at dusk, the oranges and reds and pinks mixing in the sky over the blue water; it was astonishing. The man motioned for me to come to him, and as I was walking over to him, I was awaked by a loud commotion outside my door. There had been an error at the front desk, and someone was complaining. I thought it unfortunate that I had awoken, but I figured I could sleep later.

I turned on the television and went through channels until there on the screen was the man from my dream. His name was Marshall Adams. He was a reporter. I couldn't comprehend why that man was in my dream. Why did he seem so familiar to me? He looked like someone I had known or was supposed to know, but I didn't. The disappointment of not knowing brought me to tears. All I could do was sleep and try to remember. I felt so hopeless, and cried until I drifted into a troubled rest. I saw the ocean again. I heard the waves crashing against the rocks, and standing there, almost waiting for me, was Marshall. He was very Italian looking. I strolled over to him. He took me into his strong arms, and whispered I love you. This disturbed my mind, and again I awoke. So many questions were in my head. Marshall Adams, this man I didn't know, was saying he loved me in my dreams. I was so confused. I thought to myself, it's probably just a fantasy. I saw him on the TV and now I was fantasizing about him, but I couldn't be sure. Nothing was sure to me anymore.

I decided to get out of bed and go talk to someone. I walked cautiously to the front desk to ask for help. The nice woman appeared from behind a filing cabinet and said she could assist me. She carefully stepped with me as we made our way back to my room. I sat down on my bed, feeling dizzy, and asked her who I was and why I was there. She sat down next to me and told me that I was Karen Milken, and that I had suffered from a moderate case of amnesia. She informed me that I was twenty-one years old and Marshall Adams was my fiancé. She explained to me that my family lived in Michigan, where I was originally from, and that Marshall would be here tomorrow to get me. She also said that I had moved to Florida several months before and had become a nurse. She held my hand while she explained to me all these things, and she gave me a comforting, yet unfamiliar feeling.

I didn't know what to do with my new found information. Amnesia? How did I get amnesia? It seemed like a mistake, and even though it didn't feel like reality, I somehow knew the truth. Besides the nurse telling me, I just had this sense that made me feel as if everything was wrong. Very wrong. However, I now understood why the smell was familiar and why I knew the hospital was in Vermont. It suddenly hit me that I had been here before when I was in medical school. This was all too much for my already pounding head. I asked the nurse to leave, and she did as swiftly and gently as a butterfly fluttering away. She appeared very genuine and concerned. I just wanted to sleep, and after tossing and turning for about an hour, my mind finally was at ease enough to drift into a somewhat deep slumber.

I awoke the next morning and saw the man from the television. He was sleeping on the chair next to my bed, and I wondered how long he had been there. More handsome in person than on TV, he had dark brunette hair, olive skin, and a muscular frame. He was a sight for sore eyes, although I still didn't have any recollection of him. I lay there staring at him for some time. At last I saw his eyes twitch open. He had the greenest eyes I had ever seen; they were beautiful. He smiled the smile I had seen yesterday while watching him on TV, and it gave me a warm feeling inside. I imagined things being better now, just after seeing this man smile. I couldn't explain it, but it just felt right. He talked to me in a soft voice, almost as if I was too fragile to speak to. He was sincere.

The curiosity got the better of me, and I asked him if he knew how I had gotten this case of amnesia. He sat down next to me on my bed, took my hand gently into his own, kissed me softly on my forehead, and began telling me the tale. He said I had been out with friends one night about a week ago, and that I had never returned home. He explained that he had called the police, and people had been looking for me, but nothing had appeared to come of it. Unexpectedly, he said, he had gotten a phone call from this hospital two nights ago, saying that I had been brought to Northcreek Falls Medical Center. They said that they had found his number in my wallet, and I had a moderate case of amnesia, and that's when he had booked a flight here. He informed me that the police thought that while my friends and I were out I was abducted, then beaten, and then left somewhere close to here. He said that the police also inferred that the person who brought me to the hospital must have rescued me off the street.

This was all very interesting news. I had no idea something like that could happen to me, but it was better knowing what was believed to have happened than to be in the dark. As I sat there looking confused, this man, who was going to be my husband, took me in his arms and held me, and it felt wonderful. I sat there grasping onto a complete stranger, but also at the same time, someone I knew all too well, and I felt loved. I knew the road to remembering would be long and hard, but I would not be alone, and I softly whispered thank you to this man whom I was excited to get to know all over again.

Laura Ashley Marie Oldfield
Age: 16

# LAZY

One time I got a purple, cross-eyed, wingless, ostrich on my first vacation in South Dakota. We were in Reptile Gardens. The puppet has always been my luck charm. He's been my favorite toy ever since. I named him after Andrew, Nick and Skyler. I named him Andrew Don Maybon. But I like to call him Lazy.

Joshua Mills
Age: 10

# MOLLY

I remember when my mom said, "we are getting a new dog." She looked on the Internet for one and she found a dog named Ling that she liked. Ling was a brown, prickly haired, female Shar-pei. My mom called my Auntie Taunia to pick up our dog because Ling was in Kansas City and my aunt lives in Lawrence, Kansas. She picked up Ling, paid for her and her kennel. Auntie Taunia brought her down to Saint Frances, Kansas where my great-grandma lived. We came down for Easter and we got Ling on Easter day. There were three problems. She didn't like us very much, we hated the name Ling, and she growled. My dad named her Molly after Molly Hatchet. We have had her for two years and she still growls at other people.

Cori A. Hunt
Age: 11

# THE MYSTERY OF THE AMERICAN DOLL

One day I went galloping inside to find that I had just received my first American Doll named Molly. Molly comes from the time period of 1944. Her dad is serving in World War II fighting against Hitler and his troops. That night I gently placed Molly in her case. I then drifted off to sleep...

I woke up to the sound of "Boom, Boom!" "Where, where am I?" I scarcely questioned. I dashed as fast as I could as explosions blew up right by me. I felt as scared as if I were in the war!

I finally was able to see a village. I went into the store and asked, "Where am I?" Before he could answer, I saw the date and it read January 17, 1944! I thought I must be in an antique store. But when I asked the store owner, he said it was today's date.

I ran as quick as I could to see if there was anyway to get home. That is when I saw a train loading up coal. I snuck up to the back of the train and hid in a coal department. Then I drifted off to sleep...

Beep, beep, beep, the sound of my alarm clock awoke me. I then realized I was in my bed safe and sound with Molly standing right by me. It must of just been a dream I thought to myself. But when I went to turn the alarm clock off some coal slipped off my p.j.'s onto the floor!

Anna Marie McGinnis
Age: 10

# A LIVING DOLL

As I sat in the glass case, I thought of my old life. I remember how Swift As Snake took me on her adventures so long ago, when Edna Caroline Masterson found me, and now.

Now I'm here in this dire museum that's cold and lonesome. How I wish I could be somewhere in the Cliff Dwellers' old homes (if they still exist). Maybe someday I will.

First of all, I don't necessarily have a definite name. I'm really just a doll. I've been called about every word in the English and Native American languages. So call me whatever you prefer.

When I was made, I felt special because the Cliff Dwellers made me from precious materials. Such as wooden buttons for eyes, rabbit hair for my wig, a leather scrap for a dress, charcoal-drawn mouth, and an old corncob as a body.

After that, Swift As Snake, a young Cliff Dweller girl, took me on all her adventures. Each one was different but was exciting. Sometimes Swift As Snake's mother had to fix me up a tiny bit.

Soon, though, right out of the blue, everyone was gone and I was left lying on the ground inside the cave. I had hoped that Swift As Snake would return, but she never did. After that all I could do was wait for somebody to find me.

In 1942 a young girl was passing by and saw me. She picked me up, dusted me off and carried me away.

Before I knew it, we were at a modern-day campsite. I remember the girl's mother said Edna Caroline Masterson to the young girl. It must have been her name.

I spent fifteen years in a cozy, safe spot in Caroline's room until her father took me away. He took me to a museum in Oregon. There I was placed in a cabinet with other dolls.

But in 2000 I was taken to a very famous museum in Washington D.C. called the Smithsonian Institution. This is where I am now. I don't believe, unfortunately, I will ever leave.

KERPLUNK!

Some people just dropped me in a box along with other dolls. We are being put in a delivery truck.

It seems like I've been in here for many weeks.

SCREECH!

I am now at a place called Mesa Verde. Here I am placed on an old Cliff Dweller shelf.

Wait half a second. This is Swift As Snake's old home! Wow! I can't believe it's still here! This is great. I hope I never have to leave.

Brandi Ann Krieg
Age: 10

# PRINCESS BELLE

Once there was a beautiful princess. She was very disappointed that her father, the king, would not let her go to the ball. He feared that she would get into trouble. She was tired of everybody pushing her around like a baby, especially her parents. But, one day she woke up to find her parents hard as rocks, well, they were rocks. She couldn't believe it, she was free. But that night, she woke up to find a beautiful fairy who said "Your parents have been turned into stone, aren't you going to do something?"

I looked at her weird and said "No, what do you want me to do?" Well, they were gone all right, but where was I suppose to go and what was I suppose to do?

"Well," said the fairy, "first you must go to the beanstalk forest, then you will find a queen, she'll have something to do with it." And then, in a flash, the fairy was gone.

So I dressed up in a gown which was green, to match the leaves in the forest. And with my short, stubborn dog, Puff, we headed out to the forest. I found a map in a bottle. I broke the bottle and found a map of the forest. I saw how big the forest was, but all I could keep my eye on was the queen's castle. I put the map into my bag. Before I left, I stopped and bought some bread and cheese along with some chunks of meat for Puff. And then, before I knew it, I was in the forest. I couldn't see a thing, but then I heard horse feet. It was a Pegasus with beautiful neon colored hair. She said "I know you are the princess." "Yep" I replied "looking for the queen." "Oh no" she said as she blinked. She went on to say that the queen is wicked and that there is danger in the forest. She went on to tell me all of the problems in the forest. First, there is the evil Licoriceman named Danny, then the Jammin Adam Monster, the unfriendly Kemberly lady and last, but not least; Kelli, Mother Nature. I asked her why Mother Nature was so bad. She told me that she liked to cast bad storms. She gave me some tips, then left.

I walked about a mile and a half then saw a castle made out of licorice. I looked at the map and thought that it had to be the Evil Licoriceman named Danny! There was a big gate around the castle. I looked at the front of the door and noticed guards with licorice hanging out of their mouths. I asked them to open the doors, which they did. There in front of my eyes, was King Licorice, Danny. Sitting in his throne of blue licorice, he looked at me in disgust. "You girl, come over here, what do you want?" I told him

"I want, sir, please if I could pass through your land." He asked me "What will you do in return?" Then, the light bulb came on, "I will give you cheese, it goes good with licorice." The king replied "Very well, then I will let you pass through my land, give me some of this cheese." I gave him some cheese and headed off on my journey.

I came to a spot that was warm and I lay down. I took out some of the bread and cheese and chunks of meat and me and Puff ate. The next morning, I woke up and Puff and I took off to the next place, Jammin Adam Monster's house. There, in front of my rosy cheeks, was a house made out of CD players. I pressed "play" and the "Star-Spangled Banner" played. "Who's there?" a voice called.

I replied "Princess Belle." a reggae type of guy opened the door.

"What's up man?" he said to me, then I heard the song "Hit me baby one more time."

He asked me "What do you want, man?"

I replied "Well, you see sir, I was wondering if you would let me go through your land."

He told me that I could on one condition "You have to sing "right, round" by heart. I used to jam to that song. "Start singing now, hurry and go" he said.

I started singing "you spin me right round baby..." When I finished, he let me pass.

Puff and I thought that we would lay down in Red Flower Land. I had a feeling that we were not in Kansas anymore. We settled down and I had meat for Puff, but just bread for me. I woke up and it was time to leave, time to go to Unfriendly Kemberly's home. It was about five miles, when I reached the house, I pushed the doorbell. It rang "mean, mean, hurt, hurt." "Who is it?" called a beautiful voice.

"Um, Princess Belle," I replied. "Oh, come in" and the door became open. I walked in and a girl with brown-sugar hair and red eyes said

"What do you want, dear?"

I told her that I just wanted to pass through her land, she asked what I would do for her. Now, I remembered that the Pegasus had told me to give her a rose. I had one, and I gave it to her, she let me pass, but was angry when I left. This time I didn't stop, but had food. Before I knew it, I was at Kelli, Mother Nature's house. She was sleeping outside, she did not have a home, she was lying on the ground. She said "Hola, young one, what shall you want?"

I told her that I wanted to pass through her land.

"Sure," she replied "but, remember, don't hurt my land."

I was only ten thousand miles from the castle and me and Puff had finished the rest of our food. We rested and started off the next morning. We met Gretel, from "Hansel and Gretel." She told me that she was living with the Sandman and doing OK. We had tea with them and headed off. We were at the queen's castle, I was scared, five guards stood by the door. I asked them to please open the door and they did. I saw the queen, Queen Alison. "YOU, CHILD, COME HERE NOW!" The queen said in a very loud voice.

I told her "I would like it if you would let my parents go."

"No," she replied, "I will let them go when I die, 'cause I won't be alive." She told me "If you can figure out how to kill me and undo the spell, you can have them." She locked me up in a cage and stuck me downstairs. The Pegasus came and, using her hair, broke open the cage. Once free, the Pegasus told me how to kill the queen and how to break the spell. I went upstairs and there was queen Alison, she looked at me in a weird way and said "GET BACK DOWN THERE!" I took off the mirror off the wall and put it in her face. She started melting and saying "I'm melting, I'm melting" and she turned into slime. I chanted "oolaloolaodabohla," then yelled "LIFE" and ran from the castle. I returned to town with Puff at my side and found my parents weeping. I ran to them and said "I missed you guys." It wasn't that bad.

Belinda Banuelos
Age: 10

# A MAGIC RING

One day Kayla and I were playing outside at Cole Park. I was running barefoot in the gravel. I felt something hurt my foot. I went back to see what it was. I couldn't find it at first, so I started to dig.

Kayla came and asked, "What are you doing?"

I blushed, "I felt something when I was out here." I threw my hands up and yelled, "I found it!"

It was a beautiful gold ring with diamonds in it, but a diamond was missing. I said, "I wish this diamond wasn't missing!"

Then the diamond appeared on the ring.

The ring boomed, "You have two wishes left!"

Kayla and I had a frightened look on our faces.

I made another wish, "I wish that all the starving people in the world will always have food!" I said.

"You did the right thing wishing that wish," Kayla said.

"Thanks, but I didn't use that so you would congratulate me. I used it because the starving people of the world make me sad, and look on the bright side. We'll never see those horrible shows or commercials ever again."

I asked Kayla to make the next wish. She said, "I wish everybody in the world gets what makes them happy."

"That was so kind," I said to Kayla.

"I just said that because I wanted to do something nice for people."

Kayla and I decided to go home. We were outside and we heard my mom say, "I have enough money to pay off the bills."

Then the ring said, "Get rid of me because all of the wishes have been used."

We threw the ring into the neighbor's yard. Oh. No! Here comes my cat with a ring on his tail. We went to the garden and buried it. Then the next day we flipped on the TV and heard that all the starving people in the world had food. It was a good feeling to know our wishes had come true.

Then my mom said, "I found a ring!"

Kayla and I said, giggling, "Oh, well."

Samantha Cordero
Age: 9

# WHITE WONDER

We were going home when we stopped and walked into the forest. We were walking when we came into a clearing. We looked around the clearing and we saw a white wolf. We could tell he was wild, but kind in a lonely way. Then he ran away.

"I guess he didn't want to stay," say Brandi.

"Yeah," I said sadly.

"But I want to find the wolf and say thank you for helping us. I'll find the wolf someday," I said, sadder than before.

"What good will it do? We'll never find the white wonder," Brandi said.

"What did you say?" I asked.

"I said we'll never find the white wonder," Brandi said.

" Wait, white wonder. We can take white wolf and turn it into white wonder and maybe someday we can catch him and name him. But what will we do if he got away? We could plant a transmitter and find him very fast. We could chain the white wonder up to a post. But what if he breaks the chain and gets away? We'd have to find a way to keep the wolf in a cage that is unbreakable glass. But where do you find one of those? You go look in every glass shop in town and I'll look for the white wonder. And if we can't find a glass cage and the white wonder, we'll go home and try tomorrow. We'll change jobs OK? I wonder where that wolf is. Oh, where can he be? I hope I find him soon so I can go home and go to bed early, don't you?"

"Oh yeah, she's in town looking for the glass cage. I want to go home. It's getting dark and I can't find my way out. How am I going to get home? Help! Help! Help! Oh yeah, no one can hear me in the woods. I have to find my own way out. I think I came this way. Oh no, I'm even more lost. I do have a tent in my backpack maybe I can set up camp. The white wonder, I think he wants me to follow him. Maybe I should follow him. Yeah, he always shows up in tight spots and helps us out so I'm going to follow him," I said.

The white wonder saved me from staying in the woods all night. I was very grateful. I hope I find the wolf again. We are great friends. But that's not the end of it. I was waiting for someone to find me when I see a white as snow wolf. Sure the wolf was wild but kind to me and my friend, Brandi. I made it out of the forest. Of course, I never found the white wolf in fact I never saw a wolf in my life. "I'm finally out of the forest. Where's my friend? Oh, there she is," I said.

"So did you find the white wonder?" Brandi asked.

"Yes, I did as matter of fact, he helped me out of the woods when I got lost, kind of," I said.

"You got lost? How can you get lost in a forest that's very small?" Brandi asked. We said our good-byes and went home. I told my mom and dad what an adventure I had but they never believed me. I wish I could prove to them that that did happen. Then they would believe me. But I never got the proof and I never saw the white wolf again.

When I went to bed that night I kept wondering where the white wolf had gone, so hidden that no one could find him.

Trinity Atwood
Age: 10


## MY FISH

My fish is named Spot. When you moved your finger in a circle on his fishbowl, he did a flip in his fishbowl. On our trip, he died. We were very sad. We flushed him down the toilet. A couple years passed by and my mom flushed her watch down the toilet. My mom didn't do it on purpose. Later, my dad took a metal hook and tried to find the watch. My family and I said, "Dad, you're fishing for Spot."

Sofie Marie Christensen Black
Age: 8

" All right," said Jackson. "Me and my squad are infiltrating the base. Patterson, you and your squad create a distraction. Gonzolaz, you and Miller are going to fight your way through the halls and capture Villnov. But be careful. He's a very dangerous man."

"Find Villnov?" said Gonzolaz. "But that's like finding a needle in a haystack."

Sampson said, "Lieutenant Johnson, get Gonzolaz and go check the hydro-generator."

"Right away sir," said Sampson.

When they got outside, they thought they saw an orca bomber in the distance. For this was the year 4002. Then all of a sudden BOOM! BAM! The orca bomber just dropped an electromagnetic, high-frequency bomb on Earth's base. Gonzolaz and Sampson ran back in to see a horrifying sight. Skurge's bomber had caused a mix-up. A mobile APC had dropped off thirty GI's. There were ten Americans fighting off the Skurgin's. By the time the small battle had ended, twenty-four Skurgins had been killed. The other six had been caught and were being held captive. Eight Americans had been shot by protos laser.

"What happened?" inquired Sampson.

"Those Skurge morons just attacked. What, did you think we were having a picnic?" said Lt. Johnson.

That was it. Earth had a very short fuse and Skurge just lit it.

"We are going in to attack in one week from today," said Lt. Johnson.

When that week came, Earth was mad. But before they could load onto the ships, Lt. Johnson gave a speech.

"OK," started Johnson. "Skurge has a secret weapon. Nobody knows what it is. So be on the lookout. Oh! And one more thing. Let's go get them!!!"

When Earth got to Skurge, everything was unusually quiet. Earth's troops looked around for an hour before finding Skurge's base.

Jackson and his squad got into the base, but only to find sixty Skurgins standing right there.

"Fire!" said Jackson.

And just like that everyone pulled out their plasma cannons and fired away.

"Phew," said the whole squad, when the battle was won.

But Jackson was nowhere to be found. Meanwhile, Patterson's squad was doing a good job distracting. That gave Gonzolaz and Miller a good chance to go. They ran through the surprisingly empty halls and ran into Villnov's office and immediately started getting shot at. Miller threw a flash grenade and watched the guards go to the ground trying to see, but did not prevail. Without hesitating, Gonzolaz ran over and asked the guards where Villnov was. The guards said he was in the bathroom. Right at that moment, Jackson's squad came through the door and said they could not find Jackson. Then the troop that had been talking fell to the ground. Jackson was right behind him.

"Jackson!!" shouted Gonzolaz, Miller, and Jackson's squad.

"Don't you mean Villnov?" said Jackson calmly.

Then he pulled out a protos laser and shot all of his squad.

"Gonzolaz. Miller. You idiots could never figure out I was Villnov, so I figured, hey, I'll just tell them myself."

"TRAITOR!!" shouted Miller.

Then he reached for his laser, and Villnov, being calm pulled his trigger twice. Before you could blink your eyes, Miller fell to the ground.

"NO! MILLER!" yelled Gonzolaz, and started chasing Villnov.

Villnov turned and shot at Gonzolaz. When he did this, his feet got tangled, Villnov fell, landed on his arm and broke it. Gonzolaz ran right up to him, gun in hand.

"Hey, please don't. It's me," said Jackson.

"You only wish," said Gonzolaz, who then pulled his trigger.

Right at that, Patterson and his squad ran up to Gonzolaz.

"What's up?" asked Patterson.

"Nothing," replied Gonzolaz quietly. "But someone's down."

"Who's that?" inquired Patterson.

"Oh! That's just Villnov, or should I say Jackson, supposedly my friend," said Gonzolaz quietly.

And without another word, turned around and walked off.

Alec Vasquez
Age: 12

## ON THE BUS

I hate going to school. It is mainly because of the bus. I hate the sound of the loud engine as it rumbles up to my driveway. I hate the sound of kids laughing as I walk outside my house. Every day I dread going to school. I hate when I have to get on the bus and turn sideways just to fit. I hate the bus.

As I think these thoughts, I hear the horrid rumbling of the bus. I think to myself, here I go. I walk outside, down the driveway, and I turn sideways to get through the doorway of the bus. As usual, everyone laughs. I walk down the aisle, my hips bumping into the seats. I take my seat. The bus begins to drive. I hate the bus.

At the next stop, a boy my age, who is very skinny and somewhat nerdy, sits down.

"Hi," he says.

"Hi," I reply.

He says nothing else the whole time. As I sit, trying to figure out why somebody would want to sit by me, I realize... maybe he just needed a friend.

Nicole Raelynn Hein
Age: 13

# DREAMS TO REALITY

Lizzy and her mother had an argument, an argument about dreams. Not the dreams you have at night. Not the cheesy little kid dreams. About Lizzy's true dream. Unfortunately, her mother completely disagreed. Lizzy wanted to pursue her ultimate dream. Her dream was to become a published writer, to write a text that tells the world what is happening behind their minds. Again. Lizzy's mother disagreed and thought it would be too much stress on the family. "Stupid family," Lizzy thought. "Why does everything need to revolve around 'stress in the family?' Family is always what decides Mother's final decision. I should be able to lead my own life. Why not?"

This was too much for Lizzy. She pulled her chapped hand out of her jean's pocket and flung it across her mother's face. Her mother instantly sent her to her room.

Lizzy lay down on her bed, stuffing her face into her pillow. Since there was nothing else she could do in her lonely room, she fell asleep. Obviously, when you fall asleep you have dreams. Some are nightmares that scare you out of your wits. Some are regular dreams that you will remember for your entire life. Some are dreams that you will never even know you had. Lizzy had a dream, a dream to be remembered for the rest of her life.

She dreamt about having something published. It must have been a good thing. Many people had copies of her book with a message, her message that tells the reader what is happening in the world.

Suddenly, all Lizzy could see was orange, a big blur of orange, yellow, and red. The heat was rising an enormous amount. There were beads of sweat running down Lizzy's face. All of her published books with a grand message about the first woman president were being burned right in front of her face. "Oh no!!" Lizzy screamed in the middle of her dream. Her dream that had started out as a miracle and was ending in a disaster. However, it was not over yet.

Nobody liked her opinion. People were scared of her ideas. People these days didn't want women to have any power over them. The world these days is male dominated and men don't want to hear any differing opinions. Nobody like her opinion that many other helpless women shared. People were scared of her controversial ideas. This would be why people burned her miracle books. Her books with a grand message that were finally published. Her books that she had been awaiting outcome of since age twelve.

Lizzy awoke, bewildered, flabbergasted, with sweat continually running down her forehead. There was only one thing she could do right now, analyze her dream. What was it trying to tell her?

Lizzy ran into the kitchen where her mother was beginning to cook dinner. Her mother faced the sink, not wanting to have anything to do with her daughter. Lizzy with a full and heavy heart, apologized to her mom. The mom who had refused her aspirations. The mom whom she had slapped in the face. The mom who she had loved back. Luckily, her mother accepted her apology. Lizzy then told her mother that her dream would still be pursued, just at a much later date.

Luciana Ranelli

# HARMONY

As the breeze tickled the flowers, I saw a little kitten. Yet this was no ordinary kitten, it had delicate wings, just oozing with enchantment. There were sparkling gems, sprinkled across the wings, with such dazzling colors that they shone right through my body deep into my heart and soul. This kitten's fur was a glistening peachy color, glittered with pink tones and yellow tints. A tiny crown rested on her fuzzy head. It was a gold crown with a topaz gem resting in the middle. She was singing with a stellar harmony, so I named her Harmony. She would whisper sweet poems to me. As we walked along a path, I came across a mystical white unicorn, named Misty. As we continued our journey, I saw a waterfall. Harmony peeked out from the side, and sweetly giggled. Then Misty dove in, and invited me to join her. I jumped in, but then I could not breathe, even above water, because this was very rare and magical water. It was called unicorn mist, it was the purest water, so it was harmful to any Earth mammal, like me for instance (a puppy) who went in it. Misty suddenly remembered this, so she swam deep beneath the water to free me. She got me safely to the land, where I struggled to withdraw my strength, yet no energy seemed to relieve me. As I took a huge breath, dangling for air, the slight pollution in the air revived my lungs. How would pollution help you breathe? Well, this fantasy land is so innocent pure and happy, it is immortal to any foreign body to survive with such pureness, since earth is so very unpure. Misty was sobbing with guilt, she could've killed me, yet she dashed to the magical healing springs to take me to the earth fairy, one of the many elemental fairies that live here. The elegant wings brushed against my fur, it was so warm and welcoming, I suddenly felt happiness and life. These are feelings most beings take for granted, but that changes when death creeps up to you, to take you in, but with some miraculous miracle you manage to survive with great fortune. I awoke on a fancy bed with a transparent canopy and rainbow colored lights hung around the room. This place must be blessed to have such a happy feeling within it. There was trees, leaves and flowers (fake ones), it felt like the wilderness. This was a place where happiness will be instilled into my spirit.

I, Ciera Lynn Burke, could relax, be calm and peaceful and be serene in this place. The earth fairy asked about my life, so I went on and on about events that I had experienced. She sang a song, it was in some other language, a very foreign tongue, not like French foreign, but an unearthly foreign. Then as the last word slipped off her tongue, a bright light appeared she whispered, but it was like a scream, "Close your eyes!"

I saw something in my head, it was hard to make what it was, was it a dark figure of some sort? Or an odd sign of heaven? Such decisions could not be made in this place or time period. Then a tremendous gust of wind jolted throughout the air. It felt as if I was being taken somewhere. I went to open my eyes, but then the earth fairy cried, "No you could die or get scared!" How could she tell what I was going to do next. Then she replied, "I am one with your spirit and thoughts."

Then I questioned, "Does that mean you are psychic?"

It was like I could feel her nod. Then I was back in the area where Misty and Baby Harmony first saw the river, yet the fairy was gone. Then Misty frolicked through the field of lilacs just up ahead. I chased after her, then Baby Harmony whizzed by zooming through the air. Then I tripped and fell into a hole. Misty dashed back and Harmony dove down following close towards me. Then we were in a small patch of roses, luckily non-thorned roses, and the petals soothed me. Soon we heard a strange chant almost hypnotic. Then a HUGE lizard grasped my throat and threw me at the wall. I went through, Misty and Harmony followed. We had came to a knight, like in a chess set, but real, he dashed at me with a mighty sword. He thrashed it into my leg. I passed out, the dark magic had penetrated my soul. Misty's horn went through me and cleared the dark magic. Misty was weary she had no strength, then Harmony flew her back to the flower field. Now we ran straight ahead towards a lake. This time Misty's horn illuminated, and dipped lightly in the water it flashed in different colors. Then Misty told me that the water was not perfectly pure water, but that it was safe to jump in. So I swan then a HUGE vine wrapped around my leg yanking me deeper and deeper till no air reached my lungs. Misty's horn illuminated again, but this time, it whirled a huge energy ball at the vicious vine. He let go and screeched. Now I catapulted to the shore. I hope I'll be safe again! We walked through hours of path, whispering poems, and songs. Our journey went further and further on. As we skipped along the path, I found a tiny little fox. He snickered at me, I creeched. Then his eyes became as wide as saucers, then he ran off with his tail between his legs. Then Misty and Baby Harmony told me my time has passed, it is time to let your heart lead you home.

Misty said "You must remember us, yet tell no one, do you hear me, TELL NO ONE, understood?"

"Yes," I whimpered as a tear waddled down my face. I felt that life had ended, no one was there for me, then again, I opened my eyes and saw my father saying to me how much he missed me and how he wondered where I was. Then my kitten hopped on my lap, then in my spirit I felt Baby Harmony as if she was there, then my kitten licked me then winked. So forever I shall cherish my memories with Misty and Baby Harmony.

Ciera Burke
Age: 10

# JUST A DATE

## Chapter One

"So are you going to the dance with me Friday, Jewel?" Tom asked again.

Jewel couldn't believe it; the hottest guy on earth, Tom Felton, was asking her out!!! "Sure, I'll go, Tom. I was wondering who to go with to the dance, anyhow," Jewel replied casually.

"All right, then, I pick you up for the dance at 6:30, okay?" Tom said.

"Okay, see you then," Jewel spoke.

"Love you, Sweetheart, bye," he sweetly replied as he kissed Jewel and strode down the hall.

It was hard to believe he had asked her out and kissed her!!! Friday was one short day away and Jewel had no clothing proper for the dance. She needed to shop for clothes. Good thing Friday was a no-school day.

## Chapter Two

"Mom, I'm borrowing the car," Jewel told her mother as she got home. "And some money."

"How much money?" her mother asked cautiously.

"Twenty-five," Jewel replied.

"All right, but you can't borrow the car yet because I have a two hour meeting right now," her mother said as she gave the money to her daughter.

"Please hurry back, Mom!" Jewel called after her mom who was pulling out of the driveway.

## Chapter Three

"Mom, what took you so long? You took four hours to be at your meeting!!" Jewel cried angrily. "I might not make it to the mall now to buy my dress for the dance!!!!"

"Sweetheart, I'm so sorry it took so long, but rush hour decided to come as I was headed home," her mother apologetically replied. "But there's always tomorrow, dear. Remember that there's no school then due to some teacher thing."

"But Mom ..." Jewel protested, searching for something more to say. "But --"

"Buts are waste producing things, not something to be conversing about." Her mother firmly interrupted. "Tomorrow you may drive to the mall for clothes, no later, and that's final!"

"Mother!!" Jewel cried and ran wailing to her room so she could stormily weep her heart's content out.

## Chapter Four

"Are you ready for dinner, or are you going to refuse to eat, Jewel?" Julie impatiently asked.

"I'm going to eat, Julie," Jewel replied as she trudged out of her room, red faced and puffy eyes.

"Wow, you look like Frankenstein's wife," Julie teased as they walked towards the dining room slowly.

"Shut up, Godzzillette," Jewel snapped as they entered the dining room.

"Are you done crying, sweetie?" their mother gently asked.

"Yes Mother," Jewel hotly replied.

"I've made your favorite dinner, darling, and you choose where we eat, too," her mother clarified. "Okay, then we eat in Julie's room!" Jewel said immediately brightening.

"But ...," Julie exclaimed, horrified. "That's not fair!" "I choose. You lose, Julie!" Jewel happily replied as she skipped up the stairs to her sister's room.

## Chapter Five

"Mom, I'm taking the car to the mall!" Jewel called to her mom the next day.

"Okay, sweetheart, but don't take too long!" her mom replied, handing her daughter the keys.

"I'll try, but rush hour might hit me while I'm driving home!!" Jewel joked as she hopped in the convertible and drove off.

## Chapter Six

"What to wear, what to wear!" Jewel exclaimed as she walked through the assortment of clothes. "So many things at such low prices!"

"You shopping for dance clothes too, Jewel?" a familiar voice behind her spoke.

"Yes," Jewel replied, startled as she turned around to see her best friend, Melissa, standing behind her.

"Who are you dressing up for? I've got --," Melissa said, hesitating before she continued. "I've got Zac."

"Mmm; I have Tom Felton." She could see surprise and shock painted on Melissa's face. And she knew why. Recently Jewel had been dating Zac but had broken up with him when she found out he was cheating on her. Melissa had expected a bad reaction and besides, it's every girl's fantasy to date Tom but only two (one including Jewel) had that dream change to reality.

"Now I understand shopping for clothes," Melissa managed to say after several unsuccessful attempts to speak.

"I have two words about choosing something," Jewel said.

"What?" Melissa asked out of curiosity.

"HELP ME!" Jewel responded.

"Okay, now first things first...," Melissa started, as they sorted through the clothes. From simple white T-shirts to sophisticated tube tops, to plain shorts to finely decorated jeans. They combed the entire mall in search of the perfect outfit for the dance. Now, two hours later, they took off to their own houses to get ready for the dance.

## Chapter Seven

"You took two and a half hours to go to the mall, young lady! What's your excuse this time?" were the first words Jewel heard as she pulled into the driveway and stepped into the house that came out of, unsurprisingly, her father's mouth.

"Daddy, I was looking for something to wear to the dance," she replied innocently.

"Is someone taking you because I certainly ain't," her father retorted.

"Yes, Daddy, I have a ride," Jewel sweetly replied.

"Who, then? Is it a boy? What's his name? When is he picking you up?" Jewel was flooded with all of these questions.

"Daddy, he's my date, so of course he's a boy. His name is Tom Felton and he's picking me up at 6:30. I hope I've answered all your questions, Daddy, because I have to get ready." Without further speech, Jewel strode upstairs to her room to do her things.

## Chapter Eight

"Jewel, this really hot boy is at the door asking for you and I think if you don't come down Daddy is going to kill him." These were the words that Julie was speaking.

"How do you know Julie?" Jewel carefully asked.

"He has this glint in his eyes. I don't think he likes him," Julie reported.

"Well, DUH!!! I'm coming down before Tom leaves in fright of Dad," Jewel said.

## Chapter Nine

"Tom, are you ready to go?" Jewel asked her boyfriend.

"Yes, Jewel," Tom said, slowly getting up from the chair he was sitting in then walking toward me. As they made move to leave, Jewel's father suddenly spoke.

"Wait just a moment, young man. I want you to make sure you have Jewel back by 10:30, you understand me?"

"Yes, sir," Tom said as they left. When they reached the car, Tom pulled out a red rose and a diamond and handed them to Jewel.

"Oh, Tom, they're great!!" Jewel exclaimed, running around the car and hugging him.

"I'm glad you like them," Tom said, obviously pleased.

"Like? Like? Love is more like it, Tom! But why go to the trouble?" Jewel asked.

"Because you're my precious Jewel! You mean so much to me!" Tom told her.

That's when Jewel realized that Tom really did love her and this wasn't because she had suddenly started to look good. She knew nothing was going to spoil this perfect night; and she was right.

Tryn Leigh McCardell
Age: 10

# MY SISTER KATE

Kate Rahel is a kindhearted first-rate cellist. This young lady works hard to be an excellent cellist. When Katie-o plays it sounds like a bird singing in summer.

My sibling is a grade A student! Kate is as intelligent as a computer genius! She is a kindhearted sister who plays plenty of games with me. When Kate plays hide-and-seek, I scare her and she screams like a whistle!

Kate is a fantastic tennis player. She swings like a pro baseball player smashing a home run! On the court she is as fast as a cheetah.

My sister sleeps a great deal on the weekends. If she had the chance she would sleep forever! Kate smells like flowers in summer! My sibling is as pretty as a model!

Steven Rahel
Age: 10

# FISHING

One warm afternoon I could hear the splash of water and the smell of bitter weeds and feeling the moist air in the afternoon. Having as much fun as a water park and being challenged like a video game, fishing makes me feel like superman. When I catch a humongous large-mouth, I see the water splash like a catapult flinging rocks. It is as difficult as pulling a five-ton truck with a rope. This is why fishing is my hobby.

Austin Brumfield

# THE GREAT BULLY DEFEAT OF M20

Rudi was a boy who liked to be alone. He liked to play wars by himself so he was very good with a snowball. But, what he liked best was building snow forts. He even built an igloo that he and most his class could fit in! Bullies would knock down whatever he built. Rudi didn't mind them tearing his forts down until they knocked the igloo down. It was time to stop them! Rudi went home and went straight to the family woodshop. The next day he built the biggest snow fort ever seen! It was built around the largest tree on the playground. You wouldn't even know that there was a tree there! He had a wooden door that he put on the inside and packed snow against it so people couldn't open it from the outside. Rudi climbed up to the top of his fort and saw armies of bullies coming.

The next day he built the biggest snow fort ever seen!

"Surrender the fort and you will not suffer pain!" screamed B.G. (Bully General).

"You will not get past my first soldier! Section B12, Fire!" yelled Rudi. TWANG! Ten snowballs went flying and knocked most of the first row of bullies out!

"He really does have soldiers!" screamed a bully.

Actually, Rudi had built tons of catapults. Rudi loaded the B12 catapults and fired sections of B13, C12, and A1. The kids on the playground noticed that the first of five rows of bullies was knocked out. The kids started throwing snowballs at the bullies while some other kids pulled icicles off the bottoms of cars. The bullies got to the door and were kicking at it until it came down. Then the bully that kicked over the door fell over. Behind him was Jeremiah, the famous snowball fighter. "I've always wanted to hit that guy with an icicle!" he said. "Attention all snowball tossers! Get inside the fort!" Jeremiah gave Rudi an icicle.

"Section B12, fire!"

"Pull up the gate!" Rudi yelled. Rudi and Jeremiah went to the top of the fort.

"How are we gonna get back down to the battle Rudi?" asked Jeremiah. "Rudi?"

"I always wanted to hit that guy with an icicle"

"Aaaauuuggh!" screamed Rudi as he jumped off the fort into a six-foot high snow drift. Rudi popped out of the snow drift, attacking many bullies by surprise.

"All-snowball, fire!" screamed Jeremiah. Around one hundred fifty snowballs flew and hit all but one bully. The bully took out a lighter, turned it on and ran toward the fort. "He'll melt the fort! Snowballs, fire!" yelled Jeremiah. The bully was hit by five snowballs, but he was still running. "Launch ice balls!" screamed Jeremiah. Crash! One ice ball hit the bully but he was still going. "Ice ball!" yelled Jeremiah. Another eleven hit the bully but he was still running. "Ice ball!" bellowed Jeremiah. Another ice ball flew and knocked the bully out.

"Victory! The fort still stands!" shouted Rudi.

Ten years have passed since the Great Bully Defeat. Rudi learned to like to play with actual people and grew up to be very happy. The bullies never destroyed another snow fort, and the school made up a rule that no lighters were allowed. Jeremiah became a very successful General in World War Two and still, there is a little ring of snow around that tree!

Justin Kent

-- Click!

Tracy opened the door of her car and started to get in.  She stopped halfway and listened.  It sounded like something had moved out in the darkness beyond the lighted parking lot.  She looked around, and confirmed that there was only one other car in the lot besides hers, and there was no owner to be found.

Don't be ridiculous, Tracy, you are a grown woman.  Time to stop this childish stuff.

The voice in her mind was not very reassuring.  Ever since Krissey Henderson was kidnapped three days ago, the whole town had been a mess.  Kingston still had plenty of secrets though.  It is the kind of town where no one wanted to know.  They tried to keep to themselves as much as possible.  Of course there were the usual town gossips, but even then, some secrets are not worth telling.

When Krissey's parents heard a noise coming from their daughter's room at two in the morning, they got up to check.  They found an empty bed and an open window.  Before six the same morning everyone knew.  The classrooms and cubicles buzzed with:

"Did you know her?"

"I heard her parents are hysterical."

"I wonder who could have done such a thing."

There were many questions, but no answers.

Tracy cleared those thoughts out of her head.  She started the engine of her Civic, and the radio came on.

"...No more news on the kidnapping of sixteen-year-old Krissey Henderson.  The police are baffled, having found no evidence or clues on where she is.  They are hoping they are not too late, and... "

She quickly turned the radio off.  "Don't need to hear that depressing stuff now," she mumbled to herself.  She knew, inside, the real reason was fear.

Don't worry, Tracy.  You're only a defenseless woman in a deserted place at one in the morning.  You'll be f-i-n-e.

It was amazing how the voice in her mind could scare her so bad. She reached over and pushed the lock button. The reassuring click that told her all of the doors were locked calmed her down a little. If she just would have looked in her rearview mirror, she would have seen a shadowy figure in the back seat. She put the car in reverse to pull out, and drove down the rows of painted lines in front of the Kingston Library. As she drove by, she looked at the drab architecture of the place where she worked.

At the Kingston Library, she was not even head librarian, but just an assistant. An assistant who locked up every night and did a lot more work, but still got less pay than the head librarian.

Stop this self-pity stuff. No one cares about you. You'll probably die alone in your tiny apartment and no one will find you until you have rotted beyond recognition.

"Oh great, now my own voice is insulting me," she said aloud. Pulling out onto the main road, she looked back to see if any cars were coming. Still, she was totally oblivious to her "visitor." As she drove down the deserted road, she whistled nervously to herself.

If this was a slasher movie, something would happen to me. Some guy with a chain saw would run out in the middle of the road, stop the car, and cut me to pieces. Or maybe, a lunatic is waiting in the back seat until the right moment to slit my throat.

An immense pit of fear in her stomach came, and it was so big, it almost choked her. Had she looked in the back seat before getting in? What if there was someone back there right now?

This would be the perfect time to strike. He would come out, and...

As if by some sick irony, the figure decided now was the time. He fluidly brought a rope over the seat and tied it around her head. She screamed and the car lurched off the road. It careened over the railing and landed in a ditch, knocking her out cold on the steering wheel. After a few moments, the figure could be seen running away with a huge bundle in the shape of Tracy.

She woke up slowly and very confused. Everything was blurry, and her head hurt. She was tied to a wall, with shackles around her hands and feet. Suddenly, she remembered the car wreck, and what caused it.

Oh no, what am I going to do? I don't have a clue where I am. What do these people want with me?

Slowly and deliberately, she started examining her wounds. She looked up at her hands, which were numb from the elbow up. Where the shackles touched, there was bruising and inflammation. As she craned her neck up, she could feel swelling around her neck.

Probably from the rope that idiot tied around my head.

She looked down at her feet, and groaned. They were severely blistered around where the shackles touched. She spent time looking everywhere, but found nothing else that she could see.

At least they haven't decided to hurt me yet.

-- Sniff!

She whipped her head around.

"What was that?"

She looked to her far right and saw another girl, tied up the same way she was. This girl looked a lot younger, maybe in high school.

"Who are you," Tracy exclaimed. "You scared me!"

"My name's Krissey," a feeble voice replied.

"You're the girl who is missing, Krissey Henderson, aren't you?"

"Yeah, that's me."

"Where are we," Tracy asked.

"I have no idea, but there are only two guys, as far as I can tell."

"What do they want with us?"

"Going on what I've heard them talking about, I would say it is for the ransom money."

"I can see why they would want ransom for you, but I don't have any family that lives near here. There's no reason why they would want me." Tracy said, exasperated.

Suddenly, a violent series of convulsions wracked Krissey's body. After they were over, she uttered a weak sigh. "I don't know how much longer I can last, I haven't eaten in a while and my whole body hurts..." Krissey burst out in tears.

"You have to get a hold of yourself, Krissey," Tracy said. She wondered how long it had been for her.

"Seriously, I can feel myself slip away more and more with each passing minute," Krissey said tiredly. "All this talking is making me so exhausted. I need to save my strength." She closed her eyes and drifted off.

Great, now the only one who can explain what is happening has to take a nap. I better try to get some sleep too. Maybe someone will find us by morning.

Finally, she got some reassurance from her mind. She tried to get more comfortable, but that was not going to happen anytime soon. Sleep was a long time coming for Tracy that night.

The first thing Tracy felt when she woke up was extreme pain. Shooting up her arms, the pain was excruciating. When she realized where she was, she woke entirely, and with a start. After a long coughing fit, she looked over to where Krissey was. She was still asleep.

How can she sleep that long? It has to be morning by now.

She looked again, and realized something was off. She concentrated, and saw after a while that Krissey's chest was not moving. She instantly went into panic. "Krissey, talk to me! Wake up! Please, Krissey!" She broke out into huge sobs that wracked her body. "No! Someone help me," she screamed. There was no one to answer her cries. She immediately noticed how much energy the crying and screaming took out of her. Even so, she could not stop crying, and she just let the tears stream down her face. She started drifting in and out of consciousness.

In a period when she was conscious, she noticed how extreme hunger felt. It was awful, and she almost could not tolerate the thought of food. It drove her crazy, thinking about what she could be eating. She sometimes thought of how easy it would be to let herself go. It would be so much better.

She woke up from what seemed like two minutes of sleep. Her strength was zero, and she had begun to cough up blood, her shirt sprayed with tiny dots of it. She was just hanging by her arms now. Still, she began to think much clearer. Everything seemed to become a little better, even. She felt warmer and safer. An incredible peace came over her. Now, she could accept her own death. Bit by bit, she slowly faded away in what felt like someone's safe, warm arms. Everything was going to be just f-i-n-e.

Patricia Fekula
Age: 15

# ENDURANCE

It was late in the afternoon on a dreary day. The passengers on an FBI secret mission plane were all in a fitful sleep, when the plane jerked around. Everyone awoke with a roar; all wondering what was going on. They knew that the pilot was once a fighter pilot, a much decorated one at that. He also was the type that didn't joke around much on a flight.

"Attention, we are experiencing technical difficulties. The plane has stalled. It may take some time. Bear with us."

One man arose from his seat and stormed down to the cockpit. He yelled to the innocent pilot, "What is your problem? You specifically told me that there would be no hazards or difficulties on this flight. What's your problem?"

"Sorry, sir. It seems that someone has sabotaged our engine."

"Well, tell that idiotic slob to back off or he will have to deal with me and my lawyer, OK?"

"Fine, sir. Anything for you, sir. But I have to tell you that we may not survive."

"What? This is not going EXACTLY how I planned it," said the angry man who stormed back to his seat.

"Why does he always get mad about those things?" one man asked another.

"He always wants his way."

Suddenly, everyone felt a jerk, and the plane started to take a sharp dive. No one ever thought that the plane actually was going to crash. They all thought that the pilot was a fighter pilot. But then he ran through the aisle and jumped out the back of the plane. As the plane went spiraling downward someone yelled.

"What's going on? The stupid pilot. He was the person who sabotaged the plane."

With everyone now knowing their fate, the plane hit the top of the mountain. Most of the passengers were killed on impact, but one young and extremely smart man wasn't badly hurt. When he awoke from unconsciousness, he saw that everyone but himself had perished. He looked around, trying to find a way to get out, and he saw a limb moving under the piles of wreckage. He scurried over to see if the man was all right. He frantically dug until he uncovered the half-dead man. The man found that the person under the wreckage was the snob that got angry at the pilot. He helped him up with caution, thinking that the man might try to kill him. To his surprise, he actually thanked him. They searched the plane for equipment that might help them get out. The first handy item they found was a crowbar. They used it to pry open a door to the outside. After an hour of hard work, the young man finally pried the stubborn door open.

"Finally!" he yelled.

"What happened?" yelled the other man in reply.

"I got the door open! By the way, what's your name?"

"My name is Ron Cauth, the owner of this once wonderful, extraordinary jet. And yours?"

"Mitch Wellington, the FBI's most trusty espionage officer. We really should get out of this plane as fast as we can."

They burst out of the plane and found themselves on top of a mountain surrounded by cliffs. They realized that their only way down was to scale down the rough-edged cliffs. Unfortunately, they only had the equipment for one individual.

"Hey, we only have enough equipment for one person," said Mitch.

Suddenly, Ron sprinted back to the plane. He emerged a couple minutes later with more equipment. They hooked the equipment to a sturdy rock at the top of the mountain and started down. Mitch was already half the way down when Ron yelled that he was stuck. Mitch told him the same advice his instructor had given him and finished climbing down the cliff.

When Ron got down, the thought of what they should do next left them pondering once they got down. They realized that it was beginning to get dark. Mitch started to search for sticks to light a fire. After the fire was started, they sat by it, conversing until Ron said,

"I'm thinking we should go to bed."

"Fine. We'll search for a plane tomorrow."

They went to sleep, not knowing that their life would change dramatically tomorrow.

They awoke to the precious sound of water trickling down a soft riverbed. With a little help, the two men slowly rose from the uncomfortable bed of pine needles. They realized that the soft sound of water was only their mind playing tricks on them. It was instead a roaring river. When they remembered where they were, they started planning on how to get across the treacherous river. They looked around for resources and found some twine and an old, rusty ax handle in a pile of drying leaves. Ron sat and cut the twine into strong yet small and long strands. Mitch collected the wood to make a raft. After many an hour, the two had conjured up a raft.

"Well, the raft isn't a mess and that twine is actually holding the raft together."

They pushed the heavy raft out to the sea with caution, but with a steady speed. Ron hopped on the raft, and looked at Mitch with something that said to push him. Mitch did, with a stubborn and snotty attitude. When they reached the soft banks, they sighed and stopped on the shoreline. Mitch picked up one end of the awkward raft, and yelled.

"Well, here it goes!" And with that he shoved the raft into the water and got on, though more cautious than Ron. With the speed they gained they realized that their "sea" voyage wouldn't last long. They reached the other banks in just less than two hours. They jumped off and started down the rest of the immense mountain. The rough terrain made climbing difficult, but the men went on with persistence that seemed to never end. When the tired men reached a flat acre of land, they plopped down on their knees and thanked God. They sat down on a rotted log and looked around with curiosity. They both had an eye for detail, and saw the large opening about a hundred feet away. Then, with a loud crash, a bear came stomping out of the opening, yelling and roaring with endless anger. They looked around frantically, trying to find the problem that the bear had started making such a raucous about. A little cub, no more than ten months old, came tumbling down the land the men had just climbed down. The two gawked at each other and sprinted down the mountain at speeds thought unimaginable. The bear pursued the frightened men like it would an antelope. It saw its small, helpless infant and started over to it. With this, the men ran frantically down the jagged, uneven boulders with no thought of how else to get down. When the men thought that neither could go on, Mitch halted and looked back.

They saw that the bear had not chased after them, but instead had gone back to her extraordinarily immense castle among the hills. They both thought, almost telepathically, that they were lucky to survive the crash and everything else. After their breathing slowed, their ears became more adept to the sounds of the luscious green mountain. They both heard one sound that was displaced in the habitat. Mitch set off a flare, and looked up. The pilot dove down, looking for a place to land. When it did, the men raced toward it and met the people with a look of amazement. They anxiously informed the people in the helicopter what happened. When the conversing finished they helped Ron and Mitch into the safe and welcoming helicopter. The two men sat down, still astonished that a helicopter came to rescue them. They fell asleep, glad that they might get a peaceful slumber. when they woke, the helicopter was arriving in San Francisco. The two friends departed from the helicopter just wanting to rest more. Even though the press was on them like a hungry wolf, they finally got through the mob.

The two men returned to their homes, though they kept in touch through letters and quite frequent visits. A friendship had been forged on that lonely, harsh Appalachian mountain. Their friendship was one to last forever.

Mitchell Rotunno
Age: 13

# THE DAY THE TEACHER WAS GONE

One morning I woke up and got ready for school. I brushed my teeth after I ate my breakfast. I put on my shoes and went to school with my mom. After I got to school, I was playing on the playground and then the bell rang. Everybody rushed to the door to be the first in line. But, when everybody got to the door, nobody opened it. The door was unlocked, so everyone went in. No one was there, so we sat in our desks and it was quiet.

First we sat down. It was Friday so everyone was starving. It was not even lunch yet, so we started art. We started making turkeys. We wanted to paint the turkeys, so we looked for paint. We had to search every shelf in the room. Then we finally found the paint and painted the turkeys. Then we went to recess. We played soccer and everyone broke the recess rules. We got even more hungry. When we went in, we gathered every kid's lunch money. The pizza we bought was eight bucks, and that was that.

We had a pizza party. We ate ten boxes of pizza and we felt so bad that I saw all the kids lying on the floor. They looked so sick (as in ill) I would say.

After we got sick, the teacher unlocked the door and everybody fainted and then they got up from the floor. We just stared at the teacher and then we fainted again. Mrs. Millard was late to work and now she knows not to come late again!

Antonio Gonzales
Age: 8

# THROUGH THE EYES OF A FIFTH GRADER

You are about to go on a journey. A journey through the life of a girl. Brittni Eastin, age eleven, fifth grade.

On a school day Brittni's mom wakes her up at 6:30 a.m. She gets ready for school by getting dressed, eating, brushing her hair, brushing her teeth, and starting the car sometimes for her mom.

As the time comes for Brittni and her mom to leave, Brittni waits in the car. They both leave to go to school.

Right when they get to school, Brittni's mom goes to clock in for work because she is the school's secretary. Brittni and her mom both go into the lunchroom. At exactly 7:30 a.m. the kids get to eat breakfast. Brittni's mom is the lady to whom the kids give their lunch numbers. Brittni's number is three hundred fifty, but she doesn't have to say it because her mom knows it. Her mom knows almost all of the lunch numbers by heart. Sometimes, Brittni eats. It depends on what breakfast is.

At 8:00 a.m. school starts. Brittni goes to her classroom. The first thing she does is talk to her friends. When their teacher Mrs. Lubbers comes, everyone is seated. Everybody then stands up again to say the pledge. Afterwards, sometimes they grade papers. But other times they do math.

At 9:00 a.m. they go to music and p.e. Music comes first. Brittni plays the clarinet. At 9:30 a.m. they go to p.e. Brittni's dad is the p.e. teacher. They usually play dodgeball or softball.

At 10:00 a.m. they go back to the classroom.

When they get back, they finish their math. Then, they grade more papers.

Exactly at 11:30 a.m. they go to lunch. At 12:00 p.m. they go to recess until 12:30 p.m.

After recess they go to library or computers. It depends what day it is. It is usually 1:30 p.m. when they get back to class. The kids who go to literacy lab go at that time. They finish their work. Between 2:15 p.m. and 2:30 p.m. the literacy lab group comes back.

They all do social studies until 3:10 p.m. Everyone gets ready to go home! At 3:15 p.m. everyone goes home and Brittni goes to her mom's office. They leave at 4:00 p.m.

When Brittni gets home, she does her homework, watches TV, eats dinner, and watches more TV. What do you know, it is 9:30 p.m.! Brittni's bedtime! When she wakes up, it is a brand-new day; and she does the same thing.

Brittni Eastin
Age: 11

# KING BODI

Once upon a time, there lived a king named Bodi. He even had a shiny gold sword. Well anyway, King Bodi lived in an eighty story castle in a beautiful grassy place. One day, King Bodi decided to go for a ride, so he hopped up in his cool go-cart that his dad built him and zoomed off. On his way, he spotted three little puppies. They looked sad, so King Bodi asked them, "What is the matter?" They barked and barked, so King Bodi took them home to his castle.

That very next day, King Bodi named the spotted one Bodi, the white one Sumo, and the black one Calypso. Over the years, the dogs got bigger, though the king didn't.

One day, Bodi went out for a walk when all of a sudden, a huge ugly dragon rose out of the ground. He was really scary. Bodi started to pull his sword out, but then the dragon knocked the sword out of his hands. Bodi yelled, "Help!"

Then out of nowhere, the three big dogs jumped in front of Bodi and fought the dragon just long enough for Bodi to get his sword. Bodi said, "Have a nice time in devil's land!" Then he sliced the dragon. Then he kneeled to the dogs and said, "Thank you."

And for the first time, they said, "No, thank you for helping and raising us."

Patrick Colton McKeough Larkin
Age: 9

70

PARKER 201

On January 23, 2003, in my living room, my dad told me something I'd never forget. He told me that he and his buddies worked on the biggest oil rig in North America. He worked in Wyoming, in the Rocky Mountains. While the wind hit him in the face he still worked, he drilled a 25,860 foot hole. At that time I was amazed. When he said he had to drive about two hundred miles from Riverton to the Rocky Mountains, it was a hard drive but he kept on doing it. One day he quit, now they're asking him back, I'm excited. I won't be amazed if he or his rig will be in a history book someday.

Andrew McIntyre
Age: 10

CIRCUS CLOWNS AND MORE

Fluffy, pink cotton candy; bright, happy clowns; dancing elephants -- every child's dream! These are the sights, smells, and tastes of the circus. My mom, dad, grandpa, and grandma drove me to the Barnum and Bailey Circus in Denver, Colorado, when I was only three years old.

The circus is an exciting place for all five of a child's senses. I could hear loud clapping and cheering all around me as the crowd watched many thrilling things happening before their eyes.

We saw acrobats in glittery clothes flying high on a swinging trapeze. We also saw a big round clear ball with people riding motorcycles inside of it.

I smelled buttery popcorn, salty peanuts, and sweet cotton candy. I felt my stomach growling when I sniffed the sweet smell of the cotton candy, and I asked my parents for my own. I smiled as I felt it slowly melt in my mouth. It reminded me of a pink, fluffy cloud. As the grand show ended, I did not want to go home. It had been an amazingly wonderful day. To remind me of the circus, my grandma bought me a toy. It was a clear ball with pretend motorcycles inside of it. When I pressed my finger onto a button, the motorcycles rode around in circles inside of the ball. It was a wonderfully spectacular day that I will always remember.

Baylee Markus
Age: 10

## Chapter One

When I was walking along an aisle in the library, a label on a book spine caught my eye. REBEL GENERAL, I read. It was a copy of Robert E. Lee's journal from the Civil War.

I didn't get to read any of it, but I pulled it off the shelf as fast as I could and checked it out and then went home.

When I got home, I went upstairs and read my book. It said, "Today I will lead my Confederate Army, with Stonewall Jackson, into battle against the Union Army."

I started to read into the night and fell asleep at about 9:30.

Suddenly, I was riding horseback between General John Brown and Stonewall Jackson. And soldiers were walking with bayonets and were wearing gray suits. When I looked down, I was wearing a gray hat with a gray suit and a long, gray jacket with boots. I was riding a white horse with a black mane and tail, named Traveller.

Everybody was calling me Sir Robert or General Robert and sometimes I was just called Robert. I looked straight ahead and I saw five men, each pushing a gray cannon with Confederate battle flags on it.

I asked myself, could it be? Am I leading the Confederate Army into battle at Gettysburg, fighting against Ulysses S. Grant and the Union Army?

I turned my head and Stonewall Jackson was staring at me as if I was dimwitted.

"Yes," he said.

"Yes, what?" I asked.

"Yes, you're leading the Confederacy," said Stonewall.

"Oh! Yes... I suppose I dozed off. Wait a minute! Is my accent changing?"

"Pardon me?" said Stonewall and General Brown, both at the same time.

"Union enemy ahead!" cried out a soldier in the front.

All of a sudden, gunshots and dreadful screams were heard and Traveller galloped off with me on him. And I was riding with both generals back into the woods.

## Chapter Two

While I rode up toward the Union Army, every second someone was falling by death – Confederate and Union soldiers were being shot, blown up by cannons or being stabbed by bayonets.

Stonewall yelled, "Grab your sword!" and just then, I remembered about my shiny, silver sword. But when I reached down to grab it, it wasn't there. At that moment, I ran out of luck, because a Union cavalryman was about ten seconds away from me.

My eyes saw my sword. It was hanging from the harness on Traveller's neck. So I grabbed it and charged at the cavalryman and stabbed him in his right shoulder and he dropped to the ground!

I could hear Union drummers banging their drums in the background and I could hear Confederate buglers blowing their bugles. I could hear the sweet chant music of the cannons and the dreadful screams of all the soldiers dying slowly.

I started up the hills into the woods with Stonewall and still had my sword with me in my hand.

And Stonewall said, "Keep it in your hand!"

"But why?"

"Because we're going back through."

"Okay. We shall go back through and fight for each other."

"Yes. That is true," he said.

"Stonewall, can I tell you something?"

"Yes."

"Duty is the sublimest word in our language. Do your duty in all things. You can never do more, you should never wish to do less."

"Yes. Right you are," said Stonewall. "Right you are. We should get going now."

"Yes," I said. "Good luck to you, Stonewall."

"And good luck to you, Sir Robert."

## Chapter Three

On the way back, I saw General Brown lying helplessly on the ground.

"Sherman!" he said in a low voice.

"Sherman what?" I asked.

"Sherman shot me."

"Can you walk, or can you ride?"

"No."

"I'll send help as soon as I can."

When I was riding, I heard another rider behind me. I turned and looked. It was General Grant, riding on Cincinnati, his huge, dark brown horse! He charged right for me, with his sword held high and pointed right at me! I thought he was going to kill me, but something caught his attention and he rode away.

I started riding back down the hill.

## Chapter Four

When I got there, the war was still going on and on, and more soldiers were dead. Some were propped up against trees or lying over rock walls or dead on the ground, but it didn't mean we had won yet.

So I charged. With my horse, my sword and my courage, I charged. And one by one my enemies were falling to the ground without suffering. For the moment, I was winning.

But then, I saw three horses with three men. They were coming out of the fog and mist. They were three generals -- Grant, Sherman and Douglas.

And I had only Stonewall, about three hundred men and me. But these generals were skilled and it may be their lucky day.

All three generals and their army marched. Right then, I knew I was going to lose, but we gave it our all.

## Chapter Five

At Appomattox Courthouse, where Jefferson Davis and Abraham Lincoln were standing by me, Grant wanted me to sign a paper to end the Civil War. So, I signed it and walked out of the courthouse. I got on Traveller and rode into the woods. And when I was riding, a snake scared Traveller and he bucked me off. My head hit a rock.

## Chapter Six

When I woke up, my mother had propped up me up because I had bumped my head when I fell off my bed. So that explained Traveller's bucking!

Austin Chandler
Age: 10

# LOST

One day last summer my friends and I went to the mall to shop for some clothes and a bedspread. Then we were going to get a bite to eat. After lunch we couldn't find our parents. We looked everywhere. We decided to split up. Ashley, Cassie, and I went upstairs, while Jake, Brandon, and Josh went downstairs to look for them. I tried to call my parents, but they didn't answer their phones. So, I slowly walked everywhere looking for our parents. I walked and walked but I couldn't find them at all. We met with the boys to see if they found anybody. But when we got there we asked them if they found anybody yet? They told us that they didn't see them. We said, "Let's look again, and meet back in an hour and we'll get some food and look after we eat." Then we left to go look for our parents some more. We started looking, we looked in all their favorite stores, but they weren't there. We couldn't find them. Thirty minutes passed. We had thirty minutes left, we looked everywhere we could think of. We still couldn't find them! Another thirty minutes passed, so we went to meet them at the meeting place, but nobody found them down there either. We decided to go get a bite to eat. We went to Chick-Fil-A. We all shared chicken and two pops. One for the girls and one for the boys. When we were done we went looking for them some more. We walked to Bath and Body Works. That's my mom's favorite store. So we went there because that's usually where she's at. This time she wasn't there. We went downstairs because we can't find them. I told them we should look in the Disney store, because my mom likes to buy me things from that store. We looked in there, but guess what we found. We found our parents. They said, "Finally you got done! We've been waiting for you, but you didn't come. Where have you been?"

"It's a long story," we said.

Shelby Pacheco
Age: 9

It was a glorious Saturday in autumn, and Jack really wanted to go outside and play with his brand-new rocket, but he knew that he couldn't. He had to practice his violin. Jack had promised his mom and dad that he would practice at 4 PM today, but the time had passed so quickly.

Then, he heard the nagging voice, "Sweetie, are you getting out your violin? You need to praaaac-tiiiiice."

"I sure am," he lied. Jack hadn't even washed his hands.

He had told his dad that he liked performing better than practicing, but his dad only said, "If you want to perform you need to practice." Jack knew that this was true, but he didn't like to admit it.

Jack, the boy who wouldn't practice, had two friends whose names were Jose and Maria; Jose was his best friend in third grade, and Maria had just moved to town and joined their class. Jose played the piano, and Maria played the cello. Jose and Maria liked Jack because they all had the same struggles.

"Jack, Jose is coming over in exactly one hour," his mother reminded him.

"Okay," Jack said absent-mindedly, as he opened his case and put rosin on his bow. When Jack was in the middle of one of his better pieces, a Bach minuet, he heard the doorbell ring. "Probably Jose," he thought. He knew that his mom or dad would open the door. "Hello Mrs. Stiggins," he heard Jose say, "how are you today? Uh, umm, where is Jack?"

"Jack is upstairs practicing his violin," she replied. "You may wait down here, if you'd like." Jack overheard this conversation, and knew that he had been condemned to another twenty minutes of practicing until Jose and he could play outside.

After he had finished his red, blue, yellow, and green scales -- with arpeggios -- he went on to play one of his favorite recent pieces, a concerto by Vivaldi. He looked at the clock and realized that his hour was finished. Joyfully, he packed up his instrument and put away his music stand, then went downstairs to see Jose, to play outside, to run around, and just to have fun.

Jose's dad was a pilot, and so Jack wasn't surprised when he suddenly heard his friend say, "My dad is on a business trip, so it's just Mom and I in the house."

"Where to?" Jack asked.

"He's going to New Orleans, a jazz city, and he promises he'll bring me back a music book." Jack could hear that Jose was not too thrilled.

"Why aren't you happy about getting a music book?"

"Oh you know why," Jose replied in a ninny tone.

"What, more practicing?" Jack guessed.

"Exactly," Jose sighed.

"Jack," Jose said, "did you know that you could quit an instrument?"

"Yup, but I don't really want to," Jack said.

"Why not?"

"Because it would mean that I wouldn't get to perform," Jack said.

"You know what?" Jose said.

"What?" Jack asked.

"I bet you could quit but still go on performing. See what I mean?" Jose said excitedly.

"Oh my." Jack was very excited at the idea. "Do you really think I could quit learning to play the violin but still perform?"

"Yep, that's exactly what I mean," Jose replied.

Suddenly, Jack asked, wide-eyed, "You don't want to quit, do you?"

"I sure do," Jose announced.

"Oh no! What will I do?"

"You can quit if you want to," Jose said.

"Quit?" Jack yelled. "I would never miss the opportunity to quit and still perform." Jack's cheeks were flushed, and his eyes sparkled. He could see that Jose was excited, too, so he continued, "It would be great! Let's go tell Maria!"

"Okay, let's go!"

Maria's house was across the road from Jack's, and the boys wasted no time in getting on their shoes. "Mom, we're going to Maria's for a second," Jack reported.

"Okay, honey buns," said his mother, who was working on her computer in the study, and didn't care much if Jack went across the road. "I'm sorry to ask you," Jack whispered, "but what is Maria's last name?"

"I think it is DeQuimina," Jose answered, "but don't ask me." The boys had made friends with Maria at school, but neither of them had met her parents. Jack went up to the door and knocked, clunk, clunk, clunk. Maria's mother immediately came to the door. "Hello, who are you?" she asked kindly. Jose politely answered,

"I'm Jose, and this is Jack. We made friends with Maria at school, and we just wanted to say hi."

"Hello, boys. Maria is upstairs practicing the cello. Would you like to say hi to her?"

"Thanks, yes we would," Jack remembered to say, because he was listening to the deep-toned sounds floating down the stairs.

Jack and Jose climbed the tidy wooden stairs to Maria's room, where they met a closed door with music from a cello coming out. Jack knocked softly, and the music stopped. Maria came to the door and opened it. "Hello," Jack and Jose said together.

"Hi," Maria said cheerfully, "it's nice to see you guys again. Why are you here?"

Jack looked over his shoulder to Jose and said, shyly, "We came to see if, well, if you wanted to quit cello." Maria sat down on her bed and stared blankly at them.

Then she said, "Why?"

"You know why!" Jose broke in, "it's because you don't like practicing the cello."

Maria shook her head and said softly, "I can't quit."

"Why not?" Jack said, angrily. "I'm quitting, and so is Jose." Jose nodded his head in agreement.

"Really?" Maria looked, still blankly, from one to the other... "Really? You guys are quitting?"

"Uh-huh," Jack said, "we are!"

"Really! I never thought..."

"That we would quit?" Jack chimed in, "well, we have, or, we're going to."

"And what will I do?" Maria almost yelled.

"You could quit too," Jose said.

"Yeauuuh, I could," Maria answered thoughtfully. "I couuuuld... I never thought about..."

"Thought about what?!" Jack asked.

"Well, you see, my mom really wanted me to play cello because her dad played cello in an orchestra, and it was his career. And my dad is a teacher at the college, and he also wanted me to play cello. He said he knew a man in the music department who would give me lessons. I didn't want to disappoint my mom and dad, so I started to play the cello."

Jack and Jose waited in an awkward silence, taking in this tale. Finally Jose spoke. "Gee, Maria, we never knew that."

"Yeah," Jack broke in, "we never knew that you didn't want to quit."

Maria, however, completely contradicted him. "I never said that I didn't want to quit. All I said was that I couldn't quit."

Jose had been thinking and he said, "Well, Maria... I'm sure that your mom and dad didn't know that you didn't want to play the cello. They thought you did want to play, so, you probably can quit."

Shortly after this, however, there came a bit of good news for Jack, Jose, and Maria, and that was... well, as you already know, Jose's dad was a pilot. He was going on a flight to Boston soon, because there was going to be a special concert by children musicians there and he thought that the three friends might want to go and listen. They accepted the invitation and that next Tuesday they all boarded the plane and were off. The Boston airport proved very busy and crowded. Everyone was rushing and looking for someone whom they couldn't find. At last a taxi was hailed and they went to their concert.

Just as the boys and girl go there the man at the loudspeaker was announcing, "Good evening, ladies and gentlemen. I regret to have to tell you that our cellist, violinist, and pianist have come down with the flu. Is there anybody who would like to substitute for our performers? If you would walk down the aisle to the stage, it would be greatly appreciated!" Slowly, Jose, Maria, and Jack rose from their seats and walked down to the orchestra pit, up the stairs, and onto the stage. They were welcomed with shouts of joy! After taking their chairs and instruments they played. Their beautiful music enthralled the crowd and everyone applauded.

When Jack, Jose, and Maria came back home they had changed their minds. They resumed their places practicing the violin, piano, and cello, and they played happily ever after as musical friends.

SO -- when you would like to quit something, just remember this story and think again.

Hannah Carrese
Age: 8

# THE BLAZE

Last year on Christmas Eve, my cousin and I went outside. Instead of admiring the usual Christmas lights, our eyes were immediately drawn to the blaze of fire next door in the neighbor's ditch. A strong smell of wood and leaves filled the air and burned my eyes. We bolted inside and screamed for my dad. Horrible thoughts about our Christmas being ruined filled our heads. My dad was now in a panic too! He jolted outside. Then he came racing back, shoved us aside, and scrambled to call 911! As we waited for the firemen to arrive, we returned to our own backyard to figure out more as to what was going on in the neighbor's yard. You see the boy that lives next door doesn't always understand the consequences of his actions, especially playing with fire! It seems that he wanted to see what happens when dry leaves, brittle branches and gasoline are mixed with a lit match. We all found out. The roaring blaze had now grown eight feet tall. Then the fire department arrived at the house. Within minutes the threatening blaze was out. Illegal burning is prohibited in our city. This type of offense carries a hefty fine. Luckily we noticed the blaze before our lives and houses were consumed by the fire. Since that incident our neighbor has not had a blaze, but I still watch that house every time I go outside.

Jake Bradbury
Age: 10

It was raining in New York the night the tanker carrying the nuclear bombs chugged into Manhattan. As it passed beneath the St. Matthew's bridge a silent shape leaped from the edge of the bridge and landed lightly on the tanker's immense hull.  Reaching into his pocket he grabbed his radio and dialed the frequency to his partner on the opposite end of the tanker.

"Bravo, this is Frost. I have made contact with the target and am waiting further instructions."

"Frost?  This is Bravo, I am down in the engine room, and the bombs are in the deep hull on the starboard side."

"Bravo, how many guards do they have on the starboard side?" Frost asked with a quiet whisper.

"I count approximately seven sentries patrolling the entrance to the engine room.  I'd say that there are at least five more patrolling the halls.  Frost, be careful, they have body armor so only a head shot will work."

"Bravo, I'm proceeding with preparations for plan B."

"Same here Frost, remember, place the bomb on a key structural point otherwise the boat won't sink."

"Bomb is in place.  Frost out."

"Bravo out."

"Frost stood up and pulled out his silenced SOCOM pistol.  Once he had his weapon ready, he quietly ran to the edge and surveyed his surroundings.  Several guards were patrolling the outer perimeters, close to where he had landed.  Above him, several guards were patrolling the top decks.  Pulling out his radio, he once again called Bravo.

"Bravo, this is Frost, what is the best way to get to the engine room?"

"Frost, make your way up to the top of the tanker, then find a hatch that will lead down to the engine room.  Bravo out."

Nodding to himself, he jumped up on the railing leading to the bridge.  Peeking above, he crawled through the railing and looked around.  Seeing no one, he slid through the railing and cautiously walked toward the metallic door.  Suddenly, from behind the door he heard gunshots and loud voices.

"You fool! How could you let him get past you! Bring your sentries down to the engine room, and conduct a search immediately! The Brotherhood will not allow even one mistake unpunished!"

"Yes sir!"

Hearing this, Frost quickly called Bravo. "Bravo! Sentries are coming down to search the area. Get out of there!"

"What?" Bravo questioned.

"Bravo, people calling themselves the Brotherhood know you're here. Get out of there now!" yelled Frost.

"The Brotherhood, Frost, is a terrorist group in southwestern Russia. They must be planning to attack New York! Frost, you've gotta stop them! Wait... I hear voices, Frost!"

"Bravo! Come in Bravo!" But the radio went dead in his hands.

Standing up, he raced into the door and down the hatch that led to the engine room. Climbing down the ladder, he could hear the voices yelling and more gunshots.

"Tell me, fool, what you are doing here! Answer me!" It sounded like a woman with a Russian accent. "If you don't tell me, I will make you!"

With another shot there was a shrill yell of pain. Knowing he could wait no longer, Frost leaped out and threw one of his stun grenades. Hiding in the corner, he waited for the blast. It seemed to take forever; a "pop" sounded with a bright flash.

Peeking around the corner, he saw the guards sprawled on the floor with a woman holding a pistol. Realizing that they would wake soon, he grabbed his friend and ran down the corridor to the nuclear weapons.

**\*\*\*\*\*\*\*\*\*\***

Frost gently shook his friend with a strong hand. "Bravo!" he whispered and shook him 'til he was back in reality.

"Frost? Frost, what happened?" Bravo questioned him shakily.

"You were just about to be killed by the terrorists. Bravo, I need to disable the warheads."

"Frost, you need to access the computer and get proof of the Brotherhood."

"Why?" Frost questioned.

"Because if we don't, this will look like we are the terrorists, instead of us stopping a terrorist group igniting nuclear bombs!"

"Okay, fine, how do you access the computer?" Frost said, giving up.

"Here, take this disk. Insert it for five seconds, that's it."

"Okay, where are you going to be?" Frost asked.

But before Bravo could answer, they heard voices from the hallway. "Here take the disk and go!" Bravo said, throwing it to Frost. "Now!"

Turning, Frost ran down the gloomy corridor. Turning the corner, he heard the woman yelling, and soon a shot sounded in the tanker. Running down the corridor, he thought he could hear Bravo saying quietly, "War is chaos, battle is chaos, but chaos should never be war." Tears filling his eyes, Frost fled through the corridor.

**\*\*\*\*\*\*\*\*\*\***

Peeking around the corner, Frost saw the computer complex and one guard standing nearby. "Probably his buddies are looking for me," he thought. Taking out his SOCOM, he carefully aimed and pulled the trigger. The guard fell to the ground, motionless. Frost tiptoed to the computer and inserted the disk. Counting to five he turned to see the woman aiming a gun to his head.

"Hello. Welcome to the computer center! Now I'll be taking that disk," she said slyly.

"Why would I give it to you?" Frost asked sarcastically.

"No reason, I just hold the detonator to these!" Sadistically gesturing to the weapons.

Frost couldn't stand still another minute. Jumping quickly he tackled her.

"Oomph!" she grunted as she hit the floor and the button simultaneously.

Frost staggered up and seeing her stunned on the floor, ran down the corridor. Climbing up the hatch, he ran toward the side of the tanker, readying his detonator to the explosives. Diving over the railing, he slammed his finger on the detonator button.

A resounding boom was heard. Shock waves swept over Frost, sending him under the water. Once again reaching the surface, he saw the tanker in an aura of flame slowly sinking under the beating waves. Fires dancing on the water where the tanker's gasoline had been released, he was slowly being burned by the heated water. Slipping under the waves, he knew he had saved Manhattan from disaster, quickly consciousness drifted away.

Frost woke to see the bright lights of a ship. "Am I dead?" he asked.

"No, you're not dead, but a few minutes and you would have been," said a warm voice.

Sitting up, he saw a middle-aged man with a suit of the navy. "Who are you?" Frost asked.

"I am Colonel Jack Johnson of the United States Navy. We are now heading toward Manhattan. I salute you special agent, Frost, you are a national hero." Saying this with authority, the Colonel saluted and left the room to a dazed and aching Frost.

\*\*\*\*\*\*\*\*\*\*

As Frost walked out of the ship to the city of Manhattan clapping and cheering, he wasn't really listening. He was still in that dim corridor, turning the corridor he heard the woman yelling and a shot sounding in the tanker. Running down the corridor, tears streaming down his face, he thought he could hear Bravo saying quietly, "War is chaos, battle is chaos, but chaos should never be war."

Joshua John Savage<br>
Age: 13

Smack! I hit the water and went under.

"I've got to start surfing better than this if I'm going to compete in the Halaula surf contest next week."

"We could go to KoleKole Beach," my friend Kiki said.

"Sure that'd be great!" I said.

Whoosh! My board slipped out from underneath me.

"Man these waves are awesome, but they're whooping me," I said.

"It's a nice sunshiny day here in Hawaii and the waves are awesome. Surfers, don't forget to sign up for today's competition," the announcer said.

"Mimi Kamaii; competitor," I told the lady at the sign-up booth.

"Where are you from?" she asked

"Makapala, Hawaii," I replied.

I heard my name being announced and ran down to the water's edge. The whistle blew and I jumped into the water. I saw a wave and went for it.

"8.6 points for Mimi Kamaii!" the announcer yelled excitedly into the microphone. "8.4 points for Apua Kliikakani!" the announcer yelled excitedly into the microphone

I saw another good wave coming my way so I hurriedly got into a good spot. I dipped my hands into the salty water and paddled as hard as I could. I turned my board around and waited for the right moment. I jumped up on my board.

"If I get this I could win!" I was thinking.

Wham! I slipped off my board, but got right back up.

"We have another 8.8 points for Apua," the announcer said.

"I'm still in this," I kept thinking.

A wave came and went, followed by a most definite winner.

"This is it!" I told myself.

I saw Apua my opponent.

"NO!" I wanted to scream. I went for it I was ahead of her.

"Mimi is going for it. Right behind her is Apua! Will Mimi make it?! Oh!! Apua falls! Mimi could have it!" The announcer was so excited he started yelling.

I stood up and got ready.

"Ladies and gentlemen your winner, Mimi Kamaii with 10.4 more points!!"

I walked up to shore and everyone was screaming.

"Mimi, can I have your autograph?"

Mollie Peck
Age: 12

# THE FROG NAMED BOB

One day in Cañon City, Colorado there was a frog named Bob. Bob was hopping along the road and saw a truck full of bread. So Bob jumped in then started to nibble on some of the tasty wheat. He became so full that tiredness overtook him and a nap was in order. And he went fast asleep on the remaining bread.

Suddenly he toppled over on the floor of the truck. The truck was moving really fast and he couldn't get out! He panicked and was scared to death. Bob didn't know what to do. So he just jumped back on the pile of wheat bread and hung on for dear life. Bob thought he'd never get out alive.

Abruptly, the truck stopped, Bob was tossed into an open crate. The crate was picked up and shoved into a ship, or so he thought it was. The ship ride was a long journey, Bob became tired and thirsty. Bob wished that he wouldn't have leap-frogged into that bread. Suddenly the crate was picked up and opened by a mean-looking sailor. Bob jumped out as fast as he could. To his surprise, he was on the shore of the Hawaiian Islands. That night Bob heard some hula music. It was coming out of a little grass hut.

When he scrambled in the hut the five women screamed the six men got their guns and the four kids tried to get him. They wanted to get him because he ate so much bread he was eight times wider that made him look like he was Jupiter. Finally, someone squashed him then they ate him for dinner.

Reba Garrison

# MURPHY JONES

Jack London i  )ne of the top murder investigators in New York City.  Jack has a wife and two kids. His wife Shirley is a stockbroker for the New York Stock Exchange.  They both have two wonderful boys, Pete the oldest who is a jokester and Carson the youngest.  Jack is a successful murder investigator in the Bronx of New York.  Through the years he has solved eighty percent of his cases.  Little did Jack know, his luck was about to change.

Jack woke up on Monday morning dazed and confused.  In the middle of the night he had an awful dream.  The dream was about his son Pete and a man who he did not recognize.  Trying to come to his senses he throws off the blankets and heads downstairs.  Winding down the stairs he smells the aromas of breakfast cooking.  Smells like bacon and eggs today, Jack thought.  Jack kisses his wife Shirley on the cheek while reaching for the coffeepot and his favorite purple coffee cup.

"Sorry, Honey but I'm going to have to skip breakfast today.  I have to get to the office early to finish up some work," says Jack as he grabs the paper and his briefcase and heads out the door.

Jack opens the car door and sits down and puts his briefcase and paper down on the passenger seat.  As he puts the paper down he sees Murphy Jones printed in bold letters.  Jack's heart skips a beat remembering that terrible man he locked up fifteen years ago.  Jack starts the car and drives away from his house.  Jack remembers Murphy's eyes when he was cuffed and escorted out.  Murphy looks Jack dead in the eyes, as if he was saying, "I will get you back for this."

Murphy Jones was found guilty for kidnapping and murdering children.  Murphy kidnapped and murdered five children.  A warrant was out for his arrest.  No one was able to catch him.  Murphy was a skilled killer.  After being an investigator himself he knew what they looked for.  He planned his kidnappings well leaving no traces.  After three investigators gave up looking for him, Jack London was brought in to crack the case.  Jack found one clue Murphy had left behind.  Apparently Murphy leaves notes behind for the children's parents to find.  Jack had one of the notes analyzed and to their surprise he found a fingerprint.  It was Murphy Jones.

The ride to the office was trafficless. Thoughts were overcome in his mind. He thought about his boys, mostly about Pete. Jack couldn't get that awful dream out of his head. It was about a man and Pete. Pete was in a dark alley far from home; he was screaming and trying to run from this man. Jack couldn't remember what the man looked like but was sure he had been hurting his son. At the end of the dream he saw flashing lights and many people all around. Jack gets to his office right on time. He even finds a close parking spot. Jack gets out of the car and heads for the office door. Just as he opens it his partner opens it for him.

"Hello Jack," says Monte River.

"Hi Monte," say Jack back.

"Did you see the paper today Jack?" asks Monte with a puzzling look in his eye.

"Yeah I sure did Monte."

"You still remember his eyes don't you Jack," says Monte sitting down in Jack's office.

"Yes, I do. And to tell you the truth I'm scared," says Jack while unloading his briefcase onto his desk.

"Man I would be too if I were you."

The day went on like any other day with the exception of thoughts of Pete running through his head. Something just wasn't right. Jack thought of calling the school but decided not to because Pete hates it when he checks up on him. At three o'clock Jack calls Shirley. He knows Pete is home so he can talk to Pete and know that everything is all right. Shirley picks up the phone and answers with a frantic voice.

"Jack, Pete didn't come home from school. I even called the school and he's not there. He better not be playing one of his jokes on me," says Shirley pacing up and down the kitchen.

"OK, calm down. I'm sure he's OK. I will go out and look for him. He's probably with some friend. OK dear?"

"OK. I will be right here by the phone and I will call you if he calls," exclaims Shirley.

Jack hangs up the phone and grabs his coat and briefcase, thinking in his mind that Pete knows not to go anywhere without telling them. Pete is only twelve years old and too young to go out by himself. Jack and Shirley taught him what to do if he was in trouble. Jack rushes out the door to his car. All of the sudden it all clicks. Murphy just escaped from prison today. He must be trying to get me back. How could I let this happen to my own child, Jack thinks as he hits the steering wheel?

Earlier that day Jack read Murphy's files. As usual Murphy sends a letter to the parents of the child saying he has kidnapped their child and they will never see them again. He states where they can find their child already dead and with no trace of him. Jack wiped tears away from his face as he remembers what he read. Pulling into the driveway he can see Shirley sitting by the phone waiting for someone to call. Jack doesn't know how he will break the news to her.

"What are you doing home? You should be looking for Pete," says Shirley angrily.

"I know who took him. Remember that man named Murphy Jones who kidnaps and murders kids? I locked him up fifteen years ago."

"Yes, and are you saying that man has my little boy?" says Shirley with tears welling up in her eyes.

"Yes that is what I'm saying. Where's the mail. I think he may have sent us something telling us where he is and maybe we can get there in time to save him," Jack says frantically looking for the mail.

"It's over here," Shirley points to the kitchen counter.

Jack rushes to the counter and finds what he is looking for. It's a letter that just says "Jack London." Jack thinks Murphy may have put the letter in the mail while no one was home then went to go pick up Pete. Jack rips open the letter.
The letter says:

It's too late to save your son. It's also too late to find me. I have left no clues to trace me, you can look but you won't find. You're a smart man, and I want you to go through what I have been through. Here is the place you can find your dead child. 1972 Leap Avenue. Once you find the address turn right and go to the alley. You will find him there.

Jack hands the letter to his wife and turns away from her and begins to cry. Shirley reads the letter hoping she would find some relief. Jack watches his wife's eyes as she gets to the dead child. Her eyes fill up with tears and she begins to sob.

"We have to call the police," exclaims Jack.

"OK, but maybe this is one of his jokes he's playing on us. Or maybe this is some kind of sick joke of Murphy's."

"No, I read his files and his letters are always right. He makes no errors in them nor does he joke around," Jack says as he dials 911.

Jack told his story to the police and told them to get to the scene as soon as possible. Jack knows this story will be all over the evening news. Jack and Shirley got into the car without saying a word. They drive off to where their son is. In their hearts they hope he is alive but know it's not a possibility. Jack told the police to put barriers up on all of the ports out of the United States. He also told them to tighten security at the airports.

Coming up on the scene of the crime, they see ambulances, cop cars and many people. For some reason this all looks too familiar to Jack. The sirens of the police cars are blasting; red, white and blue lights are seen from all around. Jack and Shirley pass the alleyway seeing detectives doing their work. Jack stops dead in his tracks and remembers his dream. All of this is starting to make sense. The dream was about Pete and Murphy. Jack and Shirley get to the ambulance where Pete is. They see Pete on the stretcher with feet sticking out. Four men are working frantically on this lifeless body. Jack's and Shirley's hopes raise a little. They walk towards the ambulance. They finally get to a place where they can see Pete clearly. They see one of his legs move, but realized one of the men bumped him. They spot the life support machine; they see little bumps in the line. It's a slim hope but at least it's a hope. With little anticipation the line goes flat. The men keep working on him but they fail. Jack and Shirley weep as they know it's too late for him. The men shut the doors.

The years go by. Jack London is still trying to find Murphy Jones. Jack is determined to track down this killer. Every day he gets closer and closer to the killer, but not close enough.

Julie Hinkle
Age: 18

"Adam and Lucy, it's time for bed so get your teeth brushed," shouted Mary.

"OK Mom," they both shouted.

"Hey, Lucy do you want some of my Zours?" asked Adam.

"What are those," asked Lucy.

"Zours are little sour candies, and the flavors are pink watermelon, sour apple, blue raspberry, and sour tangerine, " said Adam.

"Here, Lucy what color do you want?" asked Adam.

"Pink," said Lucy.

"Here's a pink try it," said Adam.

"Good," said Lucy.

"Mom's going to get mad at you if you don't stop eating these things," suggested Lucy.

"But they're so good," said Adam.

All of a sudden Lucy and Adam began to turn into Zours.

"Adam I think we're turning into Zours!" shouted Lucy.

"I agree," said Adam.

"What are we going to do when Mother sees us as two green and pink Zours?" asked Adam.

"I don't really know," said Lucy.

Before the little eyes on the children's heads could blink, they were in a whole different world. All around them were millions of other Zours. In the underground city it was so quiet and Adam thought he wouldn't talk because maybe they were scared of him and Lucy. Adam turned around and Lucy was gone!

"Lucy, Lucy," shouted Adam.

Then, coming from the left was a blue Zour running and calling someone's name.

"Hi, what is your name?" asked Adam.

"Cody," he said.

"I'm looking for my brother," said Cody.

"What is his name?" asked Adam.

"Brandon, and he's a orange Zour about half the size of me," said Cody.

"Ha, ha, ha," said a voice.

"Who was that?" asked Adam.

"Maybe it was the evil gumdrop," suggested Cody.

"There's Lucy and I think Brandon too," said Adam.

"I know one thing, that evil gumdrop can't live in water. Follow me and we'll get the hose and spray him," exclaimed Cody.

"There's a hose Cody," said Adam.

"Here help me spray him," said Cody.

With both of the boys pushing the knob, the water came out and hit gumdrop in the legs. Gumdrop fell and Lucy and Brandon fell to the ground with a thump.

"Lucy, Brandon," shouted the two boys.

"Thank goodness you're okay Lucy," said Adam.

Lucy said, "While me and Brandon looked in the main office I saw a sign that said 'Potions to Come Back to Normal'."

"Ya, and I saw a freeze button," said Brandon.

"Okay, let's go check this out," said Cody.

The four kids ran as fast as they could to get to the main office. They walked around but still couldn't find the freeze knob or the potions.

"Here's the freeze knob," yelled Brandon.

"Hit it," shouted Cody.

"Here it goes," said Brandon.

They all four looked out the window and saw white snowballs falling slowly down onto all of the people.

"Wow no one is moving at all," exclaimed Lucy.

"Wow, Adam look at all of this potion," exclaimed Cody.

"Here drink this Lucy and Brandon," said Adam.

"Here drink this Cody," said Adam.

All of a sudden, Adam and Lucy were in school. Diiiiiiiiinng went the school bell.

"Adam and Lucy I would like for you two to stay, I need to talk to you," said Mrs. Wanda, their teacher.

"Okay," said Adam.

"Look at this report card Lucy, all A's!" shouted Mrs. Wanda.

"Now look at yours Adam, all D's and one F. You might need summer school," said Mrs. W.

When the children got home Lucy told Ma about his report card. Ma was not happy.

Ashley Taylar Brown<br>
Age: 10

# WE WON!

"Two outs now in our six-six tie, here in the bottom of the sixth," said the announcer after the left fielder's spectacular catch. "Next batter, number twenty-three, center fielder, Logan Davisson," said the announcer as Logan stepped up to the plate.

Logan had butterflies in his stomach that felt more like termites eating his insides. He got ready for the first pitch. Here it came, a fastball, but it was high and away.

"Ball one," said the umpire.

Logan stepped back into the box and waited for the next pitch. The ball was coming way inside so Logan jumped out of the way.

"Ball two," shouted the umpire.

The pitcher took what seemed like forever before throwing the next pitch. Finally, it came, but it was in the dirt.

"Ball three," yelled the umpire.

Logan stepped in and waited for the next pitch. Here it came, Logan had to take the inside fastball for a strike because he couldn't have hit it. The count was three balls and one strike, so Logan knew that he would probably have to swing at anything that was close to a strike. Here came the pitch. Logan swung, but missed.

"What a curve ball," thought Logan.

So, now the count was full. Logan was ready for the pitch, here it came; a fastball, Logan swung and POW, there it went, down the left field line, back, back, foul ball!

"Oh," came the groans from the crowd.

Logan was so disappointed, he thought it was a home run.

Logan stepped back in and waited for the pitch. The pitcher wound up and threw a slider. Logan was ready for it and hit it far, really far. This one was even a fair ball. It cleared the fence for a home run.

Logan's team won seven to six.

"We won!" his teammates all shouted.

Logan was the hero.

Logan Davisson<br>
Age: 12

## BRUSH YOUR TEETH AND PUT YOUR HEAD GEAR ON

My mom always tells me to brush my teeth and get my headgear on. I hate when she tells me that! When I get my headgear off, I will be so relieved and happy. I probably won't get my headgear off because I don't wear it as often as I should, which is not good. My dentist will probably get mad at me for this stunt I have pulled, not wearing my headgear. My teeth would never be straight if it wasn't for mom, but do you know what? My sister Erin will have headgear on pretty soon and I will make fun of her just like she makes fun of me. So she better brush her teeth more than she does because my mom will always say, brush your teeth and get your headgear on!!

Taylor Zunich
Age: 9

## JELLYBEANS FOR GRANDMA

About a month ago my grandma and grandpa (Dad's mom and dad) came to visit. They came to help paint the garage. My grandma didn't paint; she just read and slept. One night after dinner I was rummaging through the candy jar (like I always do) and my grandma spotted jellybeans. She didn't know that they were Bertie Bots Every Flavor Beans (from Harry Potter).

"I can eat these, because they are fat free," she told me.

And so I started feeding her all the yucky flavors. First I gave her earwax then vomit, grass, booger, horseradish and so on.

"I like these!" she exclaimed.

By then I couldn't help but laugh. She was eating every flavor beans. Then Mom started laughing with me. I knew that Grandma would figure it out sometime or another.

"Can I have some more? These are fat free you know," she said again.

Finally, I gave her the sardine flavor.

"You know, this one is a little different," she said as she puckered her lips.

I told her what flavors she had eaten. After that, I started feeding them to my grandpa, but that's a different story.

Jessica Don
Age: 10

# TIGER TROUBLE

As the yellow morning sky grew warmer on the hot, dry African plains, a small Bengal tiger cub was sleeping in the untidy room that he shared with his mischievous brother. The orangish-yellow cub named Zabari was dreaming of white and brown speedy gazelles that he could chase all day on the barren plains of Africa. The dried-up auburn-tinted tall grass surrounded the fierce cub pursuing the energetic gazelles. There were oodles of places to...

"Zabari... Zabari, get up, you're going to be late for school!" yelled his mother in a grumpy rage.

"What a way to start the day," thought Zabari. "She's already yelling at us."

Calamari, Zabari's mindless brother, woke up from all the fuss.

"Calamari, we better hurry. Mom is going to kill us if we're late to school one more time!" exclaimed Zabari. "We better not get distracted by anything today."

"I know," remarked Calamari. They bolted into their camouflage jumpsuits and darted to the kitchen. Their mom had been making squishy pancakes and sizzling gazelle bacon pieces for breakfast.

"You guys are probably going to be late," stressed their mother. "And you know what will happen if you're late again. You'll be grounded to the ice-cold ground of your cluttered room and won't be able to "tiger around" outside with your friends for the rest of the year. So hustle up and start for school!"

Calamari and Zabari rushed out the door without finishing breakfast. Instantly Alfred the gazelle distracted Calamari and Zabari. "Zabari, let's try to catch that agile gazelle, Alfred. No tiger has even been ten feet close to him," whispered Calamari.

"Yeah, let's catch 'im," replied Zabari.

Calamari and Zabari camouflaged themselves in the tall grass to prepare for their attack. Finally ready, Zabari slowly counted to three and they swiftly started their hunt. The brother's plan was to have Calamari pursue Alfred on the right and Zabari on the left. They were trying to corner Alfred by having Calamari, who was faster, cut Alfred off. Calamari and Zabari desperately tried to follow their plot but Alfred was too nimble for them to catch and he had endurance. Exhausted, Calamari and Zabari decided to give up.

"Man... it's harder... to catch Alfred... than it looks!" panted Calamari between breaths.

"Let's... get back... to the path... and keep... walking to school," gasped Zabari.  Not paying attention to the extremely hazardous ground, Calamari and Zabari instantaneously fell and were stuck in some gooey, black mud by a low growing shrub.  Zabari, a quick thinker, grabbed onto a limb of the nearby shrub with his ferocious jaws and muscled his way out of the tar-like mud.

"Zabari, help...!" screamed Calamari before his head went under the mud.  Zabari frantically ran around to the other side of the mud to help Calamari.  Zabari saw Calamari's ear and grabbed it with his mouth.  Zabari struggled to find his footing then started to pull with all his might.  He jerked and tugged Calamari until his jaws hurt.  Zabari slipped once putting Calamari's head under the ground further.  Even though in great pain, Zabari managed to finally pull Calamari out of the muck.

"Thanks Zabari.  I thought I was going to be stuck forever or until I suffocated," sighed Calamari.

"It was nothing.  Now let's get moving quickly!  Maybe today we can make it on time," declared Zabari.  So Calamari and Zabari were off to the races trying to get to school.  They were hot and exhausted.

"Man Zabari, I wish that there was a lake right here for us to get a drink," thought Calamari out loud.

"Hey look Calamari, there is a lake of water over there," exclaimed Zabari.  Calamari and Zabari sprinted to the lake and started to drink the water.  They looked at each other and thought, "This is the worst tasting water ever."  They glanced down and noticed that the water was a mirage and they had been trying to drink sand.

"Let's just head for school again," sighed Zabari.  The next moment Calamari and Zabari looked back and saw the school bullies.

"They're chasing us!  Run for your life!" yelled Calamari at the top of his lungs.

"No, Calamari.  We need to take a detour to the park where we can hide," insisted Zabari.  Leading the way, Zabari turned into the tall grass and headed for Sand Park.  The bullies, who had been on their heels, had fallen further behind.  Calamari and Zabari reached the park and hid under the bamboo slide with their tiger friend Abmis, who they had seen skipping by the park.  The bullies passed by and kept running in the direction of the school.

"Thanks guys. You really helped me out," mumbled Abmis.

"No problem. Hey, since we're here, let's play on the bamboo slide," suggested Calamari.

"I don't know. I think we should get to school so we don't get into trouble," replied Abmis.

"It'll be all right. We won't be here very long and we'll get to school on time. We still have five minutes," Calamari said, trying to convince Abmis.

"Okay. But just for about two minutes," replied Abmis. So Calamari, Zabari, and Abmis played on the bamboo slide. First Zabari went down the slide and then Calamari. Finally, Abmis went down the slide but halfway down he fell off. Calamari and Zabari gasped and dashed over to Abmis who was whimpering.

"What hurts Abmis?" asked Zabari.

"My paw," replied Abmis.

"Let me see it. Ooh! Calamari, go get some extra bamboo," ordered Zabari. "Okay Abmis, I'm going to put pressure on your paw so it will stop bleeding. Then I am going to wrap your leg in the bamboo for support," explained Zabari. Calamari came back and Zabari had the bleeding stopped. Zabari took the bamboo from Calamari and made a bandage. The Calamari and Zabari helped Abmis get up and they started toward school again.

"Look," yelled Zabari, "there's our school -- Bengal Tiger Academy."

After a few more minutes, Zabari and Calamari had helped Abmis into school. They put their backpacks and belongings into the lemon-colored crates with their names in shiny letters. They also took out the supplies they needed for the school day. Then Calamari and Zabari helped Abmis into class. All of them were really embarrassed because they arrived in class late.

"You three are late again? I'm going to give you guys a referral. I think I'm going to call your parents too!" snarled Mr. Mock.

"Ah man! I told you we should have come straight to school," Abmis said. Mr. Mock called their parents. Calamari and Zabari were lucky because their mom had had a hectic morning. She forgot about grounding them for a long time and decided to ground them for just one night. Abmis' parents were not as easy on him as Calamari and Zabari's parents. He would be grounded for a week the minute he walked in the door at the end of the day. All three of them believed that the rest of the day would be horrible since Calamari and Zabari couldn't play with Abmis for a week and their teacher Mr. Mock was really
mad because they disrupted class. They actually had a great day at school and were really joyful until they all went home and had to face their punishment.

Matthew Mapes
Age: 13

# THE MYSTERY OF ROCK LAKE

There is a lake in Lake Mills, Wisconsin, where I often visit. This lake is very special to me. I go there every summer with my cousins. It's a long drive through the beautiful Wisconsin farmland. We have so much fun there that we don't mind the drive. On the way we stop at Café on the Park for a home cooked meal. Rock Lake holds many fond memories.

When we finally arrive at the lake our favorite picnic table awaits us. In only a few seconds we're in the water, splashing around and standing on our hands. My cousins and I once found a fish and kept it swimming around in a bucket. I love to watch the sailboats zooming by, their beautiful sails full of wind. When we get tired of swimming, we build elaborate sandcastles. This is one of our favorite parts of being at Lake Mills. After that we make stories about the kings and queens who lived in the castles.

Surrounding our picnic table are many large climbing trees. One of the trees has a gnarled root that curves around its trunk. This provides a perfect way to walk around the tree. Seashells and treasures can be found walking along the water's edge. Near the lake is a steeply arched walking bridge. We almost always walk on this bridge crossing a canal that flows into the lake. Sometimes boats travel under the bridge. By the bridge is a playground where there are cute, little swings in the shape of horses. We also enjoy the tall, metal slide.

That is mostly what I do at Lake Mills, but last summer I read some intriguing news. Archaeologists discovered stone pyramids on the bottom of the lake. Some believe that the Ho-Chunk tribe built these pyramids and called them stone teepees. Other archaeologists believe these so-called "pyramids" are just sand, gravel, and rock left by the glaciers. Some believe that people built the huge structures on land and then the lake expanded burying them. This is what I believe.

This discovery makes Lake Mills even more exciting. Are there really pyramids in the deep depths of Rock Lake? Most archaeologists say no. Will we ever know what lies beneath? I love the mystery of it all and choose to believe some smart people figured out how to build pyramids in the midwest. I will return to Rock lake in July and reflect upon this controversial discovery.

Johanna Christensen Black
Age: 13

It all happened last night as I was walking home from some place I shouldn't have ever even stumbled upon. But all that doesn't matter. What matters is what I'm about to tell you. So do listen and take heed to what I shall tell you.

I had just exited a typically dark and gloomy alleyway, and was standing on a street corner under a cliche lonely street lamp that flickered and buzzed adding a mundane hum to the otherwise silent night. I was waiting for the last bus run of the night when I viewed a rather spectacular sight.

Standing, actually it was more of a hovering, on the street corner adjacent to me under another street lamp was three quite unusual apparitions. The three specters were laid out as so one white, the second of the bloodiest hue of red, and the final of the blackest black.

The white phantom seemed to be female. Such a heavenly angel. In flowing robes of purity, she seemed to be a perfect spirit sent to save us all from the personal hells we had all twisted our lives into. She floated as lightly as the sun on the ripples of a pond. Such innocence so foreign in this world.

The second phantasmal appearance was such a red hue that only the flow of a wound came to mind in comparison. And it wore a muddled look upon its face. Such confusion could only be human. It must have been the human emotion we all hide from view, but are dominated by. And it didn't move around, but squirmed within its being.

The final form was the darkest of dark I had ever viewed in my lifetime. Pure evil pulsated and flowed from every ripple of his flowing figure. And it seemed to pour around instead of moving. When speech found the object's mouth it was deep and cavernous. Spoken with a force to be followed.

Well, back to my narration. I stood on the street corner waiting for my transportation when the three shapes began to argue. The darkness was declaring that he should rule the inhabitants of earth. And the angelic white was protesting in a seductive voice that was barely audible as it was close to a whisper, such as the flow of the breeze through the trees. And it went on and on. Both hurtling back and forth statements of debate trying to verbally overpower their opponent. Finally the darkened silhouette cried out in its deep and demanding voice "I grow weary of this nonsense! I will overcome all that I wish. And if you stand opposite of me I will overwhelm you and make a mockery of you as an example."

As the words were projected from his oral cavity, his center began to split with a deafening roar of ripping. From the opening, a vortex of swirling mist seeped out. Following single file in the fog was the underling armies of the doomed. What a horrible sight to witness that I am still struck speechless at the thought of those wretched evils. They carried sacks of a dust. Passing over objects they began sprinkling the powder. Everything that the grains touched drained of color and started to melt.

As the haze crept closer to the space I was standing I began to worry. Before I had a chance to react to my weakness, the virgin white whispered in her voice so lovely and light a disapproval. "You shall desist your actions this instance!" At that retort the darkness just chuckled.

The purity screamed "You shall stop or be stopped!" The dismal thing laughed some more and uttered, "I would love to see you try you mock vigilante."

With that the white princess transformed into a single white dove. After her change the dove sacrificially dove into the heart of the portal. The blacken image cried out in utter horror. The vortex had reversed its flow and was now entering the darkness of the evil. As it returned to its source the underlings were sucked back into the depths of shadow. All that had been drained and melted began to return to its original form. The darkness collapsed and imploded on itself, taking the dove with it.

All through this the reddened persona had sat and squirmed looking lost and delirious. With a look of muddled confusion it began to fold into itself until it was no more.

Feeling saddened at the loss of such innocence I began to run. As I ran tears welled up into my eyes and began to stream down my face. I ran and ran until I couldn't run anymore. As I stood crying and trying to regain my breath, I heard a flutter of wings. Looking to the sky I watched as a single feather fluttered to the ground. Staring down at the feather I reached for it to keep in remembrance of the night's events. As I bent to grasp the token, the dove landed deftly upon my shoulder and whispered a phrase into my ear. A phrase which has stuck in my mind all this time. And that phrase has drastically changed my life.

The phrase was this: Don't forget to hope.

Justin A. Rogers<br>Age: 16

# PUPPETS' REQUIEM

Two years ago I believe I saw a ghost. I'm writing this down so that I don't forget.

\*\*\*\*\*\*\*\*\*\*

The sun was shining through the window of my room. It was about twelve o'clock noon on a Saturday. I awoke with a start. It was a dream, but it was also a reality. I appeared to be the same yet I wasn't. Getting out of bed I pulled on the usual: pants, a shirt, a vest and a ski cap. I went downstairs and headed straight for the kitchen for some breakfast/lunch. After I ate, I noticed the note my parents left for me. I studied it. It stated that my parents left town for a business meeting and would be back tomorrow.

"Great." I thought to myself. "Those people who call themselves my parents are working again." This usually never affected me, but it did today. "Gee," I shouted. "First, my birthday is dismissed from their thoughts. Next my parents go out of town, and then I had that stupid dream again. I just hate that dream," I said quietly. "Why won't it stop? Wait," I said to myself, "you know that wasn't a dream. It was real, but it wasn't your fault." I never believed myself though. It had only been a year since she died, yet I'm still grief-stricken and depressed. I might look the same but I'm completely different, mentally and emotionally. So what if my eyes look as hard and cold as ice. I never have been the same since I met her. People say that I have never loved another with all my heart, but they never knew about Chloe. It happened one year ago...

\*\*\*\*\*\*\*\*\*\*

It was around six p.m. when it happened. I received a call that told me she, my girlfriend Chloe, had been hit by a drunk driver while crossing the street. They said that she wanted me to come and be with her. I asked where she was and they said she was on the corner of Pearl Street and Star Avenue, which was only a few minutes away. I left the house, running to her as fast as I could. I found the paramedics and asked how she was.

"She... she's dying and there's nothing we can do to help her. She is too badly injured to move to the hospital," one of them said. They showed me to where she was. I walked up to where she was lying and held her. Then I heard her voice "Drake... what did they say?" It took me a minute to reply. "They said that they can't do anything to help." I then looked into her eyes. Her beautiful blue-green eyes. Eyes that weren't crying. Then her last words: "Do you promise never to forget me?" I nodded yes, knowing what she meant. At that instant she died in my arms. All I could do was hold on to her and cry.

That night I met her parents. They came to get Chloe, and to make arrangements for her funeral. I couldn't say anything. A few days later I couldn't, and didn't go to her funeral. Too many people, and I wanted to be alone with my Chloe.

I snapped out of my trance. I felt there was someone else in the room besides me. I turned around and nearly screamed. There stood Chloe. But how? She looked just as she had before she died. Her beautiful blue-green eyes sparkled and her light brown shoulder-length hair was neatly brushed. She was still the cutest girl I had ever met. Then she gave me one of those 'cheer-up' hugs. I could barely ask her: "What are you doing here?"

"I got special permission to see you for a while. I have to talk to you," she said.

"Why?" I asked, fairly startled.

"That can wait because I want to give this to you so you can remember me." She pulled something out of thin air. "It's two dragons, one for me and one for you." I got all teary-eyed and started crying when I noticed she was hugging me and crying too. "I missed you so much," we said at the same time after we had cried all we could cry.

"Drake, I need to ask a favor of you," she whispered. "Anything for you," I calmly said. "The reason I came was to tell you that I love you, I miss you, and that this wasn't your fault," she said solemnly," I also need you to move on and stop mourning my loss because it would be better if you did."

I looked at her strangely. "How can you ask me such a thing? I love you and I don't want to forget you!" I exclaimed. My eyes showed how I felt now, they showed every emotion I felt. "To feel better and be happy again, you must. I know it sounds silly, but it will work if you try it," she stated softly, her eyes full of sadness. "I do promise to never forget you and to stop mourning so you can rest in peace," I responded sincerely as tears once more streamed down my face. "Thank you for understanding Drake," she cried as she gave me a sad smile. "I will miss you and I still love you no matter what," she voiced. All I could reply was, "I'll love you always Chloe," I choked out so I wouldn't cry anymore because I knew she was leaving. With a kiss good-bye she disappeared, but instead of feeling sadder I simply smiled as the weight of my sorrow was released from my being. She was right. Later I fell asleep on the couch with a feeling of great content.

That night my parents come home and woke me up to celebrate my birthday. Then they asked me why I was so happy. I replied: "Chloe came to visit me, and she gave me some good advice." My parents must have thought I was nuts but they just smiled and muttered to each other, that I must have dreamed it I heard every word. They could have been right too. I almost don't believe it myself. That night when I took off my vest the dragons Chloe gave me fell out of one of the pockets.

That is what convinced me she was here, those dragons convinced me. I'm also back to being as normal as a kid like me could possibly be.

Carly E. Dowd
Age: 14

# A LONG JOURNEY

## Chapter One

"Pay attention Bluejay! You know we need to pack for the long journey," scolded Wise One, an old man who happened to be Bluejay's grandfather.

Bluejay who was looking hopelessly lost at the clear blue sky sat up in unblinkingly surprise.

"Time already?"

Blue jay didn't want to go because they had to leave their beautiful homes that they had built, they had to leave the clear blue sky, but most of all she had to leave her mother's and father's graves.

"Oh come on Bluejay! Don't you want to go to a green land instead of staying here in the middle of a barren waste?" asked Great-grandmother Butterfly. Bluejay stared hard at her great-grandmother and then blurted out, "You never liked this place but I do and you can't change my mind!" Bluejay ran to her room and cried 'til she fell asleep.

## Chapter Two

Bluejay had a dream, a dream where there was no drought and she was climbing up the mesa to fetch some water. When she reached the top she realized that the person tending the crop was her father. He smiled at her as if nothing was wrong. Then his spirit slowly floated down to a kiva. Bluejay ran after him but he vanished down into a seepapoo. She turned to see her mother making pottery and her spirit left and was swallowed by the seepapoo too. And then Bluejay was someplace else, someplace that she did not know. Her heart leapt to hear her Great- grandmother Butterfly's voice. Blue jay then saw Wise One kneeling over Great-grandmother Butterfly.

"If she ever comes back, we will all live in peace," spoke Great-grandmother Butterfly in a raspy voice.

Then both of their spirits left through the seepapoo. A great wind blew Bluejay into a kiva so deep that the sides seemed to disappear into the night sky. Blue jay woke up in terror. She was about to call for Great Grandmother Butterfly but remembered what Great Grandmother Butterfly said. She swallowed her words. Instead she called for Wise One.

## Chapter Three

"Wise One, is it time yet?" Bluejay called out. No answer. She called out again. It was then she walked out and realized they had left without her. She watched a small dust storm wash the footprints away as if it were a sea of nothing but browness. Bluejay tried to cry but with the heat her tears dried up.

"But why did they leave me? They should have noticed that I was gone or maybe they thought I was with the other part of the troop? I should try to catch up to them now, but which way did they go"

She knelt down to pray and ask for directions from Tawa, the god of the sun. She asked Tawa because she knew that the sun would rise in the east and set in the west. Bluejay thought about asking Coyote for help but remembered that he was as trustworthy as a water pot that leaked. So she did not ask for help from Coyote, the god of all tricks.

After she had prayed she got an answer immediately telling her that, "I cannot answer that for I tell directions and bring light and people to the world but what I'll tell you this is follow your heart and seek the unknown" "But what is the unknown?!" Bluejay cried out.

"I cannot answer that either for to understand you need to experience it! Remember, follow your heart Bluejay, follow your heart!"

## Chapter Four

Bluejay quickly got up. She ran to get her buffalo skin sack. She put in a few used-up arrows that she found at the bottom of the hill, a bow and a pointed stick in case she found a place where there was food. Bluejay was running out the door when she stumbled on something soft -- it was her buffalo fur doll made by her mother and father. She placed it against her heart for a moment and then slipped it into her sack. She started to follow her heart toward what felt like home.

Hours passed. The soles of her sandals burned, but that didn't matter to Bluejay; she just wanted to go to her new home and be with her family again. Bluejay thought that she saw some water, but whenever she got closer, it got farther away. Finally Bluejay stopped looking for water because the water in the distance was only Coyote playing tricks on her. Before Bluejay knew it, it was nighttime and she was starving. Bluejay saw a few sticks lying in the middle of a clearing and right by the clearing she saw a dead cactus. She made a fire with the sticks and ate half of the worthless, dead cactus. She saved the rest for her long journey. Blue jay took two pieces of buffalo hide from her sack and made herself a second pair of sandals. Soon the fire grew dim, Bluejay fell asleep with her doll cradled in her arms.

Chapter Five

The next morning Bluejay woke up to a blazing sun beating down on her face. She slipped on her second pair of sandals and shoved everything else in her buffalo sack. Without eating a piece of the dead cactus, she started walking and followed her heart.

Whenever Bluejay saw a plant or root she stopped to put it in her sack because Bluejay knew she must risk everything to make it to her new home. She hadn't gone very far when she saw a camp, freshly built the night before. By the camp Bluejay saw a footprint. She took a good sniff of the footprint, it looked and smelled fresh. Bluejay began to run when she saw more footprints. She followed the footprints. With every step, the land became greener. Bluejay stopped at a river bank. When she looked up she saw Wise One praying by a fire. Bluejay's heart leapt with joy and she ran towards her grandfather. Wise One saw Bluejay and opened his arms to hug his beloved granddaughter. Tears fell from Bluejay's eyes as she realized that she had braved the unknown and found love, the love of her family.

Lissie Bloom
Age: 9

SALESMAN

A salesman who is very boring, a creature who is completely annoying as a baby crying. A beast so unhappy feeling like a bullfrog with his mate flattened by a car. Pretty weird but true. Like every individual salesmen have their specialties. The salesman is a talkative animal who yaps like a talk show host that cannot stop.

Personally, I believe this varmint is as greedy as the Joker with his money. The weirdest part of a salesman is how great he looks. He looks as dapper as if he is about to be married. This character is as fast as lighting darting from one door to the next. If this type of critter comes to your door, slam it in his face. Lock yourself in a room because that salesman can make you old.

Zeke Denison

It was a windy, dark, cloudy, and silent Halloween night. A little girl named Adreanna came to see her grandmother. Then she heard a sound. She wanted to go home. She didn't know the way.

Adreanna saw the word Oak. It was a street sign. It looked familiar as if she knew it well. She decided to take the trail. The street seemed different from the other streets. It was silent. A huge cloud hung over the street.

Adreanna heard a sound as she turned around. There was nothing there. She started to get goose bumps. Then, she was about to scream. Then the witch popped up in her face. Her scream pierced everyone's ears in town.

Adreanna saw the sign of her street. She was out of breath, so she stopped. The witch was catching up. She caught her breath, and started to look for her house. She went down Maple Street.

Adreanna saw her house. Her mom and dad weren't home. She surely knew that the door was locked. Suddenly she heard the witch cackle. Adreanna got frightened. Then she saw a big flash of light. It was her mom and dad's car. The witch was scared of light, so she ran away.

Adreanna crossed the street with excitement. Her mother and father ran out of the car. They picked her up and hugged her. They went inside. Her mother made her some pie. Adreanna yelled, "I'm safe, I'm safe! I will tell you my story."

Adreanna Valdez
Age: 9

I looked up at the ceiling and then down at my paper. There was a very hard problem. I knew if I did not get this problem right, I would be sent back to second grade. Jimmy, the nicest kid had told me the answer, but it was my turn to get it. I heard the clock tick. Pretty soon it got in my head, tic toc.

"Five more minutes class," said Mrs. Woarmwood. I got back to work. Jimmy saw me, wrote the answer, and started to pass it. Pretty soon I heard "Pass this to Tory." Then I got this crumpled up paper right next to my pencil. I looked around the room, nobody was looking so I unfolded it, it said to problem number sixteen: forty-eight. I looked around the room again, nobody was looking so I pretended I figured it out and I wrote down forty-eight, then I heard my tummy growl.

Mrs. Woarmwood got up and said, "You may stack up your papers nicely and line up for lunch."

When I got in line my best friend came next to me and said "What did you get for problem number sixteen, I got thirty-six."

"Um... well..."

"Tory, can you tell me what I just said?" said Mrs. Woarmwood.

"Ummm."

"Who can tell Tory what I just said? Susana."

"Make sure you walk quiet in the halls."

"Thank you Susana," said Mrs. Woarmwood.

As we walked down the hall, I saw my sister Alice. She came racing down the hall to greet me with a hug. After hugging my sister, I continued on to the cafeteria. When we arrived, I noticed that my lunch box was unzipped. This puzzled me so much that I had no idea where I was going. I was looking down at the floor and it felt like people were bowling down to me like they were the person that stole the food out of my lunch box. Then I heard my name called out from the crowd "Tory!"

I looked behind me and... whew! It was my best friend, Jack.

"Where have you been? In outer space?"

"No," I said as I pulled the apple out of my lunch box.

"Is that all you have for lunch?"

"Yea, I guess." My eyes opened wide.

"What is it?" asked Jack as he looked at me, but in a zip and a zap I was darting back to my classroom to look for my lost lunch. Then I ran square into Mr. Bean, the second grade teacher.

"What's the big rush? School is not over yet. You know the rules about not running in the halls at our school. I will have to talk to Mrs. Woarmwood," said Mr. Bean.

"Yes, sir," I said as I wondered why my day is going so badly.

"If I see you one more time running in the halls, the next minute you will be telling the principal why you went to school with the runnies." And off he went with a smug look on his face. And off I went to find my lunch. As I walked down the hall I counted the rooms. (What grade) "Fifth, fourth, third, second grade? How did I get here?" I started running backward to the fourth grade classroom. Right when I was going in "Bong!" I felt my head throb. I opened my eyes, I was against the wall. What was I doing against the wall? Was it all a dream? No, it couldn't be after the talk with Mr. Bean, how could I ever forget that. Well at least I learned a lesson.

I started towards the lunchroom, Victoria started to come out and said, "I heard you and Mr. Bean talking about running in the halls, then I came back and you fell down hitting your head against the wall."

"Um... thanks." I was speechless.

When I went back in the lunchroom I saw Jack.

"All you said was 'Um thanks' to one of the pretty girls," Jack said.

"Well, what would you have said, I mean it's not like anything happened," I explained.

"What would I have said to Victoria?" Jack started.

"Shhh, everybody can hear you," I whispered.

"As I was saying... gee, what was I saying? Oh yeah, do you want to go out to lunch with me sometime?" Jack asked.

"Sure like today," I said in big excitement.

"No, a different day," Jack said.

"Oh!" I said with disappointment.

Right then Victoria's friend came walking by waving her hand and smiling.

"Hi guys, how's it going?" she said.

"Great, wonderful how are you?" Jack started.

"Just a little hungry," replied Victoria's friend.

"You are in luck," Jack said getting my apple for my lunch, and handing it to her.

"Thanks Jack."

I coughed up my milk. I had no food and Jack just took my apple from me. I bet he wants to be "great friends."

Gee, how could I forget, today is swimming. Well I remembered my suit and my towel, but I didn't have any food so how could I have any energy. Without energy, I would drown just because I didn't have any food.

"Thanks for the apple." Yuck you have bad breath. I knew it was Jack in two ways: one because of the apple and two because of his breath.

"Man Jack, if you had given me some of your lunch today, I will have a ton of food for you tomorrow," I said as we were walking down the hall. "I mean well -- never mind."

"Hey do you want to come over today?" Jack asked.

"Only if you have food, I mean I'll have to talk with my mom and if she says yes, what would we do?"

"Come on class is almost starting," Jack interrupted. Two minutes later

"Okay only three people got the problem right, Jimmy was the only one who got the whole page right, Jimmy could you come up please, first to write problem sixteen, and then to get your award." Jimmy got up right next to the chalkboard, picked up the chalk and started to write. (This is what he wrote) 2 X n = 96. Then he got his award and sat back down.

"The next one who got number seventeen right was Victoria. Step right up here." I heard Jack clap hard. She wrote on the chalkboard 2 X n = 118.

And Mrs. Woarmwood sputtered "Tory sort of got number sixteen right, but Tory I want you to fill in number sixteen to make sure." I was amazed, this is one of the first times I went up to the chalkboard. When I got up there I forgot the answer, already. Then Mrs. Woarmwood said anxiously, "Hurry up you don't have all day." I thought hard. Then Mrs. Woarmwood said, "Class, it's swimming." Oh boy, I didn't have to do the problem! I was heading out the door, when a hand suddenly flopped down on my shoulder. I looked around and it was my mom, what was she doing here?

"Tory, come on you have a dentist appointment in five minutes."

As we got to the dentist's we had to wait five hours or at least it seemed like it. I thought I would be having more fun in the pool. Then it was my turn. I got in a big chair and had to put on sunglasses because they shined a light on me. Then they put foam in my mouth and then sucked it out. It tickled.

At the end they gave me a choice of a toothbrush and told me to brush every night. Then they gave me some stickers. I hadn't noticed what it said until she said, "remember, don't eat for four hours or something bad would happen." (In my head) "Something bad would happen if I don't get any food." When I got back in the car, I saw the clock say 3:00. We had to pick up the twins from school.

When Alice and Allison got in the car, I saw Alice had a snicker on her face. Then she spoke up, "Hey mom, I really like the food you packed for me. It was scrumptious." Alice and Allison giggled. "I liked the warm, sweet pudding and the homemade applesauce." I looked behind me. They broke out in laughter.

"Mom! She stole my lunch!" I cried.

"Now, now Tory. Just because you are hungry doesn't mean that you can bawl her out."

"But... but."

So I was left hungry for four hours because of the dentist, but then I got to eat so everything was great.

P.S. Make sure you read more of Tory's problems and adventures and much more.

Kristyn Wykert

# NOT JUST A PEN PAL

In England, September 2006, it was a wonderful morning around a small house. The early birds were chirping and the smell of breakfast filled the air. It was going to be a perfect day.

A small voice shouted, "Mom, my pen pal, Lisa is coming to visit us!" That voice came from an early teen, Amy Andrews. Amy has sandy blonde hair with hazel eyes and she is a clothes freak. Earlier, Amy received a letter from her pen pal in California. Their moms had finally let them meet each other. Amy hopes that Lisa is just like her. She wished Lisa would hate sports and like fashion and clothes and girly things.

Amy was up in her room watering the flowers in her window sill. A few moments later, the doorbell rang. She ran down the stairs like lightning. She slowly opened the door, trying to contain her excitement. When she saw Lisa she gasped. She stared at her. Lisa had on a green shirt that was meant to be green, and ripped jeans. In her bony hand she held a soccer ball. This made Amy realize that she and Lisa would never get along.

"Is this the Andrews' house?" Lisa asked.

"Yeah, what's it to you?" Amy mumbled.

"Are you Amy? Amy Andrews?" Lisa continued.

"Yes." Amy barked.

After Lisa was settled in the guest room, she went up to Amy's room. Amy was putting away her clothes. She stopped to glare at Lisa. Then picked up more clothes and put them away. Lisa picked up a wool sweater that belonged to Amy in disgust then dropped it.

"You like clothes?" Lisa assumed.

"Yes I love them! Do you?" Amy replied.

"Yuck! No. I don't care about them at all. They are dumb." Lisa argued.

"Oh yeah, well I hate sports. What can they do for your grade or future anyway?" Amy blurted.

"Whatever! I'm out!" Lisa shouted.

Lisa and Amy were not going to put up with each other. Amy wanted to see Lisa cry over her clothes so she and her best friend had cooked up a plan. At noon, Kathryn and Amy took all of Lisa's clothes and dyed them black. Lisa hated black. Kathryn and Amy giggled as they covered Lisa's clothes in black.

Kathryn had left and now Amy had to get her homework done. She was good at every homework assignment given to her. Except this one. They had to type up a report on the history of sports. They weren't even allowed to look it up on the computer! Amy was stumped. Amy was up all night pondering. Lisa came in Amy's room where Amy was doing her homework.

"What kind of essay do you have to write?" Lisa hissed.

"Sports" Amy hesitated.

"I'll make you a deal..." Lisa suggested.

"Like what?" Amy questioned.

"If you make my clothes back to the way they are meant to be, I'll help you with your assignment. Deal?" Lisa chattered.

"Yes sure... hey... so you do care about your clothes don't you?" Amy pointed out.

"Well I want to look good." Lisa admitted.

"I want my grades to look good." Amy chuckled.

Lisa helped Amy with her homework and she got an A+. Then Amy took Lisa shopping for new clothes, and they had a blast. After they went shopping they played soccer. They loved their new activity. They earned two new things: a new activity and a new best friend.

Leanne Swineheart

# THE REVOLUTIONARY TIME DIARY OF ELIZABETH DOCKSON VALLEY FORGE, PA 1773

### August 4, 1773
The move here to Philadelphia was just horrible, Lucy complained a lot, for example: her feet hurt and wanted to walk (well then get out of the wagon!) And that her doll was lost. It was just horrible!

### August 7, 1773
I'm so very excited; Mama had her baby today, another girl. We have decided to name her Abigail, Abigail Dockson. I am starting to like Philadelphia, it's growing on me. It's an interesting country; I think I shall go ice-skating tomorrow with Lucy (my little sister).

### August 8, 1773
It was wonderful until the part I fell in. It was really scary, I had no clue which way was up or down. When I finally found the top Papa said that I was blue and shaking terrible! Mama took me home immediately; she said I was lucky to be alive. She also said that I was ill horribly ill.

### September 16, 1773
I'm finally well, I'm so glad I'm able to go outside again. I want to go exploring tomorrow with Lucy.

### September 17, 1773
It's all my fault, all mine. Lucy and I were playing in the meadow and having a holly good time until we saw a bear, so we decided to run. While we were running Lucy fell and she called for me, but I was too far to hear her.

### September 20, 1773
There is a search party out looking for Lucy, I felt so bad knowing that everyone was out in the cold because of me. It breaks my heart to know that Lucy is out in the cold alone. (P.S. we found Lucy's cloak).

### September 25, 1773
We're still looking, the wait is unbearable, literally. While we wait the search party, well searches. When the search party gets back there is still no sign of Lucy.

October 2, 1773

There was a dance last night, I forgot about my worries of Lucy and had fun. While I was there I met a boy named Daniel. He's kind and considerate. I thought my family might like him so I introduced him to my family. Papa and Mama liked him very much. Mama said he would make a very good husband. Finally he introduced me to his family, turns out he has two sisters and three brothers. His sisters' names were Abigail and Emily Ann. Very nice girls but on the other hand the boys snickered at the sight of me. They were rude in my opinion, but I didn't quiet catch their names.

October 7, 1773

Lucy has been found today. It turns out she was staying in the tree house and was so scared that the bear was still at the bottom of the tree that she didn't want to come out. But when I went into the tree house I saw blueberries, raspberries and fresh stream water. I ran to the house to tell Ma what I saw, Mother said Lucy was a nature outdoorsman.

October 16, 1773

Daniel proposed to me today. Right in the middle of a meeting, it was in front of everybody. I was so embarrassed my face turned crimson with embarrassment. I said yes and Daniel said that we would marry on the twenty-third of October.

October 23, 1773

Today's the big day that I shall be wed. I'm so anxious. Later.

As a wedding present from Daniel's parents and my parents was a house that was furnished and it was even more exciting because it had pots and pans. I was so happy that I started to cry! Next thing I knew Daniel was carrying me in the wonderful new house. He said to close my eyes I did and when I opened them I saw a wonderful mirror. I hadn't seen my face in a long time. I loved it with all my heart. I also love Daniel.

Epilogue

After a few months Elizabeth had a healthy baby boy who grew up to be strong, he moved away to start a new family. Elizabeth and Daniel died in the year 1778 after their house burned down. Jacob felt so heart broken that he burned his house down with his family still in it.

Gwen Kirk

# THE MOUSE AND THE MONKEY

Once upon a time there was a little mouse, who had a family and a nice home, which is a hole with "Home Sweet Home" printed on the door. Now down the street lives a monkey who has only a sister, because his parents died. He lives in a basswood tree with green leaves all year-round (or so he says). One day the monkey set out to get some food to bring home. On that same day the mouse set out to get some medication for his younger son. The mouse took the short route to Dr. Susie Q. Squeaks, a highly intelligent field mouse. The monkey took the long route so he could fiddle around. The monkey is not a very smart animal, he saw a trap, and walked into it.

"Yowwwwwwww!" he screamed.

The mouse heard the loud scream and ran toward it.

The monkey said, "Help me you idiot."

The mouse said," No way, not if you talk to me like that!"

"OK" the monkey said, "please help me."

The mouse said, "I'll help you, if you go get my son's medication and bring it to me!"

Then the monkey agreed to get the pills. The mouse chewed through the wire and the monkey was free!

Then the mouse exclaimed, "OK, Dr. Squeaks' address is 742 No Cat Lane!"

The monkey said, "Hahahaheheheehohoho, what makes you think I'm going to get it?"

"Well" he exclaimed, "you said you would!"

"You actually believed me?" he asked.

"Yes," said the mouse.

"Hahahahehehehhohohohehe," he went on.

"You stop that," the mouse said, "you're making me angry." The mouse walked on and said, " I'll never trust you again!" After that the monkey received his bananas and the mouse received the medication and both of the families were happy. Then when the mouse got home he held a grudge.

Then the mouse said "Aw forget it, life's too short to be holding grudges against people!"

But the monkey was never trusted again.

Haley M. Orr
Age: 12

# THE WALK

One day when I lived in Lincoln, Nebraska I had just finished lunch. I was so full but I enjoyed it very much. Then we started to talk about how school had gone... I think. After that it was time to take a nap. I like my room very much because it was very big especially for a toddler. My parents came into my room to help me change into my pajamas. It had a twin-size bed, a big closet, all of my clothes and costumes, all of my toys, and best of all it was always clean. I had very nice oak floors. Then there were the nice, organized baskets for my barnyard toys, my constructive toys, and cars, pick-up, semis, etceteras basket. Thanks to my mom I now know how to put things back where they go, but I don't always use that instinct. In a while I was fast asleep. A while later I woke up to go to the bathroom. It was a good thing that I was potty-trained and that I knew the functions of a toilet or else the future would have been ruined. After I was done I felt like taking a walk because my mom always took me for an afternoon walk, but I couldn't wait (that's how I came up with the title) so I made up my mind, I was going to take that victorious walk. So I went to my room to get dressed appropriately to take a walk in public. After I was done changing I went to the front door and stepped outside. It was a good thing the fence that my mom and dad built didn't go around the whole house or else I would have met doom! My favorite animals were squirrels and blue jays and sometimes I tried to catch them and keep them as pets. I was always disappointed because none of my ambush plans ever worked. I was off, I had succeeded my master plan, and it was a prize-winning plan! My mom woke up and her heart told her that something was wrong or that something was about to happen to me. She looked in all of my hideouts but she didn't find me in any of them. I was about to get home when a neighbor spotted me. She came out of her house and walked with me the rest of the way home. My mom was very scared but then all of a sudden she heard the doorbell ring. My mom went to answer the door and when she opened it to her surprise it was the neighbor and I. My mom was so glad to see that I was fine. Now I don't know if this story is true or not but my mom told me that when I was an infant it happened.

José Ignacio van Olphen

# WHAT COULD HAPPEN IN FRANCE!

## Chapter One
### The Beginning

It all started when I was on sabbatical to France. I was playing a little game by myself when I was pushed down and I was acquainted with the sidewalk. I looked up and saw big muscular, sleek, black haired Rushed. I was mad and I mean mad as a bull. So I turned around and gave Rushed a sock in the nose.

The next day I was playing soccer with my friends when I was pushed over by Rushed's minion, Antony. Antony looked odd from where I was but he has a round face and blonde hair. It was time to act it was time for secret agent TUN TUN DUN. I crept around the playground but where was Rushed? WHOOMP! I was on the ground again. That made me really mad and

STOP! That's jumping a little far into the story. Now to make it short...

Every day I came home with a new cut or bruise. Back to the story, OK, I was on the ground OW YEE! I was really mad so I... let it be.

I told my friends what kept happening. It was really time to act so we planned tomorrow. My friends and I acted normal, so Rushed and Antony would not expect anything. Then it was time for recess TUN TUN DUN...

We got into formation then the dark ninjas appeared. I was ready for anything. WHOMP! What I was on the ground. They hit me from behind! It was straight into battle. Then there was a piercing scream from the dark ninjas as we attacked. It was a fair chase they took off running and we spread out like wolves so we could catch them. But the bell rang. Man that was our chance!

THE NEXT DAY TUN TUN DUN... another battle but this was the last we had them surrounded and they surrendered.

Off the story a little bit. But the first time I punched Rushed looked around and a girl waved at me. She had dark brown hair and was a lot shorter than me. IT WAS TOO OBVIOUS SHE LIKED ME!

## Chapter Two
### Back To Laramie

I was glad to leave France it was good to be home. One day my mom said I got a letter in the mail. Once I saw it I felt sick. It was a dark pink letter and a guy and a girl about to kiss. That moment I knew who it was from... THE STUPID GIRL!

Lucky it was winter I burned it immediately. There was a second attempt but this did not work either. A few months later I got a letter from my undercover secret agent. The dark ninjas have returned. THIS IS THE WORST NEWS I COULD GET!

## Chapter Three
### There And Back Again

On the plane ride I got connected with my undercover agent. It was worse than I thought. The dark ninjas have discovered high-tech weapons. It was time for training my agents. They trained nonstop for days. Once they were all black belts it was time to attack. While we were getting ready the dark ninjas appeared from nowhere. You could hear the clank-clanking of swords. Just kidding the dark ninjas did not attack. I'm just trying to make my story interesting. I was not even in France. That is why the chapter is called There and Back Again.

## Chapter Four
### The Moral Of The Story

To make a long story short NEVER GO TO FRANCE!!! Go to Egypt read the next exciting story... What could happen in Egypt!

Jeremiah J. Varca

# HORSEBREATHAVITIS

Once upon a time in a place not far from here, there was a horse named Holly. Holly was not a bad horse. She was not a mean horse either. But she had a problem. She had a sickness called horsebreathavitis. Horsebreathavitis is a sickness that horses get when they eat too much paper.

One day Holly was peacefully eating grass instead of paper for a change, when some poachers came around. Holly watched as one of the poachers got out of the truck. In his hand was a big apple. Holly hadn't had an apple in a long time. She ran to get the apple, but when she was ten feet away from him, he threw a net over her head. She was trapped. The man took a sniff of the air then passed out. Some of his friends loaded Holly into the back of the truck and went to town.

When they got to town, they changed into cowboy clothes then looked for someone who would buy Holly. Some doctors in the town wanted to buy Holly for $25. The poachers wanted to sell her for $100, so they decided on $50. Once the doctors got Holly into the lab, one of the doctors held out a tongue depressor and stuck it on her tongue. "Hmmmm," said the doctor named Phil. "She has breath bad enough to knock a man out and appears to eat a lot of paper. We have to study her well. She has a rare disease that no one understands. If we learn about this disease, we can name it. Start thinking of a name for the disease."

"Good night, Phil," said another doctor named Johnny. Holly looked at Phil. He was a very tall man and had blue eyes, wild hair, and wore a white suit.

The next day the doctors came in with names like "pronoses," "conticlitoses," but Phil didn't like any of those. But he did like "horsebreathavitis." "Good job, Johnny," said Phil. "We will call it that." All the other doctors, George, Sarah, Chan, and Pam, groaned. Phil said, "Start working. Johnny, find out more. George, feed the horse. Sarah, name the horse. Chan, write a paper. Pam, help Johnny, okay?"

Everyone started to work hard. Four minutes later, Sarah came back. She said, "Let's call her Holly."

"Okay," said Phil.

Six minutes later, George came back. He exclaimed, "She ate my paper! But she ate the vegetables too!"

The next day everyone brought back their homework. Phil said, "Johnny and Pam, what did you find out?" They replied, "Because Holly has this rare disease, we can see her brain waves on the computer and find out what she is thinking."

Phil said, "Chan, how about you?"

Chan said, "I typed the paper."

"Okay," said Phil, "Let's see what that horse is thinking." So they got Holly into the cage and they went to their computers. From the brain waves they learned that the people they bought Holly from weren't farmers, they were poachers! Chan said, "Their names are... Joy, Bob, Matthew, Luke, James, William, Jacob, and John. They are a well-known group of poachers." Phil said, "I think we found out enough. Let's try to help Holly first."

So for the next few days they tried to fix her problem. The doctors tried almost everything, from talking to Holly all day to not talking to her at all. Then one day, Chan said, "I quit!"

"Oh, come on. Of all times, you choose now to quit. Your whole career, down the drain," said Phil.

"I don't want to study some disease and treat it with magic tricks!" shouted Chan. He threw the paper that he was writing on the floor and stamped on it.

"Are you sure this is the right decision?" said George.

"We couldn't do it without you," said Johnny.

"I'll miss you," said Sarah.

"Why do it?" said Pam.

Chan looked around the room, then finally shouted, "Good-bye!" Then he stamped out the door.

The next day Pam came bolting through the doors, stood in the center of the room, and announced "I found the cure! I found the cure!"

Phil came in the room so fast that he broke the door. He asked Pam, "What is it?"

Pam replied, "We can't let her eat paper, only vegetables for a month. But if she eats too much paper again..."

"Don't worry, we will feed her bad tasting paper and she will learn not to eat paper," reassured Phil.

The next day, when George was going for a walk, he saw the same faces of the people that had sold Holly to them. He quickly called the police and told them where he was. He told them the poachers' names and that he could prove that they were poachers. The police were over there in a minute. The doctors showed the police their brain wave data and how they found the poachers' names. One of the policemen caught the poachers while the other policeman looked in the back of their truck. What he saw was all types of animals' skin, all from wildlife reserves. The police took the poachers off to jail.

Fifteen months later, the doctors got grants to study horsebreathavitis. They were much richer now. They planned to study a group of horses to see if they would develop horsebreathavitis if they ate a lot of paper for a long time. Then they looked at Holly and all said together, "We will miss you." They loaded her into the truck and said good-bye. Phil gave her one last apple before the truck drove out of sight. When she got back to her home, she felt like she was missing some things, but she finally felt content.

Rudi Lange Hanekamp

# PATIENCE PAYS OFF

It was a lovely day in Philadelphia in 1773. Patience skipped off to the store. She waved to Mrs. Marlock, and ran straight past Mrs. Guerdee who was talking to tall Mr. Hadestir. She slowed her pace when she entered the store.

Mr. Marcé spoke in a kind voice, "I was wondering when I would see you again. I heard about your sister getting engaged to Mr. Browner. So happy."

It was a quarter to five when Patience entered her whitewashed house. Clare was screaming, John was yelling, and in the middle of it all stood mother and Margaret.

Mother hurried towards Patience. "I'm so glad you came. I'll start cooking and you will play with Clare." Mother spoke quickly. Patience reluctantly walked over to Clare. Once William, one, Nana, two, Clare, five and John, seven, were in bed and Margaret had gone to see Mr. Browner, Mother closed the drapes. Then a loud rapping sound came from the door. Mother hurried to the door and let out a gasp.

"Mrs. Guerdee! So nice of you to visit!" Mrs. Guerdee walked past Mother into the room, ignoring her greeting. She looked skeptically around. Mrs. Guerdee was the wealthy widow of Samuel Guerdee. She now ran his large company.

She spoke fast, not looking at Mother. "Pray thee, open the window." She sat herself in Father's usual chair close to the window. Before she continued, Patience came over with a glass of water. "Our lovely Philadelphia." she gestured towards the street. She took the glass of water Patience offered without thanking her.

As all three of them looked out the window, a tall slim man dressed in black jumped into Mrs. Guerdee's stagecoach that was ready to depart for Boston with the company earnings for the week. The bandit headed out of the city.

Mrs. Guerdee jumped up in alarm. "My coach! My coach! Someone has stolen my coach!" She stormed out of the house.

Patience was just getting into her bed when her mother walked into the room looking very serious. "What happened, Mother?" questioned Patience.

Mother spoke glumly. "Mrs. Guerdee said that altogether the stagecoach and all the gold and silver and other goods were worth £3000."

Patience was amazed. "Three thousand," she cried. Continuing, she asked, "Do you think she'd offer a reward?"

Mother looked fierce. "Patience, you are not going to try to solve this mystery! It would not be ladylike." She bid Patience good night, and left. Patience sighed. How badly she wanted to solve the mystery. Then and there she became determined to solved the mystery of the missing company coach.

The next morning Patience got up, took a piece of paper and wrote:

Stagecoach going to Boston

Carrying £3000 of goods and money

Tall slim man in black

Robbed coach at quarter to nine in the evening

The same morning, after a breakfast of ham and eggs, Patience ran out to find clues. After a half hour, she found wheel tracks. She followed them quickly. It was a long way. She found that they led to... "Mr. Browner's lodging!" Patience gasped. There was no doubt. This was where Mr. Browner and Mr. Hadestir lived. She wrote,

Wheel tracks led to Mr. Browner's stable. Aghast, she hurried home. Just as she was about to tuck the paper in her nightgown pocket, Clare appeared.

"What are you doing? What are you hiding?" Clare ran to the nightgown, and before Patience could stop her, grabbed the piece of paper. She read it slowly out loud, then she stated, "You are trying to solve it. Mother won't be happy."

Patience was struck with an idea. "Clare, you could help me if you didn't tell anyone."

Clare spoke with excitement, "I could help? Great! What can I do?" Patience was pleased.

"When Mother asks me to go to the store, I'll take you. You can do the shopping while I see how much exactly Mrs. Guerdee lost."

At lunch, Mrs. Guerdee came to visit. "I'm going to my insurance company this evening to demand that they reimburse me my £3000," she said.

"Will they give you that much back?" questioned Mother.

"They've got to," Mrs. Guerdee replied.

Patience was finally sent to the store that afternoon. She dropped Clare off at Mr. Marcé's. She hurried off to the bank. She kindly asked if she could see Mrs. Guerdee's company bank statement. At first she thought that the bank must have made a horrible mistake, for the bank statement showed that they'd withdrawn only £20 on the day the company coach was to take the money to Boston. Patience voiced this sentiment, but the man checked the files and said there was no mistake. Once home, Patience wrote,

Bank account had only £20 withdrawn

Mrs. Guerdee claims a loss of £3000

So Mrs. Guerdee had only lost £20! Or maybe she hadn't lost anything! Maybe Mrs. Guerdee had spent the money some other way. What if Mrs. Guerdee had paid Mr. Browner to steal the company coach. She remembered Mrs. Guerdee stating, "I am going to the insurance company this evening." But proof, she needed proof. She was going to try to see the company coach. If it was Mrs. Guerdee's stagecoach she would call the bailiff.

The day wore on. At nightfall Patience got her chance. Patience slipped out of her four-poster bed, fully clothed. She stole out of the house alone. She traced her steps back to Mr. Browner's lodging. To her amazement the door to the stable was open. Patience crept around and looked in. It was Mrs. Guerdee's company coach! And in addition, Mrs. Guerdee was there. Mr. Hadestir was her companion. They were talking in hushed voices.

"We can paint it, and no one will know it is the same one."

"I've got the paint here, ma'am."

"Good, another £20 for you to do the job." Patience had heard enough. She ran like she'd never run before. She rapped on the door of the bailiff's house. After hearing the news, he gathered several reliable townsmen and headed for the stable.

The next day Patience was awarded £65 by the insurance company. The governor himself applauded her work. Even her mother conceded that Patience had done a good deed for the community by solving the mystery. An article in the Philadelphia Press read: Patience Pays Off

Patience Crawering, a girl of twelve years of age, caught Sybil Guerdee paying Maxwell Hadestir to steal an empty coach. They planned to repaint the coach and use it again. Sybil Guerdee would have gotten £200,000 from her insurance company for the "loss." We all owe Patience so much. The insurance company today paid Patience a reward of £65. Mr. Hadestir has a four year sentence to jail, and Mrs. Guerdee will be banished from the colony for the same period of time. Patience most certainly pays off!

Ellen M. Nye

Age: 11

124

# THE TRAGIC DEATH OF ABRILAMAN HATSHEPSUT

Once upon a time thousands of years ago there lived a young princess by the name of Abrilaman Hatshepsut, in the palace of Hatshepsut. She was sitting in her window seat, crying. Abrilaman had just been to the death sentence of her one and only boy friend, Hocus. There, sitting in her throne next to her mother and father she had watched them drag him all tied up in chains. Then her mother (the Pharaoh) had to make that choice, that one choice that would either kill or grant a man his life. Now Abrilaman was crying, her beautiful green eyes surrounded by red. A few minutes later she decided that she would go and rescue him. Later in the evening she would go and set the prisoner free and they would run away together in disguise. So after her evening meal she went back to her room and packed all of her supplies for the trip and then she waited for every one to fall asleep.

When she heard nothing but the tiptoeing of a mouse, she quietly dashed down to the dungeons. When she reached Hocus's cell she got the key from a hook and opened his door. When he saw her beautiful face with those magnificent green eyes he knew he owed her for the rest of his life. She put on her disguise and they ran through the palace gates as fast as they could. The next morning, back at the palace, a slave went to wake Abrilaman and found a horrible sight, no princess. Then the slave ran to the queen's chamber to tell her the news. When the queen heard the news she immediately sent out a search party for the princess and the prisoner who had also escaped during the night. Meanwhile Abrilaman and Hocus had just reached the beautiful Nile River with its lush bushes and its ferocious alligators swimming and basking in the sun.

Three days later the search party reached the Nile, and decided to spend the night in the bushes. In the deadness of night one of the guards heard a rustling noise and went to investigate. When he got there he saw a wonderful sight, the prisoner asleep with a straggly girl. He eagerly hurried back to camp to waken the other men. Before Abrilaman and Hocus could do anything, they were chained up and being dragged back to the palace. The guards figured out that the princess was dead anyway.

When they arrived back at the palace the next morning, the guard took them immediately to the throne room. Without any questioning Queen Hatshepsut grabbed a knife and ordered for them to be killed. Once they were ready to be unclothed they discovered the young girl was really the princess, Abrilaman, in disguise.

In the end they have her a huge burial and proper mummification. But still the queen was sorrowful that she, the queen, had killed her own beautiful daughter with her hair like the darkness of midnight, and her eyes the color of emeralds in broad day. In the end we know that Hocus's and Abrilaman's Ba and Ka live together happily for eternity in the spirit world.

Stephanie Grange
Age: 13

Susan was awakened by the tide rolling along the beach outside her window. She sat up in her bed, and instantly felt the eerie sensation lingering in her room. It was the same feeling she always had on the first of every month. Today, like all the other days, was the day her pa must leave. Quickly, Susan got dressed, and ran out of her room to find the usual scattered maps, and packed bags.

A gruff, yet kind voice spoke to break the silence, "Susie, it's time for me to go... "

"I know, Pa. Please, just this once, don't go."

"Come on, Susie, we go through this every month. You know I have to go. Besides, I love my job! I love feeling the sea breeze on my face. Just like you do."

"Yes, Pa," Susie looked up at her father with wet, teary eyes. "Please be careful, and come home soon."

"I promise. Be good, there's food in the kitchen, money in the case, and if you need anything, go to Captain," he paused, tears were welling up inside his deep blue eyes, "I love you, Susie."

"I love you too, Pa!" Susan leaped into her Pa's arms, and they embraced for a few moments that Susan wished would never end.

"Well," The man said, placing his daughter on the floor, and wiping the tears from under his eyes, "I'm off. I should be home in a month."

"Wait!" Susan yelled, but her father was already out of the door, and around the corner. A month? She thought, He's never been gone for a whole month!

Susan and her father live on the North Meridian Sea, in a small village called Leso. Her father, known as Tom, is, like many other men in the village, a crab fisherman. Crab fishing is a very dangerous job, but it pays well.

Despite the money earned, Susan and Tom live in a little shack at the edge of a cliff that reaches out from the sea towards the sky. Tom never did like spending more money than necessary.

Trying to set her mind at rest, Susan went down to the beach to fish for snails. She spent nearly two hours at the beach, listening to the waves crashing against the cliffs, and being soothed by the mist. Susan loved the sea as much as her father. It seemed to wipe all the troubles of the day, and all the pain in her heart away, somewhere far away, never to return.

"Oh look, Howard! It's little Susie. Hi Susie!" A cold, snooty voice split the silence.

Another rude voice followed, "Oh my! Susie, did your daddy have to leave again?"

It was Rose and Howard, the richest kids in Leso. Their father was the owner of the market.

"You know he did, Howard. Your father sent him!"

"Oh yeah, he did." Rose had a cruel, mocking smile on her pinched face.

"I have to go," Susan picked up her bag of snails, and trying to avoid any other humiliation, began to walk away.

Before Susan turned the corner, Rose said, "That's what happens when you don't have a mama, and your daddy doesn't care about you." Susan's heart sank, and as Rose and Howard laughed, she ran away.

I hate them! She thought, it's not for them to... to say Pa doesn't care! He DOES care! He does love me! And who do they think they are? Talking about my mom, (rest in peace,) that way? Susan's mother died when Susan was born. Although she died eleven years ago, Susan still gets offended when people talk about her mom with disrespect.

Susan's feet began to ache. She ran and ran, until finally, she reached the marina.

"Captain? Captain, where are y... "

"Susie! Susie! What be yer problem? Are you okay? What's wrong?" Captain's voice boomed from behind a tall counter. "Wait a minute, I know what're here for... "

"Hello, Captain. Is the mail in yet?"

"As a matter o' fact, it is," Captain turned to a big box, and began to dig through all the letters. He was a very large, cheery man, like Susan's father. Captain works at the marina, which is also the post office for Leso.

When Susan's father leaves, he always sends letters so his daughter will get them every Thursday of every week.

"Here it is. Miss Susan Rolle." He held up an envelope.

Susan's face lit up like a Christmas tree. She snatched the letter, and ran out of the room yelling, "Thank you, Captain!"

Susan ran, again, to the beach and read her note:

> My Dearest Susie,
>
> We've reached our destination and the crabs are everywhere! They're almost jumping in the boat! Oh you should see it! The sunsets are even prettier than they are at home. They're almost as pretty as your face. Oh, Susie, I do miss you. I'm sorry for leaving without explaining why I was going to be gone for a month. Mr. Ross, you know, the owner of the market? Well, anyways, he said there was a crab shortage all over the coast, and with the abundance of crabs out here, we figured we should stay out on the sea longer. I have to go. I love you!
>
> Love,
>
> Pa
>
> P.S. Remember, say your prayers, and let the light comfort you.

A tear fell from Susan's rosy cheek, and onto the paper. She leaned back against the rock wall behind her, and sighed. Rising to her feet, Susan began the walk home with the sun setting in the distance.

The next day, Susan read her letter again. Afterwards, she went into her father's room and stood in front of the tall bookcase. She reached up and pulled all the books from the fifth shelf. There was a safe placed in a hole in the wall. Susan put in the combination, and opened the door. The safe held several blueprints, all the money she and her father had, and a portrait of her mother. Susan grabbed the blueprints and went outside. She unrolled three blueprints that held an invention that she and her father had designed. It was a circular structure, big at the bottom, and smaller at the top. On the inside, stairs would spiral to the top, fifty feet high. In the top, there would be a big, powerful light. The light will turn in a complete circle, and shine brightly for miles. The light would guide sailors home. They called it a lighthouse. Susan's father showed the plans to the town, and they laughed at him. No one thought the lighthouse was a good idea, not even Captain.

Susan thought back to her note. Her pa had said to be comforted by the light. She thought he meant the lighthouse, but there was another possibility. Her pa was a very faithful, religious man. He believed in God and His light that must be shared to the whole world. Did Susan's father mean, "be comforted by the lighthouse, or God?" Susan tried to push the question out of her head by doing her chores, and milling around the beach. But despite her efforts, it held on to Susan's shoulders like a weight tied to her. And even though it was a heavy burden, what bothered her most was why. Why was it such a big deal? Was it honestly that important?

"Sorry Susie, no word from yer pa," Captain sighed. It had been two weeks, time for Susan's next letter. She went into town to the marina as usual, to retrieve her long-awaited note.

"Oh? The mail must be running late. It should be here any minute, so I'll just wait here... "

"No, Susie," Captain interrupted. "The mail came already. They said yer pa's ship wasn't anywhere to be found."

"What? That's silly! Pa never goes ahead of schedule! He wouldn't have gone ahead without sending me my letter, he never does. The mailmen must not know what they're talking about! That's all," Susan said in an almost snotty tone.

"I don't think you understand. They couldn't find yer pa's ship anywhere. Not at any of the ports, not anywhere. Sorry Susie, he's... lost." Captain looked at Susan for a split second, and then turned away when she began to cry.

"Lost? He can't be! He never gets lost! Never!" Her whimpers turned to shouts, "He can't leave me here! Do you know what I go through when he's gone? No! He's not lost! He's coming home!" Susan's face was red, and so were her eyes. Tears streaked her face.

"Susie... " Captain began, trying to hold back his own tears, "I know... " but before he could finish, Susan yelled, "No! You don't know how it feels!" She sprinted from the room.

She ran until her sides ached, sweat dripped down her face, and her throat was parched. She gasped for every breath. She kept running until she reached the beach, and thrust herself into the sea.

Hours passed, and Susan floated, exhausted from running. She realized that Captain was right; her father was lost. She was shocked to find herself giving in to the facts without a fight. But what could she honestly do? Nothing.

Suddenly, a thought hit Susan so hard, it was like she had heard it orally. The Light! She COULD do something! A smile began to creep onto Susan's face as she hastily swam back to shore. She ran into her house, and to the bookcase. Books were torn from the shelf, and thrown out of Susan's path to the safe. She acted as though she hadn't eaten in months, and in the safe, there was food. When she opened the safe, the blueprints, and money were snatched out of their hiding place.

The thought raced through her mind over and over again. I will build a lighthouse! I'll bring Pa home! But how? Susan's excitement immediately turned to discouragement. I can't build a fifty- foot high building by myself, and I know no one will help me! I'll build a miniature lighthouse! Leaving the blueprints behind, Susan took the money, and went to the market. She bought the biggest, strongest, brightest, battery-operated light she could find. Along with the light she bought six yards of rope, some thick boards, and other building supplies. She took all of the items, along with the blueprints, to the edge of the cliff that overlooked the sea. Then, she got to work. It took Susan nearly five hours to complete her miniature lighthouse, but when she finally finished, it was worth the effort! The little lighthouse was built like a tripod. Three boards were placed with one end of each board on the ground, and the other ends all meeting each other five feet off the ground. Susan fastened the boards together with nails, screws, and some rope. The light was hung from the boards with the rest of the rope and it naturally spun slowly in a complete circle. Another week slowly passed by, and there was still no word from Susan's father, although he should've already been back. The lighthouse was working like Susan and her father planned. Susan pitched a tent by her creation so she could "be comforted" by the light. Which, in some ways, it did comfort her. She thought her father would be home any minute.

One day, Susan had to go back to the market for new batteries for her light because the old batteries had ran out the night before. When Mr. Ross told Susan that that they didn't have batteries for the light in stock, and that it would take three months for them to come in, her heart sank. Her wonderful plan was ruined. There was no way her father would be able to survive three more months! Slowly, Susan left the market, and made her way back to her tent. She wanted to die. What did she ever do to deserve this? That night, she cried herself into a fitful sleep. Meanwhile, Tom was being tossed and turned on his ship in a terrible storm at sea. He and his crew were fighting the waves in a desperate attempt to survive! Water splashed onto the deck, making it impossible to stand, an d the foggy night sky made it impossible to see, let alone navigate their way home. But then, for a moment, a ray of light broke through the mist. All the crew saw it, including Tom, and for a magnificent second, it as like the whole world stood still, and then the light disappeared. But it came back, again and again.

"Sail toward the light!" Tom ordered. Then he smiled and said, "I see ya, Susie. We're coming home."

Meagan Bosch
Age: 14

# DIESEL

Walking into the building with my mom, I could smell the best thing I had ever smelled in my whole life, PUPPIES!  A woman took me into the back room, I saw many, many puppies who were jumping around in their cages wanting to come home with me.  Looking around for a second, I saw all different kinds of puppies that I could have taken.

I could hear their little yelps to be held over and over.  Finally, I saw the most perfect American bulldog I had ever laid eyes on.  As the puppy was looking at me and jumping around in his cage, I quickly asked the store owner if I could hold him.  The tall, blonde-haired woman carefully grabbed him out of his big cage.

Holding the small, cute puppy I told my mom, "This is the one I want to take home with us."  I was truly excited when my mom told me we could have the puppy.

As my mom and I were leaving with my new friend, Mom asked, "Do you have a name for him?"

I replied, "Yes, I think I like the name Diesel."

MacKenzie Kelley

# A COZY PLACE OF MY OWN... MY BED

You know when you wake up in the morning and everything is great:  like when you wake up after having a great night's sleep, like when your bed sheets look so colorful, more colorful than any other day and your pillow is soooo soft, so much softer than any other day and you love the fresh clean smell of your newly washed sheets, the ones your mom has just washed the night before, and the wonderful refreshed and relaxed feeling that comes from sleeping on a mattress of clouds.  Well then... the reality!  It's TIME TO GET UP!

Imagine what it would be like to never have to leave this cozy place of your own, having breakfast in bed.  "Hey, mom, I'm ready for my breakfast, I'll have three fresh pancakes dripping with butter, swimming in syrup, two pieces of crispy, sizzling bacon, and a bowl of fresh, juicy, tangy fruit and don't forget the kiwi-strawberry-mango-banana smoothie."

"Hey Meg, FAT CHANCE... get up NOW!"

Well the reality:  that could really never happen!  I wouldn't want it to happen.  HOW BORING it would be to sit in my bed all day instead of being out exploring.  I would feel like Charlie Buckets' grandparents; grandma Georgiana and grandpa George, grandma Josephine and grandpa Joe.

If I had to spend the day in that cozy place of my own, I surely would miss out on a lot of living life, but it sure is fun to dream.

Meglana Peak
Age: 11

# SNOWED IN

"Wow, it's really snowing hard!"

"Maybe we'll get snowed in!"

The excited voices of my classmates made me wonder. Would we really get snowed in?

This snowstorm was the biggest Colorado had seen in years. Plus, everything in the valley was closed except the schools. I was hungry and the candy my friends and I snuck out of our backpacks wouldn't last long.

By the way, my name is Cassie. My friends (Zoe and Scooter) and I were sitting on the floor of Mr. Bubalo's fifth-grade classroom. We were discussing what we could do if we were snowed in.

"We could sneak around the school at night!" said Scooter.

"Yea, that would be cool, but they'll probably have hallway patrols," said Zoe.

"Maybe there's a secret passageway!" I added excitedly.

We were temporarily distracted when our classmates' voices rang out once more.

"We're snowed in!" yelled Bernard.

"All right!" shouted the rest of the class.

The excitement soon died down when Opie said, "I'm hungry."

"Me too," agreed Caden. "I need food!"

"Then cafeteria, here we come!" said Franklin.

Everyone started toward the door when it flung open to a wonderful sight. The cafeteria ladies must have sensed hunger, because they brought what looked like a Thanksgiving feast! Hamburgers, fries, corndogs, hot dogs, tacos, fried chicken, milk, juice, nachos, you name it, and it was there! We all grabbed a paper plate and piled it high with food. Then everyone found a nice, cozy spot in the halls to eat. Zoe, Scooter, and I found a nice, comfy spot next to the soda dispenser. Scooter forgot to get a drink in the classroom, so he plunked in two quarters and bought a root beer.

"I wish we could sleep in a small space where only the three of us could sleep," Zoe was saying. "Then we could look around easier, without a teacher breathing down our necks."

I nodded in agreement. Then I noticed Scooter was looking very strangely at the wall in front of us.

"What's the matter?" I asked between mouthfuls of fried chicken.

"Come here," he replied, still staring at the wall.

We all got up and walked over to where Scooter was staring.

"Yes!" he exclaimed, "an opening!" He dug his fingernails into the caulking between one of the tiles. Then he carefully took out the tile and set it on the ground. There was a red button underneath. Zoe pushed it, and then stepped back, as if she expected it to launch a missile at her.

All of a sudden, black screen emerged from out of nowhere. "Type address" were the only words on the screen. Now a keyboard appeared. I typed 3224 New Moon Ridge, my address.

"Hey!" cried Scooter, "why don't we type my address?"

I made a face at him as I pushed ENTER. Just then the screen vanished and was replaced by a large crawl space, big enough for all of us to fit in. We all clambered in, and ZAP! We were transported right to my bedroom!

I was surprised to find my bed made, which I had completely forgotten about this morning. I ran to tell my parents that my friends and I had made it home safely. I didn't go into many details, so I just quickly changed the subject by asking for hot cocoa. My mom phoned Zoe and Scooter's parents to tell them that they were safe and sound at our house. That next morning my dad heard on the radio that the schools would be closed for two weeks due to the blizzard. The rest of the students and staff were still stuck at the school. It was now being torn open to rescue the prisoners trapped in the building. Of course, no one knows WE made it out, but now there's another question, what other mysteries are hidden in the school?

Brianna Castellini<br>
Age: 11

# THE THREE TRICK-OR-TREATERS

## Part One

One Halloween day there were three trick-or-treaters. Their names were Timothy, Jessica and Tyler. Timothy was eleven, Jessica was nine and Tyler was three. Well, they went trick-or-treating around their block, except to one house, because they heard it was haunted, Jessica said, "Lets go inside."

"No way," said Timothy.

"Well, are you scared?" asked Jessica.

"No I'm not scared at all" said Timothy.

"Then lets go inside!" said Jessica in a loud tone.

"I guess," said Timothy.

So they went into the house. The floors were squeaky and the walls were covered with cobwebs. Then Timothy realized, "Where's Tyler?" Tyler was standing outside the door. You could tell he was scared.

They said to him, "It's ok. Don't be afraid." But Tyler knew that mom had always said never go into the house.

Then Tyler asked, "Is there any ghost in there?"

"No Tyler, there's no such thing as ghost," answered Jessica. So they all went inside the house. Timothy was behind, Tyler was in the middle, and Jessica was the leader. When they went inside it was the same as when Jessica and Timothy went in. The three went into the next room. They saw a work table with papers on top and books with torn pages. To the right were staircases that led up and a staircase to the left that led down to a basement. Timothy said, "Let's go to the right and go upstairs." So they went up. Timothy thought he heard something, so he quickly turned around, but it was only a mouse. The three kept on going up the stairs, until they saw someone moving. Tyler screamed, "AHAHAHAHA!!!" Timothy saw that the ghost was wearing an orange T-shirt. Timothy grabbed Tyler's hand. They ran down the stairs as quickly as the three could go. When they got to the end of the stairs they heard dogs barking. They quickly ran to a door which they thought was the door out. But it wasn't, it was a dead end. "What will we do?" said Jessica.

"Let's go to the next door," said Timothy. They finally found the right door. The three ran home. "Finally, we're safe," said Jessica and Timothy.

Tyler was relieved. Tyler wondered where Mom and Dad were. Tyler looked for them. He didn't find them anywhere. Jessica called the police and told them about what they had seen in the house. The police told her about the jailbreak and they were looking around for the prisoner. Then she told them about their parents who were missing. So the policeman said, "We will send a police squad over right away." In a few minutes, the police squad arrived to see if they could find the kids' parents. They looked to see if they could find them. They didn't. Then Jessica told them, "Do you think that man kidnapped our parents?"

The policeman said, "Maybe the man is a criminal." The police squad looked around to find their parents. They went to the mysterious haunted house. The policeman said, "Is this the house?"

"Yes this is the right house," said Timothy. Timothy and Jessica went in and Tyler stayed outside. He showed them where they saw the person standing at the staircase. They didn't see the person there. They went to the staircase to the left. Timothy saw the man and ran after him. Timothy dove and grabbed the person's pant leg. They both fell to the ground. The police arrested him and took him away. Jessica, Timothy, and Tyler found their parents.

## Part Two

Three years after what happened that Halloween night. They went back to their old neighborhood to see that house because they moved to a new neighborhood. When they got there they tore the house down. They saw a different house. The house was much bigger than the other one. They looked around to see anything, it was empty. They asked their friends why no one lived there. They said, "It was haunted." They decided to look around the house tomorrow. The next day they went to the house. They looked inside. It was much spookier than the other house. There were spiders in every corner and beetles on the wood floor. They saw some steep stairs going up and down. They turned around and they saw this black figure in the shadow. They did not know what it was. Tyler threw something at it. It hit it hard and made a big thunk. They ran as fast as they could out the door. They wondered what it was. When they went back in they brought flashlights and a baseball bat for protection. They looked around to see the figure. They did not see it. They kept looking around when they saw it. It was a big man with an orange T-shirt. They thought it was a ghost, but it was someone wearing a mask. They ran after us, Tyler went out first then Jessica and Timothy. They ran to there house which was two blocks down they were safe. They finally decided to capture it. They ate a good meal. Got all their friends and went inside. They all searched when they found it. We grabbed its hands and legs. It was a man, he had a lot of hair and a long beard. It was the man that escaped from the prison, he got us all and we kept jumping on him. Someone called the cops. They came in a few minutes. We kept holding him but he would go through us everytime. He got us all. He started running, we had to chase after him. When the police arrived we was running down the block when we caught him. He tried to get us off but he was too tired. We had finally caught him. The police came and took him back to jail. We never saw him again.

Sean Johnson
Age: 11

Springtime in Paris! The sun shines brightly upon the earth, the flowers bloom and flourish, and laughter is everywhere. Riley Thompson's family has vacationed to France every summer since Riley was five years old. Sometimes Riley wished that she could spend her summer at home in Los Angeles, California. She had just turned sixteen before they left L. A. and was planning on driving to the beach with her friends every day. But, once they arrived she was swept up in Paris's beauty and mystery.

Riley also loved art. Every chance that she got she went to a museum or an art gallery. It was mid-afternoon before Riley decided to greet the day. She packed her purse with her many 'necessities'. Lip gloss, a cell phone, sunglasses, and money for, what else, shopping! She stepped out of their modest French villa and into the sweet smelling air. The house was old, yet very charming with vines running all over the exterior walls. She breathed deeply and went in search of her only mode of transportation, a bicycle that she hadn't used since the previous summer. Once she found the antique, Riley set off for an art exhibit in one of Paris' many parks. A bicycle came in handy when traveling through the narrow streets of Paris. Riley wound her way through, until at last paintings and statues were in her sight.

Surrounded by art she became lost in her dreamland, when suddenly, "Bon jour!"

Riley turned to find a small man with saucer eyes and an enormous grin crouching behind her. He mumbled something in French, then when she didn't reply he switched to his broken English.

"You like to buy a painting? Special price for a special young lady!"

She smiled and said, "They are beautiful paintings, but for now I'm just looking."

He persisted for a while, but when she still did not give in he went on to someone else. She walked over to where a man was using watercolors to paint a very fidgety little boy's portrait. The boy wriggled and whined as his mother tried to keep him still. Riley stood and watched for a couple of minutes. She saw a young girl a few feet away watching the painter earnestly. This little girl reminded Riley of herself when she first came to Paris. She used to beg her parents to take her to see more art. They would go to as many museums as they could handle, and then she went home, took out her paintbrush and notebook and would sit and draw or paint for an hour or so. She was brought out of her reminiscing by a woman's voice.

"Isn't it wonderful? Spring is here and it's the best time for young artists to improve."

The woman was older, maybe about fifty-five or sixty. She was nicely dressed with shoes and jewelry to match. Her gray hair was pulled back into a neat bun, but her hat. The hat did not match her at all. It was an old straw hat with a sash around the top and a worn bow in the back.

"Do you come here often?" the old lady asked.

"Well, I come here every summer."

"Watch how he strokes the brush. Lightly, yet just enough."

The two had turned their attention to a man in his twenties who was painting a nearby bridge. There were willow trees and no buildings behind 'his' bridge, just open meadow.

"See how he makes the picture his own. He doesn't just paint what he sees with his eyes, but what he feels with his heart."

"I'm Riley Thompson," she said.

"My name is Madame Chloe Vanderson. You may call me as you wish."

"Then I will call you Madame," Riley answered.

Over the next few weeks Riley and Madame were inseparable. Riley's parents were a little worried about their daughter spending all her time with a woman that was four times her age. But, Riley took it as a learning experience. Madame knew everything about art. She knew the different types of brush strokes and all about famous artists. She knew about Da Vinci, Michelangelo, and Monet. Madame took Riley to museums and art fairs.

One night at dinner Mrs. Thompson asked, "Riley, why do you like Mrs. Vanderson so much?"

This question surprised Riley a little. "Well, for one she loves art. And she and I have a lot in common? Why do you ask?"

"Oh, there's really no reason, it's just that before we came here you didn't want to come and now you want to stay longer. And the person that you're spending time with is in a completely different generation than you."

As she lay in bed Riley thought about what her mother had said at dinner. She thought about Madame, too. Everyday Madame wore the same hat, no matter what the weather was like, or what she was wearing. Finally she drifted off to sleep.

The next day was rainy and cool. Seeing the weather Riley thought she should call Madame to see what they would do. But her mom intervened.

"Riley!" she said. "I thought that since it's raining outside that you and I would go shopping today. How does that sound?"

"Oh, Mom I was just about to call Madame to see if she wanted to go to an art gallery today. You can come too." She saw her mother's smile fade and she replied,

"Oh, that's okay we'll shop another day. You already have plans." She felt bad, but her mom had someone that she could talk to, Madame didn't. About halfway through the day, her conscience caught up with her.

"Madame, I think I'll call my mom. You see, she and I were going shopping today." Madame cut her off.

"Well then what are you doing here with an old grouch like me, when you could be shopping with your mother?" When she finished, Riley didn't know what to say.

"I like going with you Madame. I have fun looking at art with you. But, maybe I haven't spent enough time with her."

"Riley, let me tell you a story." Madame started. "Once upon a time there were two young girls who were best friends. They both loved art and hoped that someday they could be great artists. They made other friends as well, but their strong friendship remained. The one girl, Sarah was her name, had a favorite hat that she always wore. It was a gift from her father before he died. Over the years their friendship continued. They were both married and had children. Sarah still wore her hat for everything, no matter what the occasion. Two years ago Sarah became very ill, before she died she gave her best friend a gift. The hat that she cherished so much." A tear came to Madame's eye and she looked up at Riley's face.

"I guess that's why you wear it so much, huh? You were the other friend weren't you? Riley asked.

"Yes, Riley I was. I guess that when I first saw you two months ago, you reminded me of my friend, Sarah. You're young, you love art, and I guess I just went back to those days when Sarah and I used to spend every day together. I'm sorry." There was silence for a moment and then Riley spoke up.

"No, Madame. You don't have to be sorry for anything. I had so much fun this summer and I learned a lot. I think you're a great friend." With that the two women smiled. Their friendship was true and they would never forget each other.

Riley sat on her bed back in L. A. writing a diary of all that had happened that summer.

"Riley, there's a package down here that's addressed to you." Her father called up the stairs. "I think it's from Mrs. Vanderson."

"Mrs. Vanderson? Oh, you mean Madame?! Okay, I'll be right down."

She ran downstairs and took the odd-shaped package up to her room. She ripped it open and found a letter on top of a round box. It read:

> Dearest Riley,
> These past few weeks have seemed like an eternity. I am looking forward to seeing you next summer. Inside the box you will find a token of our friendship. I pass it on to you as my friend did to me. Wear it in good health. Au revoir!
> Your friend,
> Madame.

She opened the box and inside she found Madame's hat.

Haley M. Black<br>
Age: 15

# TIGER GOES TO THE BIG CITY

One day Tiger was in his house drinking his tea in the jungle when he heard a boom! He quickly ran outside and found his brother jumping really hard. Tiger was angry because he had spilled tea all over himself because of his brother's jumping.

"You silly brother!" Tiger said loudly. "Why are you such a pain?"

"I'm sorry," said the brother. "I didn't want to cause any harm, I just can't seem to get my kite down!"

"OK then," said Tiger and he climbed up the tree and got the kite down, then walked away.

"Thank you!" his little brother shouted.

Tiger went in the house and made another cup of tea. Now it wasn't the first time his brother's kite got stuck, and it wasn't the last because the day after that it kept happening.

One day, Tiger said to his parents, "I can't stand him, I'm going to the big city for a break!"

So he did, and as soon as he got there, he was amazed at all of the wonderful places he saw. But now he had to find a place to stay, so he checked into the Wild Cats Motel 8 and he loved it! He thought it was much better than the jungle and that little brother. After he had unpacked his stuff, he went out and suddenly found out that the city wasn't so miraculous. He went and bought a dinner at a nice diner. He enjoyed his food and then got his bill.

"One hundred and eight dollars!" he shouted.

Then, he paid his bill and got out of there as fast as possible. After that he went to a shop to get a souvenir for his family. He got mittens for his mom, a flashlight for his dad, and for his annoying little brother, he got a new kite.

Then, he got a bill for twenty-five dollars and he said, "Wow! I had better quit spending and go home!"

So he did, and when he got back to the Motel 8 he went to bed. That night, he dreamed of his home, the jungle and of his family and how he must have hurt his little brother's feelings.

Then, he woke up, looked out his window, and said, "I want to go home!"

So he did. He repacked his stuff and looked at the city. "It will probably be the last time I see it," he said, and he left with that and no breakfast. As soon as he got home, he opened his gate, knocked on his door and went in.

He yelled, "Anyone home?"

His family came running toward him.

"Hey guys!" he said.

They were happy to see him. Then, he bent down towards his brother and said, "I'm sorry I said you were a pain and then left!"

"It's OK," he said.

Then, Tiger unzipped his bag and pulled out the kite and said, "I love you!"

"I love you too," said the little brother, then he hugged him. Then, Tiger pulled out the other gifts and gave them to his parents.

"Let's all go out and watch Brother fly his new kite," said Mom.

"OK, but first can I get some breakfast?" and they all laughed. Tiger told his brother about the trip while his mom and dad cooked breakfast.

Nicole Smith
Age: 10

# THE MYSTERIOUS CAR SALESMAN

Hi, my name is Kellen Bothwell and I'm a typical thirteen-year-old boy. I'm a seventh grader in middle school and I live with my mom, dad, and my annoying little sister. Most mornings at my house go pretty smoothly, with the exception of yesterday.

It was a dark and stormy Tuesday morning in my small town, my mom and I were on our way to school. On this particular morning, my mom noticed that her purse was missing and we were running late so she didn't have time to look for it. She decided to take the back roads, which she thought would be faster because there was hardly any traffic. Since we usually didn't go that way, I was checking out the new scenery when I looked behind us and saw another car. I remembered seeing that car near my house when we were leaving and at the car dealership when we bought our new car. The car, an old beat-up rusty, green Cadillac, was following us closely. He was honking and waving his hands like he wanted us to stop. He was starting to make me nervous.

A few minutes later, I looked back again and noticed the guy was wearing a ski mask. I thought this was very weird so the first thing I did was tell my mom what I saw. She didn't believe me. She looked in the rearview mirror and was SHOCKED to see I was right! We both started to get scared, so she stepped on it thinking we would lose him. We were going about one hundred ten miles per hour in our brand-new car, a white GMC Yukon. The strange man followed us as we swerved all over the road trying to confuse him. It didn't work, the man stayed right on us the whole way. We made a sharp left turn and the man made a sharp right turn. We thought that we lost him but farther up the road he met us at a four-way stop.

Right when we saw him we took off as fast as we could. We started swerving again but this time we swerved into a muddy ditch. The man was getting closer and my mom was trying to go but the wheels just kept on spinning, even in four-wheel drive. When the man got within about ten feet from us, we finally got out of the ditch. We sped away onto the overpass.

While we were on the overpass, I looked back and noticed that the man was now stuck in the same ditch as we were just in. I thought we had it made until I looked at the gas gauge and noticed that the orange indicator was on the "E." All of the sudden our car started to slow down and quickly came to a stop. The man in the other car was still stuck in the ditch. He was trying really hard to get his old Cadillac out. While my mom was thinking of a way to get going again, so was I. All of the sudden it hit me, I remembered what the car salesman said when we bought our car. He said, "This car is a great deal because it comes with one free year of roadside assistance." I told my mom right away and she called.

When the roadside assistance man arrived he filled our car up with gas from his red gas jug. We decided to play it cool and Mom only accelerated to ninety miles per hour. Apparently this was not fast enough. Before I could get the words -- "I think we lost him" out of my mouth, he was following us again. We waited for the man to get close enough and then we slammed on the brakes. The man didn't want to his us so he swerved and hit the side of the overpass and went flying. He hit the ground with a huge bang.

We waited for the cops to arrive. When they did they identified the man as Rob Johnson... The man who sold us our car! You are probably wondering why he had on a ski mask. Well the cops called his house and told his wife what had happened. They asked why he was wearing a ski mask. She told the cops that he had just gotten back from a ski trip in Vail and the heater in his car was broken and it helped keep him warm. She informed the police that he was following us because he wanted to tell my mom she had left her purse at the car dealership and he was going to give it back to her.

All in all, Mr. Johnson only suffered minor injuries and I got to school, late, but I got there. I feel kind of bad hurting the man who sold us our car, he was really nice. So if you ever see a man following you, in a beat-up green, rusty Cadillac, and you just bought a car from a man named Rob Johnson just stop and see what he has to say. If not, act cool, do what my mom did, and step on it!!

Kellen Lee Bothwell
Age: 13

# AMAZON

Down below, the sun reflected off the glistening teal sea.  Jenny Anderson and Lara Williams were flying to Brazil in a small aircraft, where they planned to be missionaries.  They both lived in Colorado and had been studying the Bible for many years, preparing for this exciting day.

Suddenly, the pilot's voice exploded over the intercom.

"Ladies, I've been notified that we'll be runnin' into a storm about twenty miles away.  So buckle up tight.  It might be a bumpy ride."  He continued, "We'll be landing in about an hour."

Then the rain started to fall.  The thunder was like many drums and crashing cymbals, all striking at once.  The bright lightning looked eerie against the dark clouds.

All of a sudden, the plane jolted hard.  At first, Jenny and Lara thought it was turbulence, but they were wrong, very wrong.  The plane's wing had been struck by lightning.  In seconds, the plane started to plunge.  Then... it went black.

When the girls slowly awakened, they peered out the window and could see only a blur of browns and greens.  As they came into focus, they discovered they were in very tall trees.  They were thankful to be alive and not seriously injured.  Other than minor cuts and bruises, they seemed to be fine.  However, when they went up to the cockpit, they found the captain was dead.  The radio was destroyed in the crash.  There was no way to call for help.  The girls slowly walked back and collected their carry-ons, which included some toiletries, a good amount of food, flashlights, blankets, two outfits, and, of course, their Bibles.

"Well, at least it stopped raining," Lara murmured.

With their bags on their backs, the girls started down the steep tree.  But, in no time, they were on the ground.

"Now what?" Lara pleaded.

"We set up camp," Jenny hollered.

By the time the trees' dark shadows appeared, the girls had made a fire and organized their belongings.

"Good thing I learned to use sticks and weeds to make fire," Jenny exclaimed.

"Yeah, I guess," Lara replied under her breath.

"We're going to be fine," Jenny reassured her friend.

"Hello!  Don't you know where we are," Lara burst. Jenny didn't answer. "We're in the Amazon!" Lara was hysterical now.

"But God will be with us, won't He?" Jenny responded, hugging her friend.

"Yeah, you're right," Lara sighed.

That night, Jenny couldn't sleep. She looked over at Lara sound asleep by the fire. The outdoors had always been exciting to Jenny. She had taken some survival classes, which was a blessing in these circumstances. As Jenny took out her Bible, she heard a rustling behind her. Jenny slowly turned, finding herself staring into the glowing eyes of a jaguar. Don't panic, she thought to herself. Then she remembered an article she had read about encountering a wild cat. It said to make eye contact, not scream, throw rocks, try to set a challenge by looking bigger, and make loud noises. Basically, I have to act like a raging lunatic to scare it off. So that's what Jenny did. She jumped up and started yelling her loudest. Then she started jumping around, picking up rocks and sticks and throwing them at the jaguar. It snarled when a rock hit it. Lara was now wide-awake. All she could do was sit and stare in horror. Finally, the big cat turned and disappeared into the dark jungle.

"Are you okay?!" Lara jumped up and ran to Jenny's side.

"Yeah, I'm fine," Jenny sighed in relief.

"I'm going to try to go back to sleep then, okay?" Lara asked.

Jenny nodded. "Okay. I'll see you in the morning."

Finally, Jenny fell into a deep sleep. The girls had quite a few scares that day, but there were more to come.

That morning, Lara was startled awake when a dark-skinned man holding a spear and wearing only a skirt-like garment made of skin was sitting, staring at her.

Lara screamed, "Jenny! Wake up!" The mysterious man quickly jumped up.

"What... what?" Jenny was still half-asleep. Yet, when she looked over by Lara, she grabbed her flashlight and started swinging it as she slowly staggered his way. By now, the confused man was even more alarmed than the girls.

"Me, Auquè," he stammered.

"What?" Jenny stopped in her tracks.

"My name Auquè!" He was grinning now, relieved that Jenny wasn't stalking him.

"You speak English?" Lara asked.

"Sssome," he carefully replied.

"What do you want?" Jenny didn't sound quite as harsh.

"Me think... you lost," his eyes wandering around.

"Well, you're right." Jenny walked back to her supplies and put the flashlight away.

"You need help?" he asked. "Me have village, not far."

"Sure," Jenny finally responded. "But how did you find us?"

"Me heard crash."

"All right, give us a few minutes," Lara told him.

Auquè nodded.

It was hot and sticky as they started their long walk to Auquè's village. Overhead, birds sang as the sun glistened through the trees. The sounds of monkeys, wild cats, and other strange sounds filled the jungle. After about an hour, Lara stopped to tie her shoelaces and noticed that a few feet ahead the ground shifted! She screamed, "The ground is moving!" Auquè and Jenny, already twenty feet ahead, stopped in their tracks. Auquè quickly turned and grabbed a little stick from a string around his neck, and blew into it. In an instant, whatever it was stopped moving. Lara stared wide-eyed at the tiny spear that had come out of Auquès stick. Then he walked over and stuck his hands into the mud and brought up a ten-foot long snake with the spear near its head. Auquè smiled, admiring the snake.

"Python," he exclaimed.

Jenny walked over and asked, "Is it dead?"

Auque' only nodded and turned around, carrying the snake.

"What are you going to do with it?" Lara asked.

"Eat," he answered casually.

Both girls were disgusted.

"At least we have our own food," Jenny whispered.

The girls ran to catch up with Auquè, who was now approaching a river. When they reached the canoe, they all climbed in. As Auquè rowed, the girls spotted many beautiful fish, the colors of exotic purples, emeralds, and blues. A half-hour later, they arrived on the shore of a small, cozy-looking village.

"Thank you, Lord, for helping us through this day," Lara silently prayed as they followed Auquè to a hut. After getting into the hammocks, the girls were fast asleep.

The following morning, Jenny was awakened by a familiar sound. An airplane! Jenny lunged out of the hut, waving frantically, but it was too late. Moments later, Auquè came to Jenny's side, holding a leaf full of what looked like blood mixed with vomit.

Jenny gagged, "What is that?!"

"Snake," Auquè proudly answered.

"Uh, no thank you," she responded as politely as possible.

Lara was now awake and changing clothes. Jenny changed too.

"I saw a plane," Jenny sighed deeply.

"What?! Do you think it saw you?" Lara asked excitedly.

"No, I don't think so," Jenny sadly responded.

Both of them slumped down on the hammock.

"What are we going to do?" Lara asked.

"I don't know."

Auquè appeared in the hut. "Hungry?" he asked, holding a leaf with the snake guts and some bananas.

"Oh, I'll have a banana please!" Lara exclaimed, and both girls ran up and grabbed a banana.

Later, Jenny and Lara helped the other women cook some worms and fish while the men hunted. The sun was lowering now, almost below the horizon. Lara looked up towards a distant hum. In seconds, a helicopter came into view. It lowered to the ground, beside the campfire where the girls were standing. Once it landed, the pilot jumped out and approached the girls.

"Are you Jenny Anderson and Lara Williams?" he asked.

They both excitedly exclaimed, "Yes!"

Then Lara added, "Just let us get our things," and they ran back into the hut.

When the girls returned and were about to board the helicopter, Auque' appeared.

The girls hollered, "Bye Auquè!" at the top of their lungs.

"Thanks for everything," Jenny added.

"Bye!" Auquè yelled and waved.

As the helicopter lifted off, they could see the villagers waving up to them, until they appeared as small as ants.

"How did you find us?" Jenny asked.

The pilot answered, "A plane searched the area where your captain reported 'Mayday' and reported that there was a small village where you might be."

After a long silence, Jenny said, "I'm going to miss this place, and Auquè."

"Yeah, I'll miss Auquè but not the rest," Lara replied. "I think we're going to have to wait a while for the mission. I just can't wait to get home."

"Same here," Jenny agreed.

The helicopter disappeared into the setting sun, taking the girls homeward, but they'll be back because they know that nothing could beat the AMAZON!

Valerie Austin
Age: 13

It was gloomy and cold, an average day at Sunshine High in Raleigh, North Carolina. Veronica, like always, was fast asleep in her French class.

"Veronica," acknowledged Gerlynn while staring off into space. "Wake up."

"What?" whined Veronica.

"One minute until the bell rings!" exclaimed Gerlynn.

Veronica's long brown hair whipped as her head turned toward the clock. Her brown eyes saw that it was 8:39 a.m. While she and Gerlynn gathered their things to go to their math class, the French teacher, Mr. Stuart, noticed that they hadn't been paying attention and told them to stay after class, along with other kids: Joe, Paul, Steven, and Ashley.

The bell rang and the rest of the twenty-nine kids emerged from the classroom.

"So," paused Mr. Stewart, "what do you have to say for yourselves?"

"I didn't do it," notified Paul using his ever popular sarcasm.

"I've had enough with the six of you!" thundered Mr. Stuart. "All year you have not been paying attention to me, not turning in your work! It's pathetic! I want to see you all after school today, or I'll hunt you down and you will regret that you didn't listen to me!"

"Take a chill pill teach," Ashley sassily replied.

"Don't you ever use that tone of voice with me missy!" Mr. Stuart angrily retorted as he picked up a desk and threw it across the room.

As the desk shattered, the fear in the eyes of the six teenagers emerged.

Veronica stood up and screamed, "I can't wait until I tell my mom about this!"

"Oh, you won't be able to; you see you won't be going home for a while much less to your other classes."

The twelve terrified eyes of the six teenagers grew wide as he said those words. Mr. Stuart was the only teacher in the school that had keys to the basement of the school because it was right next to his classroom door.

"Get up!" Mr. Stuart barked at the kids. "I've already opened the basement door. So, I want all of you to go down there and wait for me to unlock it at the end of the day, because that's when your punishment really starts," remarked Mr. Stuart.

The group hesitated for a minute not knowing what to do or why they should do it.

"NOW!!"

The sound of Mr. Stuart's voice got them hustling toward the door. Once they were all in the basement Mr. Stuart closed the door and locked it.

"How are we going to get out of here?" questioned Steven with a worry in his voice.

It was so pitch-black in the basement that they couldn't see their hands in front of their faces.

"There has to be a light switch down here," stated Joe, "find the walls and look for one."

As the group looked for the walls, they were bumping into each other. "Ouch," they were all saying as they hit their heads on the wall. Moving their hands up and down on the wall, Gerlynn found the light switch.

"Found it," she squeaked as she flicked the light on.

"Light!" sarcastically exclaimed Veronica.

"Now we can worry about how to get out of here," stated Paul.

"I have an idea," whispered Steven. "Everyone, come here, and huddle together."

Steven whispered his plan to the other five people while covering his mouth just in case there were hidden cameras in the basement.

About five hours later the group heard a voice outside the door.

"Are you still in there? Ha ha ha," Mr. Stuart wickedly laughed, "of course you are."

"OK you guys," Steven whispered, "Just like we talked about, once he opens the door..."

The door slowly opened.

"NOW!" screamed Ashley as Mr. Stuart's image showed through the door.

Joe and Paul both charged at Mr. Stuart, knocked him down, took his keys, threw them to Veronica, and dragged him inside the basement.

"Run!" screamed Steven as Mr. Stuart was getting up.

Just before Mr. Stuart charged through the doorway, Paul and Joe slammed the door in his face.

"Hurry, lock the door," Gerlynn squeaked anxiously.

Veronica ran to the door knob and luckily chose the right key first and locked the door.

"Wow, what's his problem?" questioned Ashley.

"I don't know, but we better report this," notified Steven.

"Good idea," everyone agreed.

At the police station they told the entire story to the sergeant. The parents of the six teenagers took Mr. Stuart to court and he went to jail for kidnapping. Mr. Stuart also had to meet with the school board and he could never teach again.

Rochelle Galindo<br>
Age: 13

"Bang!" The house shook as the thunder rolled across the city of Strictville like a blanket of terror sweeping across an unprepared village. Mikey Uptight, an unsuspecting teenager, leaped from his bed as the resonance echoed across his bedroom. He attempted to return to his futile slumber yet try as he might, he couldn't. It seemed to him that he had forgotten something. He thought about his dad, he thought about Principal Meany, and he even thought about old Miss Grimly. Then it hit him... he had forgotten to turn in the school assignment worth half of his yearly grade! He knew Miss Grimly didn't accept late work. What could he possibly do?

Now, he had known Miss Grimly for an extremely lengthy time. He knew she was not all there. For instance, she never slept. She would stay up all night in the school grading papers. One other thing he knew was that his dad would kill him if he failed a class. He had to get into that school. Springing from his bed, he silently pulled on some clothes. Mikey slipped down the hall, snuck into the garage, and hopped on his bike. Luckily, the garage door was already open. He was well on his way to school when he saw his dad on his way home from the graveyard shift at 7-11. Quickly, he dove into some bushes and pulled his bike in after him. He waited until he was sure his dad had passed then continued on his way. As he reached an intersection, he didn't hesitate but kept on going. He almost didn't see the ebony Escalade coming straight for him. Just in time, out of the corner of his eye, he saw the car coming and swerved before it hit him. It could have been a disaster. Finally, he reached the school and put his bike under a tree. He just had to get into that school.

He noticed the shiny red convertible with its top down that belonged to the principal. Gently reaching in the car, he pulled out the keys to the school. By the way, he noticed that the red convertible was getting ruined in the storm. Oh, well. He unlocked the door to the school and dropped the keys in the grand hallway. Now, he needed to get into Miss Grimly's classroom.

The classroom was on the thirteenth floor at the end of the hallway. As he reached the third floor, he heard footsteps coming straight for him. He leaped into a trash can full of bananas, gym socks, and any other school-related oddity you can think of. He waited until the footsteps passed then crawled out. On the fourth floor, he heard the dreadful sound of Janitor Bud's squeaky janitor cart wheels. Knowing the old janitor, Mikey decided he could just run past him. When he was well past him, he heard, "You kids cut that out!"

Suddenly, Mikey realized he needed to get a key to the classroom. He ran back and grabbed them from the janitor. Then he hid around the corner of the classroom waiting for Miss Grimly to take a bathroom break. Finally, the classroom door opened and out marched Miss Grimly intent on getting to the bathroom quickly. The classroom door clicked closed behind her. When the coast was clear, Mikey unlocked the door. He stepped into the room. Now, to turn in that assignment...

He looked around, but at first glance, the other assignments were nowhere to be seen. Finally, after what seemed to be ages, he found the other assignments and put his in the middle of the pile. He glanced out the window and saw that the red convertible was gone. Principal Meany had left for the night. Mikey made a mad dash for the stairs. He practically jumped over Janitor Bud who shook a fist up in the air. Mikey then blasted out the door of the school and into the parking lot. Now, he was almost safe.

The only matter left to attend to was getting home. "It is a long walk," he thought. Then he realized that in all of the excitement he had forgotten that he had his bike. He snatched it from under the tall oak tree and rode off for home. At last he reached his house, snuck into his room, slipped into his pajamas, and hopped into bed. In the morning, his dad asked, "So, son, how did you sleep?"

"Better than ever!" exclaimed Mikey.

Lucas Sage
Age: 13

Hello!  My name is Peak, and I am an alpine pika from the Swiss Alps.  Once, four years ago, a German boy came to the mountain where I live.  He found me easily because he liked pikas, and there are only three of us on this mountain.  He told me to go with him to Germany because the Nazi soldiers were near and it was not safe on the mountain.  When we got to Germany things there were terrible.  Everything was wrecked.  The boy (whose name is Darryl) said that he had to go to America.

***********

"I want to go too," I said.
"OK, I will take you with us," Darry exclaimed.
When we deboarded the airplane in America, Darryl's father noted that we had to move to Aspen, Colorado because they had relatives that lived there.
About this time Pearl Harbor was bombed.  The 10th Mountain Division sent sign-up sheets for soldiers to fight in the war that the U. S. just declared.  I signed my John Hancock on one of the sheets and now I am here at Camp Hale, in Leadville, Colorado.  I am starting my training to fight in Norway.  Here is a diary I kept of the war I fought in:

Weeks 1-2:  They are trying to cram the gear on me, but it is not working.  I met some new friends named Mongoose, Weasel, Fox, and Rody.

Week 5:  Camp is getting harder.  I have to ascend three mountains a day and shoot at targets.  My haystacks, which are where I store food, are getting low but Rody is sharing.

Week 6:  It is the last week of training.  A man almost trampled me.  A bazooka was fired next to me at a target.  Graduation was a bummer.

First three days of transportation and war:  I almost missed the boat.  Mongoose is ill with the flu.  My rucksack is huge and heavy.  They gave me a machine gun for my ammo.  We animals are warm, but the two-legged kind are cold.  Mongoose is well.  Our first raid began on snowy, Nazi-detained, Mount Scholuetscha.  My friends and I are positioned on the edge of the Nazi camp.  We dig holes for protection.  I shot a Nazi.  I narrowly missed getting stepped on.  Someone shot at me, but just missed.  My ears hurt.  I got some fur whizzed off.

Days 4-12:  We've had many more raids.  I have demolished a total of thirteen guys with my machine gun.  Shrapnel just missed me on the eighth day.  Bombs are detonating everywhere.

Days 12-20: Rody, Weasel, and I are making tunnels to get to the other side of the Nazi camp. Our captain gave us grenades and bazookas to blow them up along with our original guns. I do not know if we can handle the size of the weapons. We brought some food in our mess kits.

Days 20-28: Early morning at 0432 we broke our tunnel and started shooting at the backs of the Nazi soldiers. They shot back, but with our size they missed us. I almost got stepped on by a Nazi. We shot most of the enemies, then retreated. Our men on the other side took care of the rest. We overthrew Mount Scholuetscha.

Days 28-32: Mission complete! I will have to take a glacier bath when I get home. I wonder how Darryl is. All my buddies are all right. We just have nick marks on our fur from bullets. We packed our items, gathered all the ammunition, trotted to our ship, and headed home!

Days 32-34: We are home! I am welcomed by Darryl. He is in debt, but I got a $500 paycheck, so I gave it to him so he could get out of debt. The U. S. gave me a medal of honor for what I did. Mongoose and Weasel also got one. I asked all my friends if they wanted to live with me in the Alps. Darryl took all of us except Rody in the new airplane he bought.

Darryl took us to the mountain that I live on, but not before a detour over Mount Scholuetscha to show Darryl where we fought.

When we made it to the Alps, we all jumped out. I went to my burrow and set all my gear by my haystack pile along with my medal.

Darryl Beemer
Age: 10

I'm just a regular kid; well actually I'm totally the opposite of a regular kid, I like broccoli. I didn't purposely like broccoli; it was just an accident. My mom asked me if I wanted broccoli, and I thought that she said Brach's candy, so I said, "Yeah Mom, of course, you know I love it!" So, she gave me broccoli. I made a face that only my brother saw, so of course, he kept on being his tattle-tale self, and told on me for sticking my tongue out at him. The rule in my family is that you have to eat whatever's on your plate, so I had to eat the broccoli.

The next day I went to school and announced that I had eaten broccoli yesterday, and they started a chant, "Carey likes broccoli, Carey likes broccoli" until Ms. Cutler had to quiet them down, telling us that she liked broccoli too. At lunch, I told my best friend Sophie (who always understands) that I didn't like broccoli, going over the same old boring story I told you. She was understanding, and was so brave that she walked right up to Harriet (the one who had started the chant), and told her the story. Pretty soon, Harriet told Hillary, who told Elizabeth, who came up to me saying, "You better get your ears checked, Carey Canary."

"Well you better check your words." Sophie said, saving the day. I can't believe she has the courage to do that. If I ever had to (not that I ever would), I would say it really fast, then run off. I'm safe though, for I would never even think of doing anything half that brave. I'm probably the chickenest fifth grader in all of Louisiana.

Then, my older sister, Susan and I were picked up from school by our babysitter, Agatha, and we went to her house. The good thing about her house was Mr. Goldberg; the bad thing was Jiffy. Mr. Goldberg was the winner of the 1989 Olympic speed skating. I always visited him when I was at Agatha's. Mr. Goldberg always made his wonderful blueberry pancakes, and then we sat down at his rickety old kitchen table, smothered on lots of maple syrup, and Mr. Goldberg told one of his stories about faraway places.

Pretty soon, I heard my name. It was Agatha. "Carey, dinner." We had hotdogs. I put on ketchup, pickle relish, and mustard (that Agatha put on). For dessert, we had root beer floats. I put the root beer in first, and when I put the ice cream in, it overflowed. Five minutes later I heard the phone ring, and I ran to answer it. Agatha ran to answer it, too, so when we reached the phone, arms outstretched, our heads collided. Despite all Agatha's running, I got the phone first. "Hello," I said, "Hello-o? Is anybody there"

"Hi honey, it's Mom, I won't get off really, really late."

"But Mom, where will we sleep?"

"Agatha should be able to get you to bed at her house. Can I talk to Agatha?"

"Sure, here she is."

Oh my, I can't believe I didn't tell you about Jiffy, the world's most annoying dog. I think he's about to eat my ear off. As usual. Jiffy is Agatha's dumb little dog, who was named after "his favorite kind of peanut butter." I don't think dogs really care about the brand of peanut butter they get fed, though. Pretty soon, it was time for bed. In the middle of the night, I felt something on my head. "Mom, is that you?" No, it's not, Mom wouldn't bite my ear. I opened my eyes to see that it was Jiffy. I had forgotten that I had gone to sleep at Agatha's house.

In the morning, I got dressed, and had a good, big bowl of Cornflakes. I brushed my teeth, pulled my dirty brown hair back into a ponytail, and threw on my backpack. I started skipping to school. On the door of the general store, I saw a poster that caught my eye. Contest something, something, something. I couldn't read the rest, maybe I need glasses. I didn't have time to go closer; I was going to be late for school. I started running, and continued running all the way to school. As I walked past the gym, I saw that same sign: Contest, for broccoli lovers only. Now this was just perfect for me. I had grown to love broccoli.

When I came home from school, Mom made me come along to the grocery store, which I thought wouldn't be fun, but it was fine! I saw a booth with information about the contest, and ran to see. Contest, for broccoli lovers only. Winners will receive two pounds of Brach candy. Brach candy, my favorite! I kept on reading. All contestants must read show us that they do love broccoli, then read fluently from the book Barbara, the Picky Eater. Reading, easy! All readers get a copy of Barbara, the Picky Eater when they enter. Must enter by June 5th, 2003. June 5th, that was in four days! I'd better tell Mom, and fast! To enter, call Betsy Tarrings at 290-3962.

"Mom, Mom, we need to call Betsy Tarrings!"

"And who is this Betsy Tarrings?" "I don't know, this lady." "And why should you be calling someone you don't know?"

"To enter this contest, come see!" I replied tugging on her shirt. "Hmmmm..." Mom said, "No we are not calling Betsy, and we are not entering this contest."

"But Mom..."

"I don't care, you are definitely not getting two pounds of candy to rot your teeth on."

"But..."

"I don't care, you are not entering this contest. I will not hear any more about it."

When Dad came to kiss me goodnight, he stayed to talk. "I heard from your mom about the contest you wanted to enter, and I'll enter you. Please, please don't tell your mother, okay Carey?"

"Okay Dad." Before I knew it, it was June 4, and I still hadn't received my book and contest entry stuff! I thought to myself "I sure hope Dad didn't forget!" That evening, I was so worried that I couldn't eat dinner. I sat there staring at my fish, and I could almost see two fish eyes staring back up at me. When I woke up in the morning, though, I came downstairs and saw a package on the table. I looked at it and saw that it had my name on it. I tore open the brown paper and looked at its contents. Inside was my very own copy of Barbara, the Picky Eater! I read it once, twice, then three times, and decided that I was good enough.

At exactly 1:46, Dad took me to the big church, where the contest was going to be, and I sat in the very front row near the judges. I was very nervous. "Number... 18, would you please come up, eat some broccoli, and read pages one and two of Barbara, the Picky Eater."

"Dad, what's my number?" I asked in a mere whisper.

"Twenty-two." Three more people went, and then it was my turn. All of a sudden, my mouth went dry, my teeth chattered, my legs wobbled, and my hair stood up on end. I went up, though, and tried my best. After lots of people went, the judges discussed the best. I held my breath. "What about number 11?" one of the judges asked. The judges kept talking and whispering, and I listened. "Wait, 11 stumbled, but that 22 girl did awful well."

"I agree," another judge said. The judges did some more whispering that I couldn't hear. The head judge stood up and announced "Number 22, you are the winner." Twenty-two, that couldn't be possible, that was me! I was probably hearing things. No, I wasn't, it was true!

So that's how I got my two pounds of candy (which I have to hide from Mom), and remember, don't be afraid to try new things, and don't worry if your ears are a little bit funny!

Sarah McDonald

# THE ADVENTURE OF THE ALIEN INVADERS

Okay, so this is how it all started. It was an ordinary day. All I was doing was jumping on the mini trampoline, minding my own business when four-year-old Katie-Lynn stopped by for my little sister Cathleen's birthday party. She is turning five today. Then all the other kids got to my house and we were taking big, hard smacks at the giant horse- shaped piñata, when all of a sudden... a giant, humongous, stolen space shuttle landed in our backyard!

There were four, five, and six-year-olds all over the place! Some under tables, some under chairs, and some panicking running around in circles! NOT ME! Definitely not me! I was trying to gather all the kids. They were a hassle to get. It was almost impossible. Once I got them indoors, I took chances and went outside. I tiptoed quietly over to the space shuttle. Then I opened the door. Out popped a giant alien and a lot of little aliens! They were making these weird sounds as if they were trying to hypnotize me or something! I freaked out and ran as fast as a jack rabbit back into the house. The kids were going crazy! They were asking me all these questions like, "What did they look like? Where do you think they came from? Why did you go outside?"

I interrupted them saying, "Uh... uh, uh." All the children drew quiet.

"As I was trying to say... because of you, I will answer your questions first. It looks green and slimy. I think it came from outer space. And kid I went outside to see what it was."

Cathleen said, "Come on sis, why won't you tell us what it is already," she was frustrated.

"OK... OK, I'll tell you what it is you don't have to be so temperamental about it!" she said.

"I am not temperamental!" She was even more frustrated now.

"OK it is an alien!" She said as fast as she could. She did that because that is what they always did to her. She finally explained what all had happened outdoors.

Then I decided to go back outside. All of a sudden, one of them popped out from the house. I looked out the window. I saw a person walking along the side of the road. All of a sudden... a green streak of something turned her into an alien!

The aliens all just plainly disappeared! Therefore, we all decided to investigate what they had in the space shuttle. We were not amused because all there was was a laser. It was still a mystery. We went a little farther and we found the person that they turned into one of them!

We took the alien/person with us. We all went into different rooms. The kids split into groups of two. I went by myself. Cathleen and Katie-Lynn teamed up because they were best friends. That was good because they found a room with a ton of machines with lights sticking out. We put the alien/person into one of the machines and it turned back into a living human.

The aliens hadn't returned yet. However, the keys were in the passenger's seat so we drove it to the Kennedy Space Center so they could find out where it belonged. They gave us a trip home and when we got there, the aliens were back.

One of Cathleen's friends said, "Forget these aliens! Let's get this party started!" She turned on her boom box and the aliens' heads exploded and they died. The kids had a great time at the rest of the party. None of them slept that night, so in the end the aliens were dead and they had the party going all night.

Kara Sellers
Age: 9

# EVIL CASTLE

A dark gloomy night it rained. It rained forever but we never went outside because that's what the rain wanted us to do. Go outside in the cold, wet rain. We instead played "Evil Castle" a board game. Shelby, Ashley, and I were playing. Ashley was at shack of screams, Shelby at the closet of cruelty, and I on the top of the tower of terror. Ashley rolled the die, six. She moved six spaces now at the staircase of scars. Then Kyser, my little brother, ran in and said

"Can... can I play Cassie? Please! Please! Pretty please!"

"No! Kyser. We already started playing. Go play your fishing game," I answered.

"NO!" he screamed, "I don't want to play fishing! I want to play this!"

"Kyser," I said in a calm voice, "I'll let you play after we finish our game. In the meantime I'll grab you some ice cream."

"OK!" he said excitedly and ran to the kitchen. When I had gotten him his ice cream I walked back to the game. It was my turn. I rolled. Six. I moved six spaces. Huh. I gasped wishing I were anywhere but here with my annoying little brother Kyser. I had gotten to the portal in which to leave evil castle when you win, but unfortunately I nor Ashley and Shelby knew that the portal can make you enter evil castle too.

Just then was a rush of wind and a long, mournful howl. The wind started to whirl and twist in a circle around us and the game board. Everything at once became a blur. I then shut my eyes. It seemed like hours until everything was still. I was in a sitting position and I creaked open one eye. I was outside, I thought. It was very cold and windy. I stood up. Yes I was outside, but not outside my house, or even in my town, I was somewhere else, but where? Just then I realized that Ashley and Shelby were here too, and they looked the same way I did -- confused. I looked around. It was very dark but I could see fine. It looked as though we were in a graveyard of some sort, but a very old graveyard. There were crumbled tombstones with moss growing on them everywhere. It looked like the graveyard of ghosts from our board game! We started walking but close together.

Just then a dark figure jumped out. It looked as though it were only two feet tall. It had pointy ears, a pair of brown pants on, a dirty white vest, black shoes with holes where the big toe was poking out, a ragged old jacket and a little green hat. Its face was smeared with mud and a long pointy nose stuck out from it.

"Hello," it said," Whos are yous? I am Boppy."

"We-we are Shelby, Ashley, and Cassie," I answered.

"Oh," it said. "Pleased to be meeting yous."

"Come with us!" I said.

"Ok!" he said and off we went.

A while later I broke the silence and said, "I was wondering if you could tell or show us the way out of here?"

"Yes I know the way, but first let us sleep I am being so very tired," he said. So we did.

The next day we started. We walked for a while and I remembered he said the portal was at the top of the tower of terror. After a while Ashley asked, "Who's King Jordan?" when she saw the sign along the road with his name mentioned on it.

"He's the evil king of the land. Wes can't go anywheres 'til he knows abouts it," he said.

"Well then let's go see him so we can get out of here!" Shelby said. So we went straight to evil castle, but when we got there it wasn't so pretty.

"No! I can't allow it! It is simply out of hand!" said King Jordan.

"Who cares," I shouted and ran upstairs followed by everyone else including Andrew, King Jordan's guard.

Just then Andrew came running up the stairs supposedly to help us, so no one said anything.

When we got to the shack of screams Andrew said, "I'll follow you and protect you!"

"Whatever just be quiet," Ashley said.

When we got past the closet of cruelty there was a winding staircase up to the ballroom of bats which we got to after an hour.

We were almost to the hall of holler when Boom, Boom, Boom! A booming sounded throughout the corridor, and then standing behind us breathing down our necks was Exterminator. Then a dark figure with a sword shining bright in the darkness jumped out. The warrior told us to run, and we did! We ran past the hallway of holler up to the fort of phantoms and stopped there waiting for the warrior.

A few minutes later, the warrior came running up to us, out of breath. He was clad in black and a long silver blade hung at his belt. He was wearing a mask which was black also and had two eye holes and a small nose hole. He then removed his mask. His face was an oval shape, but looked young and reminded me of Andrew. Although his hair was a blondish brown, his eyes were a deep sky blue, dull in the darkness, but supposedly bright in the sunlight. He told us his name was Brandon Demoss. I, of course, was quiet fond of him, but he about me was a mystery.

"I have been following you in the shadow for a time now. Are you not going to the roof of this tower?" he asked.

"Wes are," Boppy said in a serious tone.

"Well then I'll come with you if you allow it," he said.

"We will!" I yelled but then turned red and hid behind Ashley as he stared at me but then turned.

Then no one said anything more and we began again. We walked for about two hours when we finally got to the top of the tower.

There was a door about seven feet tall and about three feet across. The doorknob was about the size of a very small bowling ball so it was very hard to turn. Once we were on top of the tower, there was a bluish-purple whirl floating in the air.

"This," Boppy said, "is the portal yous will take to get homes."

Brandon said, "I will miss you all and especially those who admire me and my coming."

"I will miss you all very dearly. Especially you Brandon, so I will visit you all from time to time," I said. Then we said "Farewell! Farewell!" and stepped through the portal.

Everything started spinning VERY quickly for a minute, then everything was still. We were back in my living room safe and sound once we put Evil Castle away. We then went to my room to get ready for bed.

Then Shelby said, "Do you think we'll ever go back together?"

"How about next week?" I answered.

"Sounds good," Ashley said, "but let's go to sleep. I'm tired," so we did.

Moral: Be careful what you wish for, you just might get it!

Cassandra Seaney
Age: 10

# A SPACE TRIP WITH MY DOG, FIDO

The crowd was cheering as my dog, or special space cadet, Fido, and I, Carl Lorensen, were departing into outer space. Fido is a brown, shaggy dog, a Pomeranian. The computer voice counted down, "Ten, nine, eight, seven, six, five, four, three, two, one and blast off." The rocket thrusters started up. I commanded, "Fido, press the green button and we will have lift off." Then I remembered I needed to put a special belt on Fido, so I could understand what he was saying. I put it on him and commanded, "Fido, once again, press the green button."

He barked, "Yes, Carl." Fido pressed the green button and we were off on our space adventure.

Once in space, Fido woofed, "I'm hungry."

I promised, "We will eat in about fifteen minutes."

Though before we could eat, a planet appeared on the radar. We pondered about this bizarre, green planet. I ordered, "Fido, get ready for landing." He whimpered, but he got ready for landing anyway. As soon as we landed, we walked around the barren wasteland. Just then, a red alien with one eye on his belly, and one on his head, little arms, and little legs, and a mustache under the eye on its belly, showed up. Even though he was an alien, he spoke English. He commented, "Greetings, bizarre creatures from the planet Ee-arth."

I said, "Uuhhh, my name is Carl and my planet is pronounced 'earth.'"

He said, "Oh."

I asked, "What is this planet called and what is your name?"

The alien answered, "My name is Ray and this planet is called Planet Nubious."

"OK, but do you guys do anything special around here?" I questioned.

"No, we do things that you earthlings do on earth." I walked around with Fido and Ray. I saw aliens playing basketball, cooking, and I saw aliens playing a game I had never seen before. I asked, "What are they doing?"

Ray replied, "They're playing galaxy-ball and it is a game where you try to get a football down to the touchdown goal or you try to get the soccer ball into the goal."

"Cool," I commented. Fido and I went back to the ship and had dinner. Then we went back outside and played with some aliens until 12:00 AM. After we said good-bye to the aliens, we left, but suddenly rammed into another ship. This was no ordinary ship. It was an alien squad car ship. "Halt earthling," someone ordered.

I yelled to Fido, "Stop the ship!" The ship stopped abruptly.

"You are under arrest for whacking a squad car ship," a voice bellowed.

"Uh-oh, we are in terrible trouble, Fido," I mused. In the alien court, back on Planet Nubious, the jury was trying to solve this arduous crime.

"Order, order," the alien judge called out, and he went on to say, "Welcome to the Alien Justice Court. Now Mr. Dylan (alien police officer), what did this earthling do to you?"

"Well, this creature rammed my ship," the alien angrily said.

I yelled, "I did not see you. You were like, like invisible." Everyone started bickering and quarreling.

The judge yelled out as loud as he could, "Order, order!" All the alien creatures quieted down. "That's better, but has the jury reached a decision about our criminal?" the judge asked. A small, skinny, red alien with black hair, a weird tail, and a squeaky voice, stood up.

He told the judge, "Guilty!"

I mumbled, "Oh no."

The judge shouted, "Then he is guilty. Put him and his dog in the dungeon." Two guard-like aliens came and grabbed Fido and me and carried us to a scary, dark place.

One of the aliens laughed, "I hope you like it here, NOT!" and they tossed Fido and me inside. A little later, we heard some moaning and saw a short, stout, blue alien. He said in a soft, but gruff voice, "I know a secret way out of here. But before I tell you, you must answer my riddles." I made a deal with him. He questioned, "I have four legs in the morning, two legs in the afternoon, and three legs at night. What am I?"

I scoffed, "That's easy. You are a person because in the "morning" means baby years when you crawl on four legs, "afternoon" means preteen years when you walk on two legs, and "night" means old years and you are an old person walking on two legs, plus a cane."

"OK, OK, you got that one right, but now how about these? I am a kind of band, but I do not play music. What am I?" he quizzed.

I gulped and answered, "You are a rubber band."

The alien looked sad, but then asked the final riddle. "I occur once in a second, twice in a week, and once in a year. What am I?"

I gleefully laughed, and said, "You are the letter 'e.'"

"Right you are, my young lad," he proudly said.

I corrected him, "My name is Carl and this is my dog Fido."

He said, "OK, but as I promised, I'll show you the secret way out." He pushed a rock out of the side of the wall to reveal a secret passageway. I thanked him. Fido and I skipped through the passageway, and discovered a few pieces of gold lying lifelessly on the ground. I picked them up and cheered, while Fido barked happily. I said, "Wow, our luck is quite good, eh Fido?" We walked through the rest of the passage, finding gold coins here and there. When we came out of the darkness, an alien marched up to us. I screamed. He calmed me down and said, "Don't worry. I'm here to help you."

"Wha-what did you say?" I stammered.

"I told you. I'm here to help you. I got a space ship ready for us to take you back." He guided us to the shuttle and "Three, two, one. Lift off," the alien counted down. He dropped us off on Earth.

I said, "Thank you and good-bye." Fido barked cheerfully. The helpful alien whizzed off in a cloud of dust. I told Fido, "Aren't you glad we are home finally?"

Carl Lorensen
Age: 11

# A TRUE FRIEND

I howled at the moon as winter blew its cool air on me. As I was walking on the beach when a cat jumped down and hissed at me its back arched back and its mouth wide-open ready to strike at any moment. I growled at it then it jumped on my back and dug its claws into my flesh. I whimpered then ran in a circle then suddenly stopped as the cat flew off my back and landed in the water with a big splash barked at it then ran with my tail flying in the breeze then I suddenly froze because I saw a man with a gun clasped in his hands aiming at the police ready to shoot in any second. I growled he turned then laughed and aimed at me as I jumped onto his chest and dug my teeth and claws into his body when he shot at me. I felt a swift pain in my leg and I closed my eyes painfully with my teeth and claws still in his flesh when I saw a light but was in too much pain to worry about it. As I awoke I heard crying and cheering worried I barked as loud as I could but the pain held me back. Someone heard me because he walked over to me and smiled then yelled "She's fine come in everyone!!!" I heard stomping and screaming I barked "What's going on!" They continued to scream and yell and dance then a strange man came in and told them to do something they hugged me and waved as they left the room. The man stared at me then smiled evilly then took off the weird cloths and there stood the man who shot me earlier today. I howled but he covered my mouth with tape and threw me into a bag I growled but no sound escaped. I heard guns being shot then I heard a weird noise and felt a fast moving movement. Then I was lifted up and thrown into the river with a great splash and saw water in the bag I felt weak and fell asleep. As awoke I saw a man leaning over me with a rag in his hands a dog was barking on the table where I lay. I weakly whimpered. The dog ran in circles chasing his tail then grabbed and threw himself on the floor with a tremendous bang. I barked then sat up slowly and wagged my tail happily the man smiled and slowly handed me some food and water I gulped down the water and gobbled down the food. I jumped off the table barked "Thank you." Then dashed out the door to freedom Even if that man was so nice to me I rushed into the field were I saw a pack of wolves. I barked at them. They glanced up and growled their teeth showing. My heart stopped and I growled. The leader walked slowly up to me and leaped. His claws slashed into my skin. I jumped and sunk my teeth into his back. He whimpered then sank his teeth into my back. I howled and slashed my claws on his mouth. As he released me to lick his wounds I ran and leaped into a river and swam for an hour cleaning my wound. Then a rushing in the trees startled me and there stood the man who shot me, and threw me in the water. He smiled and said, "This time you're dead." He took out his gun, aimed then just as he shot the dog in the house chomped down on him.

He screamed and ran. The dog barked then turned to me. "Are you okay?" It asked calmly. "Fine just a bit tired." I replied sleepily. "You should sleep I'll keep guard." It barked so I fell fast asleep thinking about the wolves. As awoke the dog was sleeping I smiled then went out searching for food my eyes were wide-open searching for any movement when I saw that man I growled then ran my fur flying my legs flew like the wind. I saw the dog sleeping still. I grabbed it with my teeth and ran my heart beating like a drum when the house came in view. I leaped and landed through the window panting like crazy when I saw the man who helped me. He smiled as I handed him his dog he petted me and went away and brought a huge bone, I barked in joy and chewed on that tasty bone for a while. He smiled with my joy and handed me some water I gulped it down then turned back to my bone and picked it up and left the house after saying thank you and good-bye. I walked a while when I saw an old man sitting on a log. He looked so sad I went over and dropped the bone into his lap. He looked at me and grinned picked me and the bone up and took out a gun I gasped as he shot me. The only thing I felt in my leg was pain I fell down acting dead 'til he slowly walked away I jumped up and limped into the woods. The hours slowly went by as the blood dripped on the ground the pain still strong I then saw a river. I followed it towards a small town. I limped up to houses but they kicked me away so I went into an alley and feel asleep the pain sharp as ever. I awoke to find myself in a house a bandage was around my leg water and food was placed under my face. I lapped down the water and gobbled down the food I tried to get up but the pain held me back I howled in pain. A man walked in, smiled and gave me more water which I slowly sipped. That moment I knew I had a true friend.

Lidia Kamionka
Age: 11

# THE PAIN

Tom got out of the car at the funeral home. It was raining and had been, for a few days now. He and his family walked across the rough parking lot to his uncle and two cousins. He was tall with blonde hair that was shaved. He was crying and talking to Tom's mom. Tom and his three brothers went over to Joey, their cousin. He said a quiet and labored "Come on." He led Tom and his three brothers into the funeral home and down a hallway. Joey was brown-haired and brown-eyed, just like his mother. He was about eight years old and was normally always cheerful and ready to play, except for now. They met up with his older sister, Deanna. She was ten with blonde hair and green eyes, just like her dad. Deanna and Joey led them to a table. On it were their mom's most prized possessions. Her violin, her kayak paddle, her stethoscope, and her nursing school degree. Pictures of her with her family were also scattered amongst the treasures. The distant sound of organ music played and they could smell the strong flowers as tears began to dance in their eyes. Joey led them into a room where her casket was open and flowers were everywhere. Family members and friends were there paying their respects to her as were they. They went up to the casket and looked at their aunt. She looked just like she was sleeping but there was something missing, something that wasn't there that they could feel. They knew she was gone but there was some shred of hope that this was all a joke, it wasn't happening.

Cancer had taken her life. Nobody spoke because they felt words weren't needed right now. They were speaking a new language. Not sad and not happy, just emotion as all their hearts were one with each other and as inner peace was achieved in all of them and they knew they would all be together again somehow.

Joey said, "It's better for her to be gone."

"Yes, I guess so," Tom agreed.

They all went and sat down to talk about the memories they shared with her and Tom could almost hear them laughing with her again.

They sat and talked as guests came and left. They all shared a common binding spirit with each person in that room. It was happiness, love but the most felt was pain. The pain was surreal that whole evening and would be imprinted on their souls for the rest of their lives. A life was taken and they knew it was gone. Yet somehow they knew that laughter would be the ointment and care would be the bandages for all their broken hearts.

Her last request was for Joe (their dad), Deanna and Joey to move back to Colorado and be with the rest of the family.

**********

Tom went back to Colorado with his family and went back to school, waiting for his cousins, uncle, and grandma to call on the phone and say that they were coming. The plan was for their grandma to go back to Joey and Deanna to her house back in Colorado. Once their dad finished school, he would move out and find a house.

The day finally came when they arrived in Colorado. But whenever they would play or visit they would always remember that this is what Aunt Denise wanted and she knew that their laughter would be their ointment and their care for each other would be the bandage for their broken hearts.

Tom Lyman
Age: 13

# CATCHING UP WITH MYSELF

MaryJane who is a very good writer indeed, had just finished a book yesterday and the most fascinating event happened, but not to MaryJane. The next day when she awoke fans and people who had read her last book were outside her house bellowing, "Write another book! Write another book!" However she tried to ignore their demands because MaryJane was happy with what she had and what she already accomplished. Then she got calls saying the same message, write, write, write, but the letters quadrupled the phone calls. Finally she saw herself on the news and she burst, "Fine I'll write another book," MaryJane exclaimed.

She sat down that night with her p.j.'s on, a cup of coffee in hand, and a ready mind, but no matter how hard she tried she could not come up with an idea for a new book. Then finally at twelve o'clock she gave up and went to bed. Next morning when MaryJane went to open the living room curtains, out the window she saw a new girl she had not seen before. She was headed in the direction of the neighborhood school. With her she had a brown lunch bag in one hand and an apple in the other (I'm guessing the apple was for her teacher) and her book bag on her back. She had on a grayish light blue dress with pink flowers. With that she had Velcro black shoes. Then MaryJane closed the curtain because that new girl brought back bad childhood memories and went back to thinking about what she would write about in her big wooden chair. The miniature girl came back gazing at MaryJane's house in midday. Her whole body was covered in gooey mud. She was bawling her eyes out. Then she kept on trudging down the sunny road. MaryJane felt depressed for the tiny girl, but was also upbeat and felt as rich as a million dollar millionaire because a brilliant thought popped in her head! She would write about the little girl she saw slumping back and forth in front of her house every day when she went to open and close the curtains and the girl who cried like she herself used to when she was new to the town and school. The girl who had long brown curly ragged hair. The girl who had a freckled face and brown eyes. Could it be herself MaryJane when she was small? Ya right! Naa! MaryJane thought about the thought for days passing. Once in a while the idea popped back in her head, but she would just shake it away. Over the weekend MaryJane would cry and cry so she wouldn't convince herself yes the girl was her when she was in elementary school. She also saw the girl who came walking up the road with her head down until she reached MaryJane's house. She would stop trudging and look up with her brown eyes, freckled face, and then put her head down again and keep on walking. MaryJane loved to watch this girl. She watched her every day thinking what will she be like when she grows old and gray as me. With children gone to college, and a husband in Heaven as the same as me, MaryJane thought, and with her own families. Could this be the time when she herself MaryJane gets to watch just one more poor and sad child grow up once more... her mind was right the girl was her!!! Way down deep inside of her she knew it all along, the girl was her when she was small. MaryJane made her mind make an illusion so she could write another book better than the last. MaryJane finally finished the book about the girl, published it, became even more famous, she also added what happened to her how her mind made an illusion so she could write another excellent book, and she named it CATCHING UP WITH MYSELF. A few weeks later crowds and fans again were outside yelling, "Write another book! I loved your book!" And clapping for MaryJane too!

Elizabeth Burger
Age: 9

"Please! We have been really good this week! So you can tell us one of the stories from when you were a kid? Please!" There were many pleas coming from the children who at the moment were in their nightgowns and pajamas sitting cross-legged with their eyes the size of round eggs. "Please Grandma Ellen?"

"All right, all right, settle down," I said in a mothering voice, "I'll tell you a story from when I was twenty-three and was living in Moscow, Russia."

"Thinking back"

Hearing my heart racing faster and faster as I went to the door, I turned the knob, and the chilled night air began to seep into the apartment. Now realizing two outlined figures had knocked on my door, I stood there a moment, peering into a pair of eyes, cold, dark, black, and full of hatred. The figures stepped forward into the candlelight. I could now see the shiny boots and buttons they wore. They were German soldiers! They came in and said they were going to search my apartment to look and see if I was hiding any Jews. The soldiers began rummaging through my belongings!

When they had looked enough, they started going for the door, but right then they caught sight of a picture of Paul, my husband. One of them took the picture, held it up to the candlelight and gave a sly smirk. Then he lit the picture on fire. I watched in terror as it fell to the floor. The red and orange flames spread across the floor. The moment the Germans finally left, I fumbled around to find a pot or bowl for water and threw it on the dancing flames. The flames lessened dramatically until they were out.

My husband came home around 11:00 PM. I asked him how well he did at the Resistance. "It was a good night to bomb the German factories, since most were out looking for Jews!" replied Paul.

"Where did Tom and Ema go?" I asked as I went to make sure the black drapes across the windows were closed tightly.

"We have given them a safe hiding spot, so the German army can't find them. After all, you know they are Jewish!" he replied.

"Where did you hide them, Paul?" I asked curiously.

"I can't tell you, the soldiers could be listening to us talking!"

After those last words a silence fell upon us like a spell, but I could understand why we had to talk in a sort of code, since it was World War II! I began to miss Ireland, where I was born. "Oh yes, and Paul, " I said, "We must wait until tomorrow to take the Jews to the free land, meaning Sweden, since Sweden is a neutral country. Why don't you call Natalie and Tom to let them know about tomorrow's plans?"

"Alright, it has been a long day we better be off to bed. I shall call Natalie and Tom in the morning," Paul said.

When I awoke, I could see a glimpse of pure brilliant light peeking through a crack in the window. I pulled on some clothes, and then started preparing breakfast. Suddenly an ear splitting sound started. It was a siren, "AIR RAID" Paul and I shouted to each other. We ran for a bomb shelter. As we ran the door slammed behind us. A few German soldiers spotted us. They stopped us dead in our tracks! Then they dragged us into the street where we had to stay until the raid was over. It was one of their rules, when they caught you heading for a shelter; they make you stay above ground with them! I closed my eyes, thinking about the green hills and misty valleys of Ireland. When the siren stopped I opened my eyes, there were fires burning everywhere. Then, we were let go and we started for our house.

Once we were back at the apartment I finished making breakfast. We ate in silence.

That afternoon we left for the train station, where we bought tickets for St. Petersburg, Russia. As we boarded the train we saw a few soldiers making their way up the aisle towards us. We sat down quietly but then they came and asked us who we were, where we were going, and why. I answered, "I am Ellen Wied and this is my husband Paul, we are going to St. Petersburg to visit my sister and her husband, we are Irish!" The soldiers moved on to the people seated in front of us.

The train came to a halt in front of a huge brown building, which was our exit. As we got off, a man in a blue uniform checked tickets to make sure everyone was at the right station. We had to call a taxi to take us to Natalie's house. We traveled awhile, along the muddy road. As we reached the outskirts of the city, it seemed as if civilization barely existed anymore! We stopped in the driveway of what seemed to be a tan colored house that was once white. Paul paid the driver and we headed for the house with a couple of bags.

When we got to the door it opened and a smiling face stood behind it. "Natalie!" I shouted. After the warm welcome we sat down for a cup of tea. Since the Nazis had taken most of our resources and used them for their army, we were forced to be resourceful and use herbs and grain for tea. It seemed as though someone was watching us. Then I felt a hand on my shoulder, I was afraid to move. I realized it was Jon, my brother-in-law. He was in the resistance with Paul. "You startled me, Jon!"

"Sorry," he said, "I just couldn't resist."

"I don't care, you know better than to do that!" I said with a smile. Jon made his way across the room and started talking to Paul. "When will we leave?" asked Natalie, "We can't stay here all night, while the weather is perfect for Sweden!" Natalie stared up at the starless, diamond clouded sky.

"We shall leave around ten o'clock tonight," Paul answered in a stern voice.

Natalie and I ran silently through the forest with some Jews struggling behind us towards the docks where Jon's boat, The Batel, was. Paul and Jon were together somewhere. There was a rustling in the bushes, when suddenly four soldiers appeared in front of us, two of which were holding Paul and John, who had been knocked out! Another soldier was holding the leash to a snarling dog. The last soldier had a stern face that was half hidden in shadow. He had a horrible accent; it was hard to understand his Russian. He was asking me what I was doing, leading so many people toward the docks.

I whispered into Natalie's ear, telling her I'd distract the soldiers, while she got Paul and Jon. Instead of answering the soldiers, I kicked him in the shins as hard as I could. Natalie and a dark haired man stepped forward quickly. They took Jon and Paul from the surprised soldiers, running as fast as they could off the path and into the brush. The soldier, filled with hatred, punched me hard in the stomach; I fell to my knees gasping for air. The soldier pulled me up by the shirt and told me I would suffer being relocated to a place of many horrors! He and another soldier took me by my arms and dragged me to the truck that was parked just outside the thick forest grove. They threw me inside and locked the doors! I pushed, pounded, and kicked, but it was useless!

After four hours or so, we arrived at a place of torture! The German soldiers were running around yelling. I had to face it. I was terrified! It seemed my whole world had turned upside down. I felt as if I had stopped breathing. I was pulled from the truck out into the mud. When I stood up again they shoved me through an open gate. I was inside the gates with a large crowd; the guards pushed the gates shut. I noticed there were many tear stained faces. There was much yelling and crying at this place.

All day without food or water, but now it was night and soldiers were coming for us! We had no idea if they would give us food or torture us. I happened to think that it was the second, since they came armed. As they drew nearer, everyone became tense. One woman with a baby began frantically wailing. Then there were an outburst of shouts, and a shot was fired in the air to reclaim silence, which it did! "Men to the right, women to the left, elderly and women with children straight to the furnace!" yelled one of the soldiers.

It was as though war had broken out, right in front of my eyes! Prisoners broke out in fury, some ran at the soldiers, but were shot down. The Nazis pushed the frightened crowd in every direction. More and more soldiers were coming to sort out the prisoners. I was being pushed back and forth.

A soldier came over and dragged me through a gate and into a building. There, women were sewing uniforms for the Germans, others were stuffing blankets and pillows with soft white cotton. I was still being held by the soldiers, who now were dragging me towards a smaller table where another soldier was waiting, seated behind it. They spoke in German, so I couldn't understand. The seated soldier stood up and looked me over. He pointed at the long table where women were stuffing the blankets and pillows. The soldier who was holding me pushed me towards the table. Then he stopped pushing me and ordered me to sit and start working! I gave him a scowl as he stamped away. Only the woman sitting next to me said anything, "Be careful," she said, "if they catch you doing that they could shoot you!"

It was a nightmare there! All I did is what the soldiers told me. Finally we could go to bed! Since there wasn't much to think about that day I thought about an escape plan. I thought about the plan every day I was there, but I was too afraid to use it!

I was there eight long years.  Then one day the soldiers opened the rusty gates to let the prisoners go!  At first we weren't sure we could leave, we thought they might be testing us, and if we headed for the gates they would shoot us!  Soon one by one people began to leave.  I was one of the first!

About a month after I was released, I went back to Natalie's house.  When I arrived it seemed nobody was there until I made my way inside to the kitchen.  There I found Natalie with her back to me humming to herself as she was washing the dishes.  I stood in the doorway waiting for her to turn around.  After a few moments she turned around, slowly but surely.  "Oh thank the Lord, Ellen," Natalie said,

"I thought you were dead all this time!  Whatever happened to you?" I explained everything that happened all those years ago!

"Paul still thinks you're alive," said Natalie.  "A lot of people thought he was crazy."

"Speaking of Paul," I began slowly, "where is he?" Natalie told me he had gone to live in Sweden.  She also gave me his address and some money for a train ticket.  I gave her a hug, thanked her and was on my way!

About a week later I had bought a train ticket for Stockholm, Sweden where Paul was living.  It took a day and a half to reach Stockholm.  I took a cab from the train station.  I went to Paul's house.  As we pulled up, Paul was standing on the porch of a small cottage.  The cottage was brilliant lavender with bluish-white trim.  I jumped out of the cab and ran towards him.  He recognized me and ran towards me.  We hugged each other for a long time until the cab driver yelled that I hadn't paid him yet!  We were laughing, it felt so good to laugh again.  Then we had children, those children had children, and those children are you!

"That's the end of the story; wow it's time for bed!"

"Do we have to?" whined the children,

"Yes, your parents will be very upset with you and me otherwise, now off to bed with you all!"

Lauren Wied

# HEALER VS. NANOTECH
## A YOUNG BOY'S DISCOVERY OF FREEDOM

My name is Elijah and this is my story. I have been a healer for ten years now, and live with my grandfather in New York. We own a little healer's shop, and that would have vanished if it were not for my grandfather. My story may be insignificant except for the fact that a simple person with a twelfth-grade education toppled the United States Supreme Court. Please, all who hear this story, take heed for someday it may be you in the same position.

My grandfather, who was also my legal guardian, is one of the greatest healers alive. The ancient race of the healer has long since died, but my grandfather and some others read the old scrolls and learned the art of healing people. Unlike a normal doctor that uses nanobots, a healer uses herbs, spices, and other natural products. The nanobots seem to be a favorite for many people because they save on health bills.

Several years ago, before I was born, some doctors took my grandfather and other healers to court saying that their practices were unsafe The doctors did not win that time, but since the boom of nanotechnology and nanobots the doctors have won. In the mid 21st century nanobots and nanotechnology became the popular thing. If it was not nanotech, then it was outdated. A once great country had been turned over to the scientists that control the nanotechnology. The old saying, "Those that have the knowledge have the power," came true in the mid 21st century. The scientists and doctors had the United States government pass a law that prevented healers from working in an indirect way. The new law stated that every child born after January 1st of 2075 had to be implanted with nanobots. Those born before that date had a choice. My grandfather always said, though, that the choice was never really there. The insurance companies would not accept anyone who did not have the nanobots. They said, "It is just safer and cheaper than the old medicine of the 2000's." The latest that a child was to be inoculated was their sixteenth birthday.

But I digress, to get to the point, it all started on my sixteenth birthday in the year 2898. For most people this day was a great day, but for me it was a totally different day. The nanobots were fine with most people, but they actually block a healer's ability to feel, and sense problems. This means that I would not be able to sense where a health problem was and how to heal it. I had been trained as a healer for sixteen years of my life and now I was about to lose all of it just because the public school would not let me attend if I did not have insurance coverage. Maybe a high school diploma was not a big deal for me, but for my grandfather it was a big thing. He was from the time when education was your only real security. My grandfather was going to fight it all the way.

Most teens get their driver's licenses, nanobots, and cars on their sixteenth birthdays. Not I. I got a trip to my grandfather's lawyer. We met with him that morning. That's when it hit me. We were not just challenging the state courts or the insurance companies. We were challenging the United States government! We were about to do something that would be in my children's history books. My grandfather told me that night, "Elijah, this is going to be a long hard road, but we are going to win. Then you can be a healer and take over the shop. I want you to know that no matter what happens in the courtroom, you and I will always be healers, and if we have to move to Canada to be healers, then so be it." I don't think that I will ever forget that night. It was that night that I took the rites to become a healer, in the service of God and my grandfather.

It was a full six weeks later that my grandfather and I walked into the Supreme Court building in Washington, D.C. It was huge! I had never seen anything like it before. Sure, in New York there had been skyscrapers that reached all the way into the stratosphere. They were built with the nanotechnology. This building, though, was massive. It was made with human hands, not machines and robots. One could just feel the power radiating from the building. The columns towered above my head, and seemed to reach for the sky. If the Supreme Court judges were like these columns, with all their power and might there was no hope for us at all. For my grandfather was a simple healer with no Ivy League degree, and I was just a sixteen-year-old boy. In the entryway I found something that sparked my interest. It was the first paragraph of the United States Constitution. Finally, I grasped the meaning of the day! I understood why we were here. It was not only for me; it was for the betterment of my country, and thus myself. This document had seemed only a thing of the past to me in school, but now it was my life, it was my reason for being. The government could not force us to do anything that would hurt our right to freedom and blessings. I was going to walk into that courtroom with my grandfather and challenge those great column-like judges, and I was going to win. If not for me, then for the world that I was now vowed to serve.

My grandfather walked over to me and said these few simple words, "We are Americans and it is our right to secure the blessing of liberty for us and our children." Still to this day, I wonder if it was that obvious what I was thinking. The media portrayed us as traitors for disobeying and challenging the law. Now I saw that we were different; we were true Americans because we took our right to challenge that law. As I thought about this we walked into the courtroom. There, seated at the bench, were the judges. It surprised me to see that they were normal people just like our lawyer. In fact, they probably had nanobots and wanted a true choice, too. The room soon filled and the session was underway.

The lawyers battled back and forth, one saying that the nanotechnology was saving the country billions of dollars in medical bills. Our lawyer came back saying that the government had no right to make us use nanotechnology. It should be our choice and the government should protect that choice. The day went on and on. The judges would ask questions, and the lawyers would fight. My grandfather and I were called to testify many times, along with doctors and scientists. I thought that it would all be over in a day, but the one day stretched out to weeks and then months. Finally, the last day came.

We all piled into the courtroom for the decision. The most senior judge stood up and gave the verdict. She pronounced, "After much time and consideration this Supreme Court of the United States of America find that the law requiring the placement of nanobots in the bodies of American citizens is unconstitutional, and this Court will be requiring that the Congress and House of Representatives revoke this law. The Court will also be recommending that Congress and the House pass a law protecting those that choose not to be inoculated with nanobots by making sure they are given an equal chance to secure their blessings of liberty. No company, including insurance companies or governmental agencies in the United States, can deny this right to any citizen of the U. S."

That very day I walked back into the school and a year later graduated. I then went on and graduated from the University of Scotland and Wales with my Ph.D. in Herbology and Natural Medicines. I even studied under a Druid priest for a summer. I eventually came back to New York and helped my grandfather in the shop. Our business is doing exceptionally well. I think that first day at the Supreme Court building will live on forever in my mind.

Jennifer Crandall
Age: 17

Ever since I was little I have always wanted to race cars. My name is Bryan Renneisen... I race many cars. I don't know their names. I race for speed and money. My first ever racer was a homemade go-cart which was made for my birthday. My dad used to race cars to support his family. When I turned eight, my dad died in a race. My dad was driving a souped-up Lamborghini Diablo SV, the other opponent hooked my dad's bumper and threw him into the wall. As soon as his car hit the wall it exploded. By the time the rescue team got there, Dad was dead.

## Manhattan Speedway
### 12:00 a.m.

"Ha, Bryan are you going to lose today," asked Coupe. "You're the one that always loses driving that Mustang Mach One. You might as well dress up as a hippy. Well, well nothing, it's the new age."

Welcome to Manhattan Speedway's Race # 10. Today's racers are Bryan Renneisen and Coupe. There are the cars coming to the starting line. Bryan will be driving a Ferrari F-50 and Coupe a Mustang Mach One. The race is about to begin.

Beeps...beep...beep! Off goes Bryan, Coupe right behind him only a couple of feet. "I wonder who is going to win the race," yelled the announcer. Oh my, Bryan has won the race. He has just won the race $200,000.00

## Home
### 1:00

"Hey Victoria and Veronica my Ferrari twins, I won once more. We'll see you girls later. Let's see what's on the news.

"Hi, welcome back to two o'clock news, I'm Tom, let's see what is going on in cars today. Today at Manhattan Speedway at twelve o'clock, a racer named Bryan Renneisen won the race.

"Whatever," said Bryan. I guess I will see what is in the paper. Here we go, I have found my new mechanic and his name is Spud.

## Next Day
### 8:00 a.m.

"Hi, welcome to Bob's Car Repair. My name is Bob."

"Good for you," said Bryan. "I'm looking for a person, his name is Spud."

"He is in the back of my shop."

## Back Of Bob's Car Repair
### 8:10 a.m.

"Hey, is your name Spud?" said Bryan.

"Ya you have something to say about it?" said Spud Rudly.

"I'm looking for a mechanic. If your name is Spud I will pay you five thousand a day. Plus if you start right now, I will give you a Mustang Mach One and ten thousand dollars."

## Back Home
## 10:00 a.m.

This is you will work and see that out there that's where you will live. Oh one more thing, here is ten thousand and a Mustang Mach One with a 316 Hemi V8 and a Hemi blower and you can get it painted any color you want it. It also has a hydraulics system and turbo muffler.

## Speedway Oregon
## 12:00 p.m.

Hello, today's racers are Bryan Rennenisen and Ben. Today we have a pro racer from the year 1985. So Roger who do you think is going to win today's race. Well, Ben has an addition in control, but Bryan numbers in speed. Well the race is about to begin so we can just see who wins today. Beep... beep... beep off they go. Boom! What is wrong with Ben's car, he is drifting toward the wall. Ben's car has just exploded.

## Back Home
## 3:00 p.m.

Hello, this is Tom on three o'clock news. Today a racecar driver was shot while driving his car at Speedway Oregon. It happened about one p.m. The bullet missed Bryan just by an inch. It hit Ben in the neck. He had been going two hundred three miles per hour when he hit the wall. His car exploded right away. The gun that was fired was a 30-30 with a scope. They had found that the gun was fired from two hundred yards.

## One Race Before The Championship
## 4:00

Well today it will determine who will win the championship. Today's racers are Bryan Renneisen and the three time national champion in the world, Zeike. Bryan will be driving his father's Lamborghini SV and Zeike will be driving his favorite McLarne. The race will begin in a few minutes. I guess not, here they come to the finish line. Beep... beep... beep, off they go. They're almost to the end of the race. What is wrong with Bryan's car. It is on fire! Oh no Bryan's car has just exploded into little pieces.
Bryan is not going to the championship CHAMPIONSHIP 2003

Today's races are going to be dedicated to Bryan Renneisen and all the others perished in a race this year.

Bryan Renneisen

# DILEMMAS OF LIFE!

Most of my life has been spent being the best criminal lawyer I could be. For twenty years I had been a well-respected lawyer. I had cherished each and every minute of it. I had defended hundreds of suspects, such as O. J. Simpson. That was a hard case, but I was up for the challenge. Then I decided to move forward and become a judge, but since I'm a blonde-haired woman it is a little harder than I expected.

I had all the experience and knowledge I needed to become a judge, however; to become a judge, a committee had to elect you into the field. Unfortunately, this committee that was chosen to interview me was made up of chauvinist males. What luck! The committee would not even hear me out, every time I would go in to meet with them, I had to put up with sexist comments and the conversation would stay away from the topic of me becoming a judge. It was the most frustrating thing I had ever experienced.

Finally I had enough of this bigot board and stood up for my constitutional rights by complaining. This was a bigger deal than I had ever predicted. Every time I would try to make complaints regarding the committee to another agency, they would direct me to another organization. This was a never-ending process! After I spent two years of my live trying to override this committee, I finally got so frustrated that I ended up going to complain to the President of the United States of America. I spent about seven hours in a conference with the President. The President and I talked about what an extremely qualified lawyer I was and my potential to become a phenomenal judge. His breathtaking comments really meant a lot to me. Even if my dream of becoming a judge did not come true, such fantastic remarks being said about me from the President of the United States of America meant a tremendous deal. The President was so disgusted with the committee's proceedings that he went and personally spoke with them. The president told the committee that they needed to be more respectful in choosing lawyers to become judges. He fired every member of the committee who selected judges and forbid them all from ever becoming part of a national committee. They each had to pay a $1,000 fine and apologize to me and all other women that they denied the right to become judges on national television. They were very humiliated because they had to apologize for being sexist, opinionated pigs. This also ruined their reputation, which meant everything to them.

After he fired the committee, I got the chance to interview with a fair judge hiring committee, and they hired me right away. The new committee told me that I was a fantastic candidate to become a judge and that I'm one of the most highly qualified lawyers that they have ever seen. Roger, the president of the committee, told me that they could never understand how anyone could deny me the right to be a judge with all the qualities and experience I had.

I now have been a well-respected judge for about five years and I have cherished every minute of it. I don't take a solitary second for granted, because I put so much effort in becoming a judge. I encourage all women to: fight for their human rights, do what they desire with their lives, and not let anyone impede them.

Patricia Dawn McConahay
Age: 16